MARIËTTE WHITCOMB

FORTIUS

This novel is a work of fiction. Names, characters, places, and incidents are the product of the author's imagination. Any resemblance to real persons, living or dead, events, or locales is entirely coincidental.

ISBN Paperback: 978-1-77628-231-9
ISBN eBook: 978-1-77628-237-1

I dedicate this novel to every person who has been abused, assaulted, or preyed upon by a predator in a position of power.
May you find the strength to rebuild your life and more than anything may you have your day in court. Your life and voice matters.
You deserve to see justice served.

Also, to the brave men and women who have lost their lives because they were willing to stand up against abusers, for themselves and/or others.

The truth will come out.

One

Marcel
Saturday, 23 January, 7:30 p.m.

Not the most questionable thing I've ever done, but there I stood outside Aidan's office. I listened, waiting for the perfect moment to march in and state my case, to stake my claim as a member of the organisation. I had been on the sidelines for far too long, and I wanted this investigation. No, I needed this for me, but most of all for the victims.

"No," Aidan said.

Rowan exhaled hard. "Mom needs a break, and this is what Finley does best. You can't deny the victims justice because you don't want to risk putting your wife in danger."

"You will not discuss these murders with Finley. That's a direct order."

"Too late, it came up when I showed her my new tattoo."

I didn't need to see Rowan's face to know he smiled. He loved taunting Aidan by flirting with me. Harmless play between a brother and sister-in-law who share a deep, indescribable bond. He's a younger brother in my eyes. Rowan and I had grown close since I learned the truth about the man who carried me out of the bunker where I had been held as a prisoner of war. Or so I thought at the time. The only thing we can't agree on is flying. Rowan loves it. I never will.

To help Rowan out, or to eavesdrop longer? I waited. He's a big boy and has always stood up to Aidan.

"I showed my sister my new tattoo, so what? And during the ensuing conversation, I mentioned the murders to her. We need her help on this one, Aidan. I get why you're reluctant, but you need to make peace with what's inevitable."

"How much longer are you going to eavesdrop, Mrs Walker?" my husband asked.

Busted. I sashayed into the office, as if I've never put a foot wrong in my entire life, until I saw the emotions duelling in Aidan's eyes – anger and fear. "You knew this day would come, my love. It's here, and I won't back down from this fight. Not with you, or with the person responsible for the murders of at least four people." Placing my hands on my sides, I stood my ground.

Aidan held my stare. "Rowan, please leave us. Close the doors on your way out."

Rowan did as his brother, his superior in the organisation, commanded. When he reached me, he pressed his lips to my cheek and said, "I'm not going to apologise, we need you. He knows it."

I nodded and as soon as Rowan closed the doors, I pressed the automatic lock. Not even a bomb could open the doors. On this side, an explosion was about to erupt.

Aidan placed his hands on the desk and leaned forward, bowing his head. "Where's Ainsley?"

"She fell asleep even before I put her down. Your mother suggested she sleep in their room tonight. I think being around Ainsley is helping her decompress. And she wants us to have some alone time, seeing as this is your day too."

My husband walked around the desk and pulled me against him. Aidan pressed his lips to my forehead. "You did an amazing job with her party. You must be tired, Fin. Let's go shower, sleep, and continue this discussion tomorrow."

I pulled back, staring up at him. "No." Resting my head against his chest, I drew a deep breath, filling my soul with his scent. I know Aidan Walker well enough to know if we didn't continue this discussion now, there was no chance of getting my way come daylight. "Aidan, you need to get over what happened and accept that I'm returning to work. I want this investigation."

He released his hold and walked to the window. Bullet-resistant glass blocked out the sound of the waves crashing on the shore. "You promised to give me a year."

"It has been a year." I tried.

"No, it hasn't. On the twenty-third of April last year, when Ainsley turned three months old, you made a promise. Therefore, it has only been nine months. You owe me another three."

"Semantics." Again, I tried.

Aidan laughed, the sound making me smile at his reflection in the window. "Three entire months aren't semantics, Wife. A promise is a promise."

"Your mother's exhausted. She can't continue working the way she has this past year. It's time I take over as head of profiling and interrogation. The position they offered me when I signed on."

"You could die, Finley." Aidan turned to me, his eyes filled with nothing but fear.

"So could you." I closed the distance between us and lifted my hands to his face. The familiar tickle of his stubble against my palms. The same storm raging in his eyes whenever the day of Ainsley's birth came up. "Aidan, I could die of a heart attack any minute. Cancer might be spreading through my body. I can slip and fall down the stairs. You knew who I am when we got married. You and I both promised Ainsley, even before she was born, to make this world the safest place for her and as many children as we can. I will not go back on our promise to her."

I stepped away from him, crossing my arms over my chest. "Three people have been brutally murdered, another's death remains undetermined. They were daughters and a son. Their parents deserve to know what happened and why, but more than anything *who* took their children from them. I, we, can bring them closure, and the killer to justice."

"Nothing the police can't handle. We can hand over what Rowan uncovered." Aidan turned his back to me.

No matter how much I ached to touch him, to hold him,

even beg him to let me run this investigation, I didn't. His reason for acting like this, I understood. Almost losing Ainsley and me, on this very day a year before, had turned Aidan into an overprotective Papa-bear. Not the cuddly, honey loving kind. The kind who will fight until his last breath to keep us safe, even if that meant keeping me locked in our home. We weren't fighting each other. We fought for us, for our daughter, and for our life. *Protective Aidan is sexy.*

There was only one way for me to get both of the things I wanted more than anything in that moment. With his back still turned to me, I began my last attempt to win this battle. I removed the Glock 43 Gen 4 holstered at my right ankle and placed it on the coffee table, careful not to make a sound as I did so. Inside the fortress we called home, I didn't need to carry more than one gun. Of course, multiple weapons were hidden throughout the house, out of Ainsley's reach. It would stay that way until she's old enough to carry, or at least handle her own.

"Aidan, don't force me to go over your head. Your father is still head of the organisation, and he'll side with me. Your mother needs to decompress after what happened in Columbia."

Aidan spun around, the heat of the fire in his eyes changing the instant our stares locked. "What are you doing?" The corners of his mouth lifted, his left eyebrow raised.

I grinned; victory was so close I tasted it. "I'm going to lay it all out on the table for you, and you'll agree that it's time I start working again. Then we'll bury the hatchet. Deep."

Aidan shut his eyes, drawing his bottom lip between his teeth. "It's my birthday too. Can we please continue fighting tomorrow?"

I lifted myself onto the mahogany desk and tilted my head to the right. "Did I not wake up the birthday boy by blowing his candle?"

The sound of Aidan's laughter filled the room. "Really, Fin?"

"My bad. It just popped into my head. Now get over here so we can make up." Without taking my eyes off his, I leaned back and arched my body as I stretched my arms out above my head.

"The desk is too hard for what I'm about to do to you."

"Not as hard as you appear to be, Mr Walker." My eyes followed Aidan's every move as he changed into his birthday suit.

"This discussion isn't over." Aidan lifted me up and carried me to the couch.

Brushing my lips against his, I ran my fingers through his hair. Not a grey hair in sight, despite being married to me. "It is. I'm starting work tomorrow. Your mother will take care of Ainsley until we can find a suitable nanny. I'll ask Eli to run background checks on the nanny, and her entire family and friends."

"Let me guess, Mom has already agreed to this?" Aidan lowered me onto the couch and followed me down.

"No, but she will. She needs time with her granddaughter, it will do her good, and I trust no one more to take care of our baby." The perfect lines of his triceps and shoulder muscles played under my fingertips. I focused on his mouth, waiting for the explosion.

Aidan pressed his lips to the spot below my left ear. "You promised me three more months, Mrs Walker."

"It's not my fault four people were murdered, and I'm forced to go back on my promise." I lifted my hips and pressed against him. "How can I ever make it up to you, Commander Walker?"

With his body, Aidan pressed my hips down and settled himself between my thighs. "By promising you won't put yourself in danger, *if* I allow you to investigate these murders."

"I can't promise you that. I am who I am. However, you have my word that no matter what happens between now and when I gift this killer with a hollow-point bullet between his eyes, I'll be careful. No charging in anywhere guns-a-blazing without your direct order to do so. And wearing Kevlar."

"Not good enough." Aidan brushed his lips against mine.

My back arched on its own. "What will it take, Captain Walker?"

He laughed against my mouth. "How did I go from Commander to Captain in mere seconds?"

I pressed my head back into the couch and stared up at him. "Why are we still talking?"

The conversation seized. The discussion over. *For now.*

Two

Marcel
Saturday, 23 January, 9:16 p.m.

The moment I unlocked the doors and pushed them open, it struck me. Aidan agreed to let me run the investigation, but it meant I would have to leave Ainsley in someone else's care. My mother-in-law as good a person as any; she had done a fine job raising four sons. Eighteen months after Nathan's birth, she had started to work again and continued after Liam was born. If not, they wouldn't have had Rowan.

Nausea crept out of unknown places and lodged in my throat. *Is this how all mothers feel when they go back to work when their maternity leave is over?*

I ached to see my daughter. Her sweet face reminding me of the love parents have for their children. Four who had been murdered. As I always did, I hoped the victims were loved. And I prayed for their parents. Losing a child is a pain no parent should ever have to endure. When they did, I couldn't ignore the darkness' call to seek justice and vengeance for the victims, and their loved ones.

In the guest bedroom I found Heather sitting on the bed reading a paperback novel. Our eyes met as I opened the door. "What's wrong, sweetie?" she whispered.

"Nothing, Mom. I just need to see Ainsley." My beautiful, perfect daughter lay on her back, her arms stretched out above her head. Her favourite soft toy, a stuffed tiger Aidan had bought, lay against the side of the cot. I bent over the rail and moved it away from her face. Never in my life did I feel the need to protect as fiercely as when I looked at her innocent face. We have the means to protect her against almost anything life might throw at her. But what about all the children, and parents, who aren't as lucky?

I understood Aidan's reasons for not wanting me in the field, but I could bring a killer to justice. If I didn't, I wouldn't be true to who I am. Dr James had said as much during my last session. He had helped me win the fight against the post-natal depression which attacked me out of nowhere. Jimmy said I would need to work again, for my own sanity. *A mother who works outside the home isn't a negligent mother, as long as her work isn't illegal.* Then again, that's a grey area – what if she doesn't know a different, or more legal way to provide for her children?

"Finley?" Heather whispered and placed her hand on my shoulder.

I wiped my eyes before I turned to her. Heather motioned with her head towards the balcony door and I followed her out. The air warm; the sound of the crashing waves a reminder that Aidan and I had created a new and better home. It stood on the rubble of the house which had been here before. We built on the ruins of our past, not only in a literal sense.

To my right, Lizzie and Eli lived with their son, Levi. Ainsley's cousin. Aidan and my godson. To my left a safe house owned by the organisation I now worked for. All three homes impenetrable. Fortresses. The lengths we went to in order to ensure our family will be safe. As safe as we could be in this cruel and dark world. One I would now re-enter at the cost of spending time with my daughter.

"What's wrong?" Heather pulled me close, wrapping her arms around me. She rubbed a hand up and down my back; the way a mother comforts her child.

"I need to ask you a favour. Do you mind staying for a while and taking care of Ainsley? Rowan informed us of four murders and Aidan has agreed to let me run the investigation."

Heather hugged me tighter before releasing me but kept her hands on my shoulders. "That's not a favour, it's my honour as her grandmother to take care of her. No matter how long you need."

The destruction Heather had witnessed no longer lingered in her eyes, or in the exhaustion audible in her voice. This would be good for her too. There's only so much one person can see in their lifetime. What happened in Columbia was the last for Heather. An entire town burned to the ground. Its people slaughtered with machetes, all because of a turf war between rival cartels. I had known since Heather walked through the door two days before, her days at Fortius were over. Which meant mine would start.

"Thank you. Can I ask you something?" I turned away from her and stared out over the dark mass in front of me, except for the sporadic blue flashes of lightning on the horizon. "Was it difficult for you to go back to work?"

Lizzie and I discussed it countless times. She had returned to the office when Levi was twelve weeks old. Of course, my sister opened a day care on the grounds of Williams Pharmaceuticals, much to the delight of her employees. Little did they know about the background checks Eli conducted on every person who took care of their children during the day. Not only on the day care's employees, but on any and every person they had ever been in contact with. None other than Duvall Construction, a company owned by my in-laws, had done the construction. Their employees all ex-military. The Walkers' way of helping soldiers adapt to civilian life.

"It's difficult for every mother, but I kept my focus on the good I did. The same as what you'll do. Ainsley won't lack in any aspect if both you and Aidan work. Quality is far more important than the quantity of time spent together. When she's old enough, she'll understand the importance of the work you do. Is Aidan okay with you being out in the field?"

"No, but he can't keep me locked up here forever. Neither can we keep Ainsley here for the rest of her life. Death will come for all of us."

"You won't be in danger every day, not like a police officer is, or if you still served in the military. Aidan understands the risks and the safety precautions in how we operate better than anyone. Include him as much as you can in the investigation, and in time he'll make peace with it."

I leaned my head on Heather's shoulder. From the first day we met, I saw her as a mother. So similar to my own, yet even more similar to me. Might be our shared lust for vengeance and stomachs for torture.

"My darling girl, I think the question is, are you going to be okay?" Heather pressed her lips to my hair.

"Yes, as okay as I can be. As you said, it's a sacrifice every working mother makes. To be honest, I know I'm not the best person to take care of Ainsley. I don't have the patience to teach her the way a qualified teacher or nanny can."

Heather laughed, the bullet-resistant glass of the sliding door kept the sound from Ainsley's ears. "Do you have any idea what a wake-up call it was when my two-year-old started reading stories to me and telling jokes? I always thought myself intelligent enough to get by in life, and then along came Aidan. You might not have the patience or know how to teach Ainsley certain things, but you'll teach her to shoot a gun, hand-to-hand combat, evasive driving. Skills she'll need in this world, Fin. Just leave it to Aidan to teach her how to handle a rifle. He didn't build the indoor shooting range for the two of you. Oh, and let him teach her about explosives, and whatever else he has written on the list you two created."

Again, Heather laughed. "You're both amazing parents, and will continue to be so, despite not being with her every second of the day. Now, tell me about your first official investigation working for Fortius."

I turned to Heather and shook my head hard. "No can do, Mom. You're on leave, slash the impromptu nanny, full-time grandmother, and caretaker of a busy one-year-old." I pressed my lips to her cheek. "But, if I need your help, I will ask."

Before I opened the sliding door, Heather spoke, "You won't need my help, my girl. I've got our baby girl, and you've got this investigation in the bag. A murderer is a murderer, no matter where in the world he kills."

At the time neither of us realised how wrong her statement would turn out to be.

Three

Marcel
Saturday, 23 January, 9:47 p.m.

Aidan and Rowan both turned when I stepped into Aidan's office. The smile on Aidan's face, I knew all too well. Not his post-coital smile, but the one he wears when hunting human prey. Perhaps our conversation earlier, before I had left his office to check on Ainsley, reminded him we are, and always will be, stronger when we hunt together.

Rowan held up his hand, and I slapped mine against it. "Told you you'd know what to say to him."

I wrapped my arms around Aidan's waist and pressed my cheek to his chest, his heartbeat strong against my ear. "Perhaps I did some showing and not telling."

My brother-in-law dragged a hand down his face. "I don't need to know that about my brother. Sure, thinking about you like that, now that's – hot."

Aidan cleared his throat. "You showed my wife your penis?"

Despite no longer practising medicine, Aidan preferred to use the correct terms for body parts and never resorted to the crude words his brothers used. *Or me.*

"Rowan's is so small, I wouldn't have seen it even if he had pulled his pants down all the way. Come on, Mr Walker, if you've seen one you've seen them all."

Aidan had seen countless female sex organs the years he practised as an obstetrician and gynaecologist. It never bothered me. This was Aidan's attempt to lighten the mood. When he would much rather lock me in a tower, and commission a dragon to guard me, than allow me out to hunt the person responsible for at least four deaths. Perhaps more.

"I can dismantle a bomb with one hand tied behind my back while blindfolded. I assure you, I showed your wife my tattoo without even giving her a glimpse of what she's missing out on." Rowan winked at me and I couldn't help but snort a laugh.

"Before we sit down to discuss murder, and I'm not talking about yours, Rowan, do you want to tell me what the hell happened between you and Quinn?" I took Aidan's hand and led him to the couch we almost broke hours before. Twice.

I waited for Rowan to answer, knowing he would evade my question. Quinn had done the same when I cornered her before she had left and returned to her undercover assignment.

"My murder?" Rowan took a seat across from the couch. Aidan glanced at me out of the corner of his eye, the exact moment I looked at him. We both grinned. Rowan shot to his feet. "Where's a safe place to sit, on which you didn't have sex since the last time this room was cleaned?"

I rolled my eyes. "The balcony, but we need to discuss our plan of action, so let's say the other chair is safe." I lied, but at least four people had been murdered. This was not the time to remind Rowan that he was all big talk for a man who could count his sexual partners on one hand. The things I know about my brother-in-laws no woman ever should. Then again, our relationship isn't what any other family would term *normal*. Death and destruction surrounded all of us, every single day. Our bond reminded me of the one I had with the members of my squad. When you face war daily, and your own mortality, you form a different connection with those around you.

"You haven't answered my wife, Ro. What happened between you and Quinn?"

Rowan leaned back in the chair and retied his long, dark brown hair at the back of his head. Most women would give anything for hair with a natural curl like his, myself included. The reason he always wore it tied up, or in a despicable man bun, only he knew. I had asked him once, and he mumbled something about 'damn Rob Granger'.

With his hair in place, Rowan looked straight at me. A devilish grin on his face. Mischief played in his dark eyes. "I will answer any and all questions, *if* you rub beeswax on my tattoo."

I took a deep breath and sighed. "Youngest Mr Walker, eldest Mr Walker will skin you alive if you don't stop teasing. Let's be honest, Ro, you won't know what to do if I got down on my knees in front of you, and rubbed that close to your, uhm ... thingy."

Once more Aidan's laughter filled the room. He pressed his mouth to mine and grinned. "Woman, I love your wit."

I grabbed the back of his neck and returned his mouth to mine, forgetting we weren't alone. It wasn't often we could be Aidan and Finley, instead of Daddy and Mommy. Like all parents, we made the most of the time we could steal. When we weren't too tired because the saying 'sleep like a baby' is the biggest lie ever. Whoever said that never had a child. They don't sleep through the night when they cut teeth or go through a growth spurt. I had loved breastfeeding. But doing it every two hours, for an hour because Ainsley used me as a dummy and not just as a walking, talking, breathing constant supply of milk, left me more exhausted than I've ever been. Perhaps the birthday party, and having the entire family over for the day, was getting to me.

I forgot the reason we were in Aidan's office. I called it his office even though command centre would've been a more adequate description. At that moment, it didn't look like it did when Aidan ran an operation. *Why are we here and not in bed? Oh yes – murder.*

"I'll make you a deal. Once I've put a bullet between *this* killer's eyes, you'll answer all of my questions. Don't you dare come with some spiel about the two of you having a history. You've both moved on since your short-lived relationship when you were eighteen. What ever happened, it was recent. Sometime between Christmas and today." I closed my eyes, rubbing my temples.

"You're profiling the wrong thing, Mrs Walker. Focus on the murders. We need to get to bed before Ainsley wakes up at 0500 hours tomorrow morning. Do you accept the terms of the deal, Rowan?"

"There's nothing I won't give Fin, if I can see her pull the trigger on whoever buried two people alive, hacked off a young women's hands, and killed the last victim in a way the medical examiner is unable to determine."

The darkness festering inside me once again flapped her majestic wings. She rose out of slumber as goose bumps rippled across my skin. Without her, I can't hunt those who indulge in their darkest desires. The darkness and I thrive on hunting them – human predators. I rubbed the orca tattoo on my left wrist, a predatory sneer on my face. A groove formed between Rowan's eyes as he stared at me.

Aidan placed a hand on my knee and squeezed. "Fortius welcomes you, Mrs Walker. Are you ready to hunt a non-territorial serial killer?"

I turned to Aidan. The sound of flapping wings seized, the goose bumps remained. "This will be our first time hunting together. Are you ready to stand back and let me be who I am? Are you ready to make any and all of your resources available to me? I need to stop him before he kills again." *Seventeen faces.*

The ringing of Rowan's mobile phone broke the rising tension as Aidan and I stared at each other with raw, unbridled lust. We've never been oblivious to who the other is at our core. Two vigilantes. Although, now we hunted with military precision and more fire power than most of the militaries in the world. Fortius lurks in the grey, waiting, ready to strike in either the black or the white. Our hands not bound by red tape, only the simple laws of what's wrong and what's right. When we can't agree, we put it to a vote. A family. A unit. A warship which will be mine and Aidan's to command once his parents retire at the end of the year.

"Eli, what do you have for us?" Rowan said and turned on his mobile phone's speaker.

"Your hunch paid off. He placed another call ten minutes ago." Eli's words sucked the air out of my lungs.

"Where?" Aidan asked.

"Vienna." The familiar sound of Eli's fingers pounding away at a keyboard in the background.

Rowan lifted his eyes to mine and swallowed hard. "How?"

"He said the bodies will still smoulder by the time the police got there."

I pushed to my feet and paced the length of the coffee table. Aidan lifted his bare feet onto the couch to save his toes. "Bodies? Two victims. This time he killed by burning them. The only reason we know these murders are committed by the same person is because of the phone calls he makes to the police in each city."

A man and a woman were buried alive inside a coffin in Majorca. In Malta he hacked off a woman's hands. The death of the young woman in Budapest remained undetermined. It appeared as if she had died in her sleep. As if any person would willingly go to sleep in the dead of winter in Normafa Park.

My pacing stopped, and I turned to Aidan. "Do you have contacts in the Bundespolizei?"

"Your pronunciation needs work, but I give you ten out of ten for knowing the name of Austria's National Police." Aidan's palm connected with my bum. "Yes, I do. What do you need me to do?"

"I want to see the bodies, and where they were found." I shook my head. "Ainsley, I can't leave her. No way I'm taking her with to hunt down a serial killer. Not until she's at least sixteen and can handle a SIG better than any of us. Eli, is it too early to teach her Krav Maga?"

Eli laughed before Aidan did. "Finley, you're losing focus. Ainsley can stay with us; I can assist with the investigation from anywhere in the world."

Aidan got to his feet and cupped my face in his hands. "My parents are already here, and Mom agreed to take care of Ainsley. This is her home, she's safe here. Not that she won't be with you, Eli, it's just my mother needs to be around Ainsley right now."

"I get it. I saw what Heather did in Columbia, just not in real life. With the matter of Ainsley's care resolved, what do you need from me? I can be there in five minutes."

"For now, keep monitoring any calls made to the police across Europe." Aidan's eyes narrowed. "What is it, Fin?"

I started pacing again and did something which used to freak out my sister. "You killed before Majorca. How many people have you murdered? Why call the police to inform them, especially the couple you buried in Majorca? Each murder is different, why? What are you trying to tell us?" The killer didn't answer.

"Eli, can you send out one of your worm thingies? We need to know whether he has killed before Majorca." I stopped pacing. "Don't limit your search to Europe, include any country that keeps electronic case files of homicides. He may have started on a different continent."

"What are you thinking, Fin?" Rowan asked.

I'm not sure why I asked Eli to expand the search beyond Europe. Something about this killer struck me as odd. To be so brazen to call the police after each murder, he may have started somewhere he thought the police wouldn't catch him. With each murder, his confidence grew.

The couch cushion made no sound as I slumped down and asked Rowan, "Your tattoo artist in Budapest said the guy had sixteen female faces tattooed on his back. Your guy added number seventeen. Why not include the men?"

Four

Marcel
Sunday, 24 January, 8:00 a.m.

A strange sensation wormed itself into my being. Not dread, nor nausea, or fear. Perhaps a mixture of isolation, anticipation, and a growing uneasiness, all of which collided inside me. No matter how hard I tried, I couldn't recall a single word which describes it. With Aidan next to me, I couldn't feel alone, yet knowing my daughter would be thousands of kilometres away broke my heart. My in-laws would take care of Ainsley, lavish her with love and attention while Aidan and I hunted. Our precious, babbling one-year-old hadn't even given us a second glance when we kissed her goodbye. Her focus on her grandfather, as Ryan had made aeroplane noises while feeding her cereal. *Aeroplane equals flying.* Could what I felt be because of my fear of flying?

"We're ready for takeoff," Rowan said. "Fin, you've never flown with me, I promise to make this the best experience of your life and get you over this silly phobia of yours once and for all." He placed a big hand on my shoulder.

"I'm not afraid of flying." Petrified would be a better word, but I needed to downplay it and remind my brother-in-law that I'm a badass. Even more so as this was my first official operation with the family business. To phrase it like that makes us sound like an organised crime syndicate, when in fact, we hunt criminals. After all this time, I was finally in the field with them. At the cost of leaving my daughter behind.

"Sure, you're not. Maybe once we reach cruising altitude, you can come inside the cockpit. You know, have a look around, touch a few things. See the world the way I do, from up front."

"I would love to, but where will you and your co-pilot be?"

Rowan frowned; Aidan laughed. "Don't worry about my wife, Ro. She has enough work to keep her busy for the duration of the flight. You just focus on getting us to Vienna and I'll worry about Finley."

"Okay." Rowan shrugged and headed for the cockpit.

"I can't figure him out. All innuendoes, but when I bat one back at him, he misses it." I fastened my seatbelt and glanced around the interior of the Boeing 787 9 Dreamliner VIP. From the outside it looked like any other, but the interior reminded me of the command centre, which is Aidan's home office.

"If it gets too much for you, we can always renew our mile high club membership." Aidan pressed his lips to my neck.

"Didn't you say I have too much work?"

"That you do. Eli found more unsolved homicide cases. Once we're airborne, we can run through it together."

I turned to Aidan and placed my hand in his as the Dreamliner started to taxi towards the runway. "I will review the case files on my own, and once you've slept a couple of hours, we can discuss it."

"I don't need sleep." The red veins in Aidan's eyes had been there since he brought me my morning coffee. For the first time not wearing a towel wrapped around his waist. To be honest, the SIGs holstered at his thighs might be even sexier.

I ran my hand up his thigh, over the black cargo pants he now wore daily instead of the suit pants he had worn when he brought new life into this world. The thigh holsters were a recent addition, which I hoped would turn into an everyday thing. Aidan lifted my hand to his mouth. He smiled, the same emotion I felt flashed in his eyes. Still, I couldn't put it into words.

"I love you, Aidan Walker. Thank you for allowing me to work again."

"You didn't give me much of a choice. You're rather persuasive when you want to be."

"I'm sorry, my love." I wiped the wetness from my face

with the back of my hand, not releasing his. "This isn't easy for you, but it's time."

Aidan leaned his head back and stared at nothing, memory played on his face. "I need to apologise. For everything I've put you through since the day Ainsley was born."

I understood more than any other person ever could. I told him so.

"That's why I love you, Finley D. Williams-Walker. You understand me like no other person ever has, or ever will. You sense my emotions, as I do yours."

"I think it's part of being married, more so when there are no secrets. We can't go back and undo what happened. I'm here, Ainsley survived. We've been through so much since we met, I think we both forgot we're only human. Despite everything that has happened, bad stuff can still happen to us."

If the accident had been any further from the hospital, we would've lost Ainsley that day. Neither of us would've survived losing another child. Least of all Aidan, when he had already lost one child because of a car crash. It was a miracle Ainsley survived when my placenta had ruptured from the impact of the head on collision. Going against protocol, Aidan delivered her, as Dr Brown had been busy with another patient. The paramedics had called him en route to the hospital, despite me begging them not to. They knew Dr Walker from the years he had worked in the ER. Part respect, part fear of his wrath, had made them go against my wishes. They saved my daughter's life by ignoring my pleas to first find out if she was okay before we called Aidan.

On his fortieth birthday, Aidan held his daughter for the first time.

"Why are you crying?" Aidan wiped my cheeks with the back of his fingers.

I shook my head, but kept my eyes on his. "We've been through so much. I'm beginning to think things will never be easy for us. There will always be some sort of enemy around every corner, and me going into the field puts our life in even more danger."

Aidan smiled, the sweetest smile I've ever seen on his face. "I will do everything, and anything within my power, to keep both my girls safe."

He had. Our home, in the middle of the street, can withstand an aerial strike, even an explosion. Every room a panic room. Aidan had gone so far as to have my new G-Class reinforced with steel bars, the windows and tyres bullet resistant. I swear if it would've looked less conspicuous driving it around Marcel, he would've bought me a Gurkha, or a Humvee. At one time I suspected to see a tank drive through our gate. As with everything else, we overcame, together. Even seeing Dr James for therapy sessions, together. Here we were, husband and wife, parents to the only child we can ever have. The future leaders of an organisation I never even knew existed, as most of the world doesn't, including some presidents, and heads of state.

"Why didn't you sleep last night?" His cheek warm against my palm.

"Keeping my girls safe. You have a meeting with the detective assigned to the Vienna murders first thing tomorrow morning. We're at cruising altitude."

As always, Aidan kept my mind busy, and my focus off my irrational fear of flying. I wondered if this time, knowing the pilot helped a little. No, it was all down to the magnificent man I get to call my own.

"Why don't you sleep while I work through what Eli found since we spoke last night? If you don't want to leave me to go sleep on the bed, at least rest your head on my lap."

Aidan lowered the overhead screens and handed me the controls. He showed me how to use it, knowing I would wake him up by throwing it across the cabin when I failed to get it to do what I wanted.

His hair soft between my fingers, his breathing calmed, and I got to work. The first time I hunted a serial killer since the Sophia Blake case. Of course, Quinn and I hunted down the men who had raped the young women of Pepper Gorge. Quinn had all the fun taking them out, while I wasn't allowed to join in. Aidan refused his pregnant wife the privilege of taking the lives of monsters masquerading as upstanding citizens in their countries. Aidan Walker is a party pooper, but he loves me, and I him.

Eli had found twenty-five unsolved murder cases in different countries across the world. I read every file, memorised the crime scene photos, and made notes on my mobile phone as I didn't want to disturb Aidan by getting up to search for a pen and paper. I prefer old school ways to make sense of the depravity of those who indulge in their darkest fantasies.

Twenty-five unsolved murder cases. Seventeen female faces tattooed on our unsub's back. Why did our unidentified subject not get the faces of his male victims inked into his skin?

Rowan took a seat next to me and stared at the crime scene photo displayed on the overhead screen. "What's the deal with the snakes and the leaves?" he whispered, in attempt not to wake Aidan.

Without opening his eyes, I knew Aidan was awake. I checked the time to destination at the bottom of the screen – Aidan had slept for five hours. Five hours I spent trying to understand the violence captured in the crime scene photos. Death is never pretty, even when the victims' bodies showed no visible signs of trauma. Not considering those who were burned.

I continued playing with Aidan's hair, but turned to Rowan. "I have a theory but need more time before I share it with the team."

"Do you think all the cases Eli found are the work of our unsub?" Aidan asked, his voice alert.

"No. Unless he hid any earlier victims better or didn't contact the local police. My professional opinion? The murder in Playa del Carmen was his first. Or perhaps he perfected his MO before he headed there and didn't bother with the calls. But I think our killer was born this cocky. He called the Policía Federal Ministerial because he thought he had a better chance of getting away with murder there. He travelled to Mexico with the sole purpose of ending a young woman's life. The dress was a size too big for her, but the detail he put into it is meticulous."

Aidan got to his feet and returned with two coffees and handed Rowan a bottle of water. "I scanned through the case files on the way to the airport. Phyllobates terribilis are endemic to the Pacific coast of Columbia; they aren't found in Mexico. In captivity they lose toxicity and are endangered."

"Did you research golden poison frogs during the short drive as well?" I smiled before taking a sip of the delicious caffeine.

Aidan stared down at me, rolling his shoulders without spilling a drop from his mug. "No. Learned about them when I was five."

With even ten percent of his eidetic memory, life would be much easier for me. Aidan Walker is a fountain of knowledge and I knew, staring up at a man more handsome than he is brilliant, that my thirst for him will never be quenched.

"The question is – how did our killer get the poison from Columbia to Mexico?"

I placed the mug down and started pacing around the cabin. "You're either a pilot, a flight attendant, or you work on a cruise ship. Although, the murders in Budapest and Vienna shoots that theory out of the water. Perhaps you're on vacation now."

"Why a cruise ship?" Rowan asked, leaning forward and resting his elbows on his knees.

"Every murder I suspect he's responsible for has been in a port city, except Budapest and Vienna."

"Of the twenty-five Eli has found, how many do you think is his work?" Aidan watched as I moved around the cabin.

"Seventeen cases, make it eighteen if we include the Vienna murders. Eighteen cases, twenty-four victims. The other eight murders aren't his. The victims are older, and the crime scenes, or rather stagings, don't have his touch. I can't call it a signature, not yet. Each murder is different, but it isn't. It's as if he cycles through them."

Rowan stood and stretched. "What do you mean he cycles through them?"

A rhythm, a flow. "To give you a definite answer, I need to go old school and write this down. Where on this futuristic aircraft might I find good old-fashioned pen and paper?"

Aidan reached into his backpack and handed me what I needed. He asked Rowan to join him in the onboard kitchen and left me to create an A4 sized murder board. Some call it a crazy wall, I prefer a more adequate description.

Five

Vienna, Austria
Sunday, 24 January, 10:00 p.m.

It shouldn't have surprised me when we landed at a military base. Neither should it have come as a surprise when we walked through the base with our weapons visible. Rowan greeted the man who met us as we stepped off the aeroplane. Despite not understanding much of their conversation, it sounded like they were talking the way friends do.

The first chance I got, I asked, "What the hell just happened?"

"What do you mean?" Rowan glanced at me in the rear-view mirror and returned his eyes to the road. The black SUV waited for us on arrival.

"People don't just land on a military base and walk through better armed than any of the soldiers. Who owes you what favour?"

Aidan, riding shotgun, turned to me. "We foiled the kidnapping of the previous Chancellor's family while they were on vacation in Egypt. His gratitude is passed down to every Chancellor who follows him. The head of Austria is one of very few in his or her position who are aware of our existence."

I laughed aloud. "How dare you look your wife in the eyes and lie to me? There was no attempted kidnapping."

Mischief played in Aidan's eyes, but his face remained serious. "The family returned unharmed to Austria after seeing the pyramids, riding camels, and scuba diving in the Red Sea."

"You people crossed the line there, and Ryan is so proud of sticking to the grey." I snorted a laugh and stared out the window, seeing Vienna for the first time. Why our killer chose this time of year, I didn't understand. It was freezing. Unless he came for the snow, which was breathtaking. Perhaps a bad choice of words, as that's what the killer had done – taking the last breaths of two people. No, he ended the lives of twenty-four human beings.

"You people? Fin, you're one of us now. Everything we do is for the greater good. We live by the same rules you do – no matter what, as long as the end justifies the means." This time Rowan kept his eyes on the road.

I reached forward and placed my hand on his shoulder. "Calm down, Ro. This is a lot to take in. I've seen you work." The laughter bubbling out of me, not joyful. "I'm one of the people you've saved. Twice, if we consider the matter none of us ever speak about."

Rowan covered my hand with his. "You miss Ainsley. This killer is different and as you mentioned before, the chance of him still being in Vienna is slim."

I missed my daughter. The ache in my heart the worst I've ever experienced. As I stared out at the passing storefronts, and the snow falling on the other side of the window, only one thought came to mind. *The sooner I catch this killer, the sooner I can hold my precious child.* A luxury the victims' parents will never have again. No matter how much I longed to hear Ainsley laugh, or watch her try to walk on her own, hunting down a serial killer was worth the stabbing sensation in my heart. I had promised to make the world a better place for her, and by being on the other side of the world meant I kept my word. I had to stop more innocent people from being murdered and seek justice for those who already died at his hand.

Where the killer would strike next was anyone's guess. Frustration and anger sparred inside me; I glanced down at the SIG holstered at my right hip. *How many bullets will I have to fire before the killer takes his last breath?* No way I would allow him to rot in prison for the remainder of his natural life. In which of the seventeen countries would he serve his time?

***

For the duration of our time in Vienna, we stayed in an apartment utilised whenever Fortius operatives need a place to stay. A safe house. I had learned a long time ago to stop asking questions when it came to how my in-laws acquired their wealth and resources. The story remained the same – someone owed them a favour, a past acquaintance, shares in a hotel Heather had inherited from her parents, payment for rescuing a high-profile hostage, or helping a government take down an enemy without causing an international incident.

A substantial amount of their wealth came from Heather's inheritance. Both Heather and Ryan had worked hard to grow the companies she took control of after her father's death, and kept using it to better the world. Of course, there were also the times they took what they needed from the crime syndicates, cartels, and individuals they took down. Money, weapons, whatever they needed, the rest destroyed in order to keep it out of the wrong hands. *We* operate in the grey. Rather in our hands than those who will use it to destroy the lives of innocent people.

Rowan walked out of the bathroom, his hair hung past his shoulders, even more of an envy-inducing curl when wet. He caught me watching him and tied it at the back of his head, and winked at me. "Are you ever going to accept it has to be long, but I don't need to enjoy wearing it down?"

"When it's down, you appear even more formidable, scary even, despite you being a marshmallow on the inside."

"And that, my dear, is the point. When are you going to share your little murder page with us?" Rowan laughed.

"She's armed to the teeth. Don't mock her." Aidan pressed his lips to my hair and placed a plate in front of me on the dining table.

I didn't want to eat, but I forced myself to. This killer wasn't making it easy for me, and I suspected he left Vienna soon after informing the Bundespolizei of his most recent murders. First thing the following morning I would meet with the detective assigned to the case and see the bodies of the two victims.

I wish it would be the first time I saw human beings burned beyond recognition. *War spares you nothing.*

Aidan and I tried to do a video call with Ainsley before turning in for the night. She couldn't care less about our faces and tried to grab the mobile phone from Heather's hand to taste it. Heather said their day was going well. She laughed when she mentioned Ainsley didn't even ask for us once. It might be a good thing our daughter didn't realise her parents weren't home. At least Ainsley was having more fun than her mother. An elusive international serial killer – who killed following a distinct pattern Aidan and I had found – sucked the joy right out of me. Although, the darkness shivered with anticipation.

A killer like this one wasn't found in any textbook. Perhaps when he took his last breath, I might write a paper on him, in case there were more like him. I doubted it even as the thought came to mind. I couldn't write a paper, not without alerting the world to our existence. Fortius doesn't exist, which means neither do I.

Mr Walker and I both knew sleep wouldn't come easy; our bodies still ran on Marcel time. However, we perfected the art of tiring each other out. For Rowan's sake, I hoped the rooms were soundproof. If not, he wouldn't be able to look either of us in the eye over breakfast.

Six

Vienna, Austria
Monday, 25 January, 7:00 a.m.

Rowan dropped us off at the Medical University of Vienna and said he would be back before we were done. The wind burned my skin and made my eyes water. Not to mention my nose's reaction. I tried my best not to look as cold as I felt, Aidan moved behind me to block the wind. As we stepped through the morgue's front doors, I removed the layers of clothing and thanked the detective for the coffee she placed on the table.

Aidan's accent flawless as he spoke and laughed with Detective Wagner, while I warmed myself with the coffee and tried my best to appear as if I followed their conversation. The caffeine welcome; jetlag had never been my friend.

Even though Aidan and I had made a superb attempt at tiring each other out the previous night, it only made us hungry. Rowan hadn't been in the apartment when we went in search of the leftovers from dinner.

Detective Wagner pulled out a chair across the table and nodded. Younger than I expected a homicide detective to be, or perhaps her anti-wrinkle creams worked better than mine. Her dark hair tied in a tight bun at the nape of her neck. I would've thought her an attorney if we were to pass each other on the street.

"We have identified the bodies. The female victim is twenty-two-year-old Dana Ichilov. An Israeli national, here on a student visa studying at Universität Wien. The male victim is Franz Brandstätter, twenty-six. He planned to emigrate to Canada. We identified him through his fingerprints, for the Canadian criminal record check."

"It's a sad irony," Aidan said and reached for my hand under the table. "Brandstätter sounds like fire starter, but it means fire city, implying a city worker."

"Your German is good." Detective Wagner smiled at my husband.

"How did you identify Dana Ichilov?" I asked. "I thought the bodies were burnt beyond recognition."

Detective Wagner gave a stiff nod. "Yes, they were. As you will see when we go to the autopsy room, Franz's right hand isn't burnt. It stuck out of a hole the killer made in the drum. We suspect, for ventilation for the fire, not the victims. Miss Ichilov, we identified through the serial number on the plate in her skull. She was in a motorcycle accident four years ago."

"Did you know Herr Brandstätter?" I brought the mug to my lips and studied her over the rim.

"Nein." Detective Wagner shifted in her seat.

Next to me Aidan remained quiet, so I continued. "No? You referred to the female victim as Miss Ichilov but called Herr Brandstätter – Franz. It seems personal to call a murder victim by his first name, *if* you weren't *freunde*." The few German words I knew came in handy. Aidan would correct my pronunciation later and thank me for not including swear words to any of the questions I directed at Detective Wagner. One slipped out when I stood next to the bodies.

Aidan and I followed Detective Wagner to the autopsy room. I considered asking her again about the nature of her relationship with *Franz*, but it didn't matter. This killer was mine to hunt and bring to justice, not hers. No point in suggesting she recuse herself from a case which would lead nowhere. The killer was long gone.

Over the years I've witnessed more than enough death, in various forms, but a burnt body, or a floater, is something I doubt anyone can ever get used to. I took a deep breath before we stepped through the doors of the autopsy room, knowing the bodies were already waiting for us. The smell familiar, yet different, to the burn victims I had seen during the war.

I wondered what type of fire exhilarant the killer used, and how long it would take the forensic laboratory to answer this question. Perhaps we would also have left Vienna by then, hopefully heading home and not to see more victims.

As Detective Wagner had said, Franz Brandstätter's right hand was the only part the flames didn't touch. Dana Ichilov hadn't been as lucky. The medical examiner confirmed what I already knew – both victims were alive when they were forced into the 200 litre drums. They had breathed in the flames, their lungs burnt. I asked permission to take my own photos of the bodies, and the drums standing in a corner of the room. With no serial numbers, we couldn't trace where the killer purchased the steel drums. I doubt he brought it on a flight in his carry-on.

Aidan thanked the medical examiner and Detective Wagner for their time, and for sharing details about the case with two detectives from a country he didn't name. They didn't ask any questions, and we offered them no lies. Someone high up gave them explicit instructions that any information they uncovered during their respective investigations be shared with us.

Rowan waited for us where he dropped us off earlier and asked, "Where to?"

"Meierei im Stadtpark," Aidan said. His accent made my spine tingle for all the right reasons and chased away the images of the two bodies which were added to the reel of my mind.

Rowan glanced at me in the rear-view mirror. "Can you eat after what you just saw?"

"You have no idea who I am, do you?" I smiled at him.

"Apart from the perfect woman for me?"

Aidan punched his brother's shoulder; my laughter filled the SUV. It's a strange world we live in, and those who face death and destruction every day. As Aidan had said years before, compartmentalising is the best way to cope.

"After breakfast we need to find the local tattoo artist our unsub visited. He wouldn't have left without adding Dana Ichilov's face to his back. Also, we need to find out how the killer finds his victims, not just the two here. From what I've read, nothing indicates the male and female victims were acquainted. Their paths never crossed. Why kill them together? Why them?"

At the exact moment Rowan glanced in the rear-view mirror, Aidan stared at the side mirror. "Do you think they realise they're being followed?" Aidan removed the SIG from his thigh holster and checked the chamber.

The atmosphere inside the SUV became electric. Deep inside me, the darkness lifted her head. A predatory grin spread across my face.

We were being hunted.

Seven

Vienna, Austria
Monday, 25 January, 9:18 a.m.

Rowan yanked the elastic band from his hair and slammed his palm against the steering wheel. "I'm going to kill him." The controlled anger in his voice caught me off-guard.

"Who?" I asked.

"First Ludwig Schneider, and then Liam Walker." Rowan's thumb played over a mobile phone I never saw him use before. He spoke too fast in German for me to follow what he said. The only words I caught – Anna and Maria.

"Where's Liam?" Aidan's voice low and hard.

"With Maria."

Aidan swore. *Never a good sign.* I placed my hand on his shoulder, grateful to feel the bulletproof vest snug against his body. Mine didn't make me itch; I barely even knew it was there.

"What's the plan?" I've never been in a position like this before, not with them. Despite all my years in the military, and the time I spent as the Hangwoman, in this world of covert operations I was as green as one newbie operative can be.

"Keep you safe and ensure Theo doesn't kill Liam before I get my hands around his neck." Rowan's knuckles turned white as he gripped the steering wheel. He kept driving at the same speed he had since we left the Medical University of Vienna, except when he adhered to the traffic laws.

"As soon as we get to the restaurant, you go to the ladies' room and you'll stay there until I come for you." Aidan said to me, keeping his eyes on the side mirror.

No deal. I wanted in on the action. It had been far too long since I last gifted anyone with a hollow-point bullet. Whatever trouble Liam got himself into, I might just thank him later. "No."

"Finley, that's a direct order from your commanding officer. As your husband, one of us has to return to Ainsley."

Rowan growled. "If Liam followed orders, we wouldn't be in this mess."

"Once the situation is contained, I will deal with him." Aidan reached back and placed his hand on my knee without taking his eyes off the road. "I need you safe."

"Yes sir." This wasn't the time to fight with my husband, or Fortius' second in command. If bullets started flying, as I expected they would, nothing could stop me from protecting my Aidan. Not even defying his direct order, or the consequences of doing so.

The cold didn't register. My senses were in overdrive. Flanked by Aidan, and whoever Rowan was when he wore his hair down, we walked through the park towards the restaurant. It would've been easy to take us out as we made our way through the park, but Rowan knew a shortcut and I hoped whoever followed us was too dumb to think of following the footprints we left in the snow.

Aidan palmed my bum and ordered me to wait in the restroom as we walked into the restaurant. A quick scan of the ten patrons seated inside, and I knew why we weren't gunned down while we made the trek through the park. Whoever followed us had people waiting inside the restaurant. People think they don't give off certain tells, but it screams for attention the harder they try to hide it.

I didn't have time to tell Aidan there were more than the two men he and Rowan saw in the car which had followed us.

No, I didn't follow Aidan's instruction. But I stayed out of sight and kept my eyes on the four men who tried their best not to stare at my husband and brother-in-law.

Rowan nodded at the waitress and returned his attention to Aidan, who didn't remove his newsboy cap. Since he put it on earlier that morning, I wanted to do many things to him. Things I couldn't do in a morgue or being followed by an enemy I had no prior knowledge of. Or with his brother in the vehicle. This wasn't the time to wonder why I found that silly hat so attractive on him. *Liam, what did you do?*

I removed the SIG and attached the suppressor. With my shoulder pressed against the wall, I waited. My heartbeat in my ears, my hands remained steady.

Aidan and Rowan shot to their feet. Their chairs crashed to the floor. Time stood still. A single bullet from each of their guns; both found their mark.

Movement to my right. Instinct.

I stepped forward, lifting the SIG in one fluid motion. Two pops. Two men fell, their HK433s never fired a single round.

Aidan turned to me; emotions duelled in his eyes. I shrugged, realizing the expression on my face resembled that of an apex predator. *I'm back*.

Hastened movement in the corner of my right eye. I sighted down the barrel of my gun. And I lowered my weapon as recognition slammed into me. *Detective Wagner.*

Rowan walked over to her, holstering his weapon. They stood too close to each other. The proximity of their bodies mirrored mine and Aidan's as he came to stand next to me.

He slid his hand down my back and squeezed my bum. "Is it weird that I'm really turned on right now?"

I glanced down at his crotch and stepped in front of him. "You need to control my not-in-the-least-little, friend. Detective Wagner is heading this way and I don't want her to realise she's been sleeping with the wrong brother."

Behind me, Aidan drew a deep breath. "We'll discuss you defying my direct order later."

"Thank me now for saving your life. And spank me later for defying your order. What's done is done."

Detective Wagner came to an abrupt halt, her hands behind

her back. I didn't give her a chance to talk. "Those two over there, aren't yours, are they?" I shot my chin out towards the bodies of the two men I shot.

"Nein. Lucky for you." She turned to Rowan. "They are with you?"

"Yes, Anna." Rowan smiled down at her. "Where's Ludwig?"

"Being taken to the base, as you requested."

"And Theo?" Rowan asked.

"Er ist tot," Detective Wagner said, and nodded before she turned on her heals, her hands remained behind her back.

Rowan followed her, and I studied them as they spoke. I couldn't hear a word, but the tension between them struck me as odd. It was far more than us killing four criminals in her city. Or giving her something to do while I returned my focus to hunting down a serial killer. First, we needed to deal with Liam.

Eight

Vienna, Austria
Monday, 25 January, 10:42 a.m.

Liam shot to his feet as we boarded the aeroplane. He moved towards me but stepped back as Aidan and Rowan were on my six.

"Sit." Aidan ordered and threw his coat on a chair before disappearing into the kitchen.

Unsure of what to do, I checked my phone for messages and sent Heather a 'thank you' message for the photo she sent of Ainsley. Our daughter had slept while Aidan and I were in danger. Neither of us would lose any sleep over taking lives. Rowan had told us who they were, and yet again, by pulling the trigger we made the world a better place.

Rowan didn't say a word when Liam spoke to him. The tension between them building to fist-punching point. Instead, Rowan tied his hair at the back of his head and told me he needed to complete his preflight inspection. He trusted no one to do it for him, and the thought put me a little more at ease knowing we would soon take to the sky. Where we were headed, I didn't know. No point in staying in a city when the killer was no longer there.

As I wondered where he went, I received a text message from Eli. I pulled on my coat and went looking for Rowan. Our flight plan had just been confirmed. *Twenty-five.*

The wind chill factor made my decision for me, and I returned to the warmth of the aeroplane. Liam sat with his head in his hands, while Aidan towered over him with his arms crossed over his chest. "Your coffee might be cold," Aidan said without looking at me.

I made myself a fresh cup and took a seat next to Fortius' second in command. It wasn't Liam's eldest brother talking to him. "Your recklessness not only put my wife in danger, but also Rowan and me. Not to mention the years Rowan has spent creating this cover. The things he had to do to become Rob Granger. You better hope you didn't blow it for him, Liam. You're benched until I decide what your punishment will be."

Liam opened his mouth, but Aidan held up a hand. "Dad's on leave, which leaves me in full control of Fortius. You'll be lucky if you still have a position with us once I've informed Dad of what you've done. It's as if you *want* to screw up, Liam. Dad has been more than patient with you. I won't be. So, either get your ass in line or you'll find yourself unemployed. I won't risk my team's safety because you think with your penis."

I covered my mouth, trying to hide the smile. Somehow the way Aidan used the biological word, instead of what the rest of us would've said, made a harder impact. Liam lowered his eyes to his shoes. "I'm sorry."

"You're sorry?" Rowan growled, stepping forward and yanking off his coat. He tossed it on top of Aidan's and stared at Liam.

The moment I caught sight of Rowan's hands clenching, I stood. "Rowan, sit down before you beat your brother to death. Commander Walker, if I may?" I asked Aidan.

"The floor is yours, Fin, don't hold back."

I didn't. My handprint would've been visible for hours if not for the stubble on Liam's face. "Aidan, *your brother*, was almost killed today because whoever followed us mistook him for you. Your niece could've lost one or both of her parents. And what about Rowan? *Your* brother, Liam. Your family."

The similarities between Aidan and Liam were striking at a distance, but there was no mistaking them up close. Aidan's eyes the colour of the sky after a storm, his hair a sun kissed brown. Liam's hair darker, his eyes the same rich brown as their mother's. Aidan five centimetres taller than Liam, but shorter than Nathan and Rowan. Although Rowan's DNA wasn't that of his brothers, he's more Walker than Liam ever tried to be.

"You chose to leave the military and join the family organisation. You, Liam. No one made the decision for you. Now, I don't know what the hell you did to put a target on my husband's back, or threaten Rowan's cover. The fact is – you screwed up. Is that woman the reason you missed your niece's first birthday? No one-night stand, or month-long fling – whatever – comes before your family. Ever." I paced, waiting for him to answer.

"I had to get Maria away from Theo. She doesn't deserve the way he treats her."

Rowan dragged a hand down his face. "By bringing her home? Liam, this is the first place they looked for her. And you, idiot, took her out to dinner. I saw you last night."

"This is about Anna, isn't it?" Liam lifted his eyes to Rowan's. "She's a brunette, ergo mine."

Rowan's nostrils flared as he rolled his shoulders, shaking his head. "Your dick is going to get you killed. I'm done with you, Liam. You will never work with me again."

"Not with you, never *with* you. Always *under* your command." Liam stood and headed for the kitchen. He returned with two bottles of water, tossing one towards Rowan. Liam didn't move fast enough, the bottle crashed into his face. "What the hell, Ro?"

"You were under my command. My operation. One I've been running for years. All you had to do was provide back-up *if* necessary. Not abduct Theo's wife, after screwing her."

"Language," Aidan said.

Rowan and I both frowned as we looked at him. "It's not like Liam made love to her, and I think Rowan meant abducting her screwed her chances of survival."

"No, but thanks for trying, Fin." Rowan's smile one of defeat.

"Theo's dead. Anna's team took him out, and I'm sure they'll now find the evidence to prove he murdered his first wife." Liam rubbed where the water bottle had connected with his forehead.

"Theo might be dead, but you didn't listen when I told you how his gang works. His second in command is already out looking for Maria."

"She'll be fine, I bought her a train ticket to Bucharest."

"Maria isn't going to Bucharest. She's going to spend the rest of her life in prison for drug trafficking. You think you saved a damsel in distress, she's as bad as Theo. It won't surprise me if Anna finds proof that Maria was complicit in the murder of Theo's first wife. After all, at the time she was his mistress. *One* of them."

Liam shook his head. "No, Maria's a victim in all of this."

Rowan laughed, his eyes turning darker. "No, you're too gullible for undercover operations. All you had to do was go to the party with me and keep Maria busy while I made a deal with Theo. Dammit Liam, Anna was right there with you. For once in your life couldn't you have just talked to a woman instead of..." He glanced at me and I burst out laughing.

"Everybody calm down." I carried the coffee mugs to the kitchen and picked up the bottle of water Rowan threw at Liam's face as I returned. The men still glared at each other. The controlled calm on Aidan's face I knew hid his true emotions.

"Boys, listen up. Rowan, is your cover blown?"

"I don't know. It depends how fast Anna and the Bundespolizei can arrest the members of Theo's gang. To call them a syndicate is a grave exaggeration."

"Okay. Here is an idea: kill Ludwig Schneider. Put it out there that you don't take it lightly when one of your employees sleeps with your clients' wives, girlfriends, or whatever." I walked over to Rowan and placed my hands on his arms. "Make it a spectacular and grim death. It can be your statement to the world that Rob Granger is not to be messed with."

"That reputation is solid." An unknown sadness flashed in his eyes but he smiled and hugged me. "Thank you for having our backs today."

"Of course, there's nothing I won't do for my family. Why do you think I slapped Liam? It's time he understands what a privilege it is to be a Walker and a part of Fortius."

To my back Liam said, "I'm sorry, Fin. For missing Ainsley's birthday, for screwing up yet again."

I turned to him, understanding why he had been a decorated soldier, but couldn't find his feet in Fortius. The huge chip on his shoulder would prevent him from doing so, and I wanted to help him get rid of it once and for all. "Stop saying you're sorry. Change your behaviour. You took orders while you served, it shouldn't matter now if those orders come from your younger brother. In Fortius, Rowan's your superior."

"What you're saying is one should never defy a direct order?" Aidan's left eyebrow raised as he turned in his seat to look at me.

I walked over to Aidan and dropped to my knees between his legs. "Thank me for saving your life."

He pushed his fingers through my hair and brought my mouth to his. "Later," he murmured.

I rose and turned to Liam. "Your stunt has wasted hours of our time hunting down an international serial killer. Rowan, are we ready for takeoff?"

"Yes, ma'am. One day, Fin, I want a wife just like you. If Aidan won't thank you, I will." He winked before heading to the cockpit.

"Where are we headed?" Aidan asked as I fastened my seatbelt.

"Zurich. His victim count now stands at twenty-five."

Nine

Zurich, Switzerland
Monday, 25 January, 1:22 p.m.

From Dübendorf Air Base we drove to Zurich. I booked us two suites at Baur au Lac, while Aidan contacted the local operative to help us track down the detective assigned to the most recent murder case. I considered giving the killer a nickname, but I've always been against the idea of giving them a name the media uses to sell sensationalized stories. It isn't stories when people are brutally murdered, and it doesn't matter what the final victim count is. Until I could call him by his actual name, I continued referring to him as the serial killer, or killer.

Rowan wasn't happy when I told him he would share a suite with Liam. Instead, he proposed we book Liam on the longest possible flight back to Marcel. I refused. Until word got around of Ludwig Schneider's death, I couldn't risk having Liam in the same city as my daughter, or my sister and nephew.

While Aidan showered, I stared at my murder board. Its puny size mocked me, as did my inability to profile this killer. I checked the time on my mobile phone and smiled at the image I chose for the wallpaper – Aidan and Ainsley. Their eyes the same, but where her red hair came from was a mystery. If not for the security measures on my phone, I wouldn't have something so personal on it. Without my retina, it can't be unlocked. Not even if my eye is removed or my last breath taken.

A soft knock on the door brought my mind back to Zurich. In the span of two days, I went from my daughter's birthday party to Vienna and now Zurich. I opened the door to find

Rowan, anger pulsing off of him. I stepped back to let him in.

"Where's Aidan?" he asked before slumping down on the couch.

I walked to the doors leading to the balcony and gazed out over Schanzengraben canal. No swans, despite there being no snowflakes in sight. "What happened in Vienna?"

"You were there."

I turned to my brother-in-law, a man I grew to love as if we shared the same blood. "I'm not one of your brothers, Ro. Let me in."

Rowan shook his head but kept his eyes on mine. "Anna's number five."

I understood the implication. Rowan can count his sexual partners on one hand, but he only ever loved one.

He leaned back on the couch and stared up at the ceiling. "I know which number she is, but Liam has no idea. The fact that he doesn't understand why that bothers me, scares me, for him. I get why he has hated me since we were both in diapers, but since joining Fortius he's different."

"Liam doesn't hate you." I sat down next to Rowan and leaned my head against his shoulder. "He hates himself. I'll make it my personal mission to find the root of his hatred and help him deal with it."

Rowan pressed his lips to my hair. "Thank you for your willingness to try, but don't take it personally if you can't get through to him."

"You underestimate my power, Ro. I understand Liam better than you think. A long time ago I was him. Lived in my sister's shadow all my life, but once I joined the army, all that changed. Liam needs to see his worth within the family, and sooner or later he'll find a woman he won't be able to toy with."

Rowan laughed, the sound warm and familiar. "I can't wait for the day he falls in love again. He's doing all of this because she chose me. Liam's afraid of women he can become serious about because he doesn't want to get his heart broken again.

It's been almost two decades; I can't believe it still bothers him."

I made a deal but was in the mood to probe. "When last did you and Quinn have sex? The tension between the two of you on Saturday spoke volumes. By the way, leave the profiling to me. If you don't, I might be out of a job."

Rowan placed his arm around my shoulder and hugged me to him. "Do you see a bullet between the killer's eyes?"

Worth a shot. At least I came to the correct conclusion. "Speaking of, the tattoo artist you met last night in Vienna, does he also have a criminal record?"

"Yes. The unsub knows who to go to, not only for their artistic skills, but people who'll be reluctant to go to the police. Janos has been an invaluable informant to me over the years, and even though he's out of the game, he knows what goes on in Hungary's underworld."

I kissed Rowan's cheek and stood; Aidan came into the living room wearing nothing but a towel. "I'll get dressed, didn't expect company."

"Sorry, bro, I'm either here or strangling Liam. If I have to listen to him say Maria is innocent one more time, I will snap. Dammit, I have footage of her taking a delivery from Theo's main fentanyl supplier. The world's a better place with Theo dead and Maria incarcerated. Although, she won't be for long. Theo's men will find a way to get to her."

"How does he know who to go to?" Both brothers looked at me, so I elaborated. "Our unsub, he goes to tattoo artists who have criminal records. Janos was incarcerated as a teenager, got out before his twenty-first birthday. He's been living on the straight and narrow ever since."

"We might be looking for a hacker." Rowan offered.

Aidan closed the bedroom doors and returned dressed in more clothes than I wanted him in. Perhaps the newsboy cap, and nothing else. I shelved that request for later. He was about to add something that I hadn't considered yet.

"A pilot. Someone who works on a cruise ship. A

businessman who travelled to all nineteen countries for work. We've considered these possibilities, but what if our unsub has extensive financial means? An inheritance, or he has a lucrative business with a CEO or MD who runs the day-to-day operations, leaving him with time to indulge in his fantasies."

"We need Eli's help," I said. Aidan retrieved his mobile phone from the bedroom and called Eli.

"What was Theo going to buy from you?" I asked Rowan.

Rowan stood and walked to the minibar. He removed three small bottles and emptied each in a crystal tumbler. He added ice to mine and his, leaving Aidan's neat. He held the tumbler out towards me, and I sipped the Johnny Walker Blue Label, savouring the taste of my beloved liquid Walker.

"It doesn't matter anymore." Rowan lifted the tumbler to his lips.

"Humour me. And what party?"

"The party is a story for another day, and *party* isn't the best word to describe it. Theo wanted long-range rifles."

The whiskey lodged in my throat; I swallowed hard and ignored the burn. "Your cover is as an arms dealer?" Rowan shrugged, but the wink he gave me confirmed it. "So, this *party*, what is it if not a party?"

Rowan drained the remaining content in the tumbler. Ice clinked as he placed it down and refilled it. "Let's just say, while we talked business, a woman went down on Theo's business. And there I sat, watching her head bop up and down, and tried to negotiate a price in between his moans." I gagged. "That's how I felt."

"Okay, so he's allowed to do whatever he wants, but his wife isn't? Did Liam sleep with her at the party, event, sex-whatever?"

"Yes, and with Anna. Same time." Rowan lifted his tumbler into the air. "He claims he and Anna did it to gain Maria's trust. Anna has been trying to find evidence of Theo's dealings for years, but she is who she is. She had a brief affair with your murder victim in Vienna, after she learned about her husband's infidelities."

"He's a few years younger than she is. I can understand why she doesn't want anyone to learn about their past. If he's her ex-lover, with him leaving for Canada, and being found with a woman younger than her, it puts Anna straight at the top of the list of suspects. Means, motive, and opportunity. She has all three."

"Yes, well, it's all in the past now. As is she in mine."

I marched up to him and wrapped my arms around his waist. "You will find your fairy, Rowan. I promise you."

He hugged me back. "Aidan told you about that?"

"Of course, it's sweet."

"Do you two want a room?" Aidan asked. "Eli's running with the information and will get back to us as soon as he finds something."

I released my hold on Rowan and turned to Aidan. "What if he travels on different passports?"

"I've asked Eli to run facial recognition of all the footage he can access at any ports, or points of entry."

The rhythm of the murders bugged me. There was something there and I couldn't figure it out. If only the hotel had an indoor shooting range instead of a gym and spa. I asked Aidan for permission to shoot something in the room, he denied my request.

One, one, two. One, one, two.

Ten

Zurich, Switzerland
Monday, 25 January, 4:35 p.m.

If the killer stuck to his pattern, I knew what the local forensic laboratory would find once they conducted a toxicology screen. Victims one, seven, and thirteen all died the same way – toxin from the golden poison frog. The last excruciating minutes of the women's lives had been spent wearing the same dress. The killer stuck to the same six ways of taking lives, not once deviating from this pattern. I stared at Aidan as he stood motionless in front of the television; his back offered me no answers. The sight of his gluteus maximus in his dark blue jeans made me wish we were alone, but it was better for Rowan to be with us rather than strangling the other Walker brother. Nathan the most stable of the three Walkers I didn't call my husband.

Rowan stood to open the door and cursed under his breath when Liam walked in. I wasn't in the mood for more of their verbal punches, and even less for cleaning up blood. Aidan turned to me. The look in his eyes said he felt the same way.

"When can I see the victim's body?" I asked, trying to remind everyone we weren't in Zurich for the fun of it.

Aidan shook his head. "Not going to happen. I can get you copies of the crime scene photos, but that's it. Our local operative hasn't made a solid informant since the previous one retired a few months ago."

"Whatever isn't handed to us, Eli can find."

Liam joined me at the window as I stared out into the dark. European winters aren't for those who suffer from Seasonal Affective Disorder. "Why does he call the police, directing them to the bodies of his victims? Finley, didn't you once say serial killers don't want to be caught, because they don't want to give up playing the god of death?"

"He's doing it to prove a point, that's why he gets his female victims' faces tattooed onto his back. It's more than just a trophy for him. It might be a timeline, the story of the murders. Yet, he never gets a tattoo of the male victims. They aren't important after the fact, only as part of the murder itself." I rubbed my temples, desperate to get my grey matter to work.

My stomach growled. I realised we didn't have anything to eat the entire day. Breakfast had turned into an action scene. Some might call it a crime scene. But is it really when those who died were criminals? The time we were on the aeroplane, both on the ground and in the sky – a soap opera. With the way the two younger Walker brothers had acted over a woman. "I need food."

"We can go out for dinner, there's a great restaurant not far from here." Liam headed for the door.

"No time for it. I have a serial killer to annihilate and a daughter to return to."

"Annihilate? You make it sound so *murdery*." Liam leaned back against the door.

My fingers played over the custom-made grip of the SIG holstered at my hip.

"Finley, no."

I turned to Aidan and rolled my eyes. "You never let me do anything fun."

"If shooting Liam is your idea of fun, count me in." Rowan removed the Glock 41 from the holster at his lower back and smiled down at it.

"Twenty-five victims and Liam wants to go sit somewhere to eat dinner. I should punish such blatant stupidity with a small piece of lead. I'll ensure the bullet just grazes his skin, and you have extensive experience with bullet wounds, so it doesn't matter if my aim is a bit off." I forced out my bottom lip.

Aidan laughed. Liam didn't.

Rowan slid his Glock back in place and crossed his arms over his chest. "I'll order room service, and you can keep working. What can I do to help, Fin?"

Liam opened his mouth, but one look from Aidan left his words unspoken, and his body hole-free where it needed to be.

"I need a bigger murder board; this piece of paper isn't cutting it. Problem is, I can't stick up multiple pages on a wall if we might leave any second. Eli might call any minute informing us of another victim."

The names of the countries in which the killer had struck played in my mind. I closed my eyes, forgetting I wasn't alone. "You killed for the first time in September two years ago, in South America. Playa del Carmen, followed by Buenos Aires and Santiago. For three months you didn't kill again. January last year you killed in Singapore, Hong Kong and Da Nang, Vietnam. Followed by four months of nothing. Then in June you killed twice in Australia, then in Cape Town, South Africa. Last July you killed in Edinburgh, London and Paris. Since then, it has been a murder a month until this January. Four people killed in less than two weeks; three crime scenes."

The killer didn't answer. They never do. Not until they sit across from me, and their lives lay in my hands.

Someone in the suite had spent time in South America. I turned to Liam who lingered by the door. "Why Mexico, Argentina, and Chile? Why start in Mexico, despite the obvious reasons? If he killed in Los Cabos, Acapulco, or even in Tijuana, it could've been made off as part of their high murder rates. He calls the police because he wants them to find the bodies. However, he hasn't once let slip about murders in any other countries. His words are always the same – a body or bodies, the location, and that's it. I stand by my theory. Serial killers don't want to be caught."

Liam stepped away from the door. "Playa del Carmen is considered a safe tourist destination. The same for Argentina and Chile. Most South American countries aren't ideal holiday destinations, not if you haven't travelled before, go alone, or live under a rock."

As most people do. "The other murders were also in what's considered *safer* destinations. Cape Town, for instance, if you don't get lost or walk around at night. He buried the two bodies in a remote area not far from the Koeberg Nuclear Power Station."

I knew someone who had spent time in South Africa. I started talking before she even said hello. "If you were going to dump two bodies in Cape Town, where would you do it? Before you answer, you're going to dig a shallow grave for a coffin with two bodies, two snakes, and three leaves. Okay, go."

Her laughter caught me off guard; she seldom laughs. "What type of snakes and leaves? Male or female victims? Do I have help? Digging a grave isn't a quick job, not even a shallow one. What kind of vehicle am I driving as I take it the coffin isn't the self-assemble on-site type?"

I walked into the bedroom and closed the door. "Victims are a male and female. Two puff adders and three protea leaves. When did you last have sex with Rowan? Nothing special about the coffin, except that it's big enough for two adults."

The ensuing silence made me regret slipping the question about her and Rowan's most recent fornication in. "Quinn?"

"There are a lot of places to dump a body. The best places to do it are all in gang territory, so unless you can blend in, no go. From experience I can tell you the area from Melkbosstrand to the Koeberg Nuclear Power Station is as good a place as any. Lots of sand dunes, very isolated, chances of someone spotting you while playing in the sand are minimal."

"Experience, you say?" I asked.

Quinn sighed. "Yes. And that's all I'll say on the matter. The snakes and leaves aren't strange for that part of the country. Ask Aidan about the snakes, he'll be able to answer any question you can think of. Is that how the victims died?"

"No, asphyxiation. I'm sorry, Quinn, I shouldn't have

asked." I slumped down on the bed. Since first meeting we had grown close, yet Quinn remained one of the most private people I ever met.

"I don't mind sharing my knowledge of body dumping or South Africa. If you have more questions, let me know, as long as it relates to whatever you're working on. How did you get Aidan to agree to let you work again?"

"We're hunting an international serial killer; he knows better than to stand in my way." I smiled at the lie. It took much more than my doctorates in criminal psychology to convince him.

"Where are you?"

"Zurich for now. Ryan and Heather are taking care of Ainsley." My heart clenched as I said my daughter's name. I missed her but kept focusing on the parents who will never hold their children again.

I thanked Quinn, ended the call, and returned to the sitting area. "He has help. No way he can do all of this on his own." The men turned as one. "Aidan, puff adders. Why?"

"For the fear factor. If being buried alive isn't scary enough, adding two snakes, in this case puff adders, into an enclosed space would do the trick. On average, a person can survive up to two hours in a buried coffin, one hour for two adults. No way they stayed calm, and their oxygen levels would've depleted much faster. The snakes were nothing more than psychological torture. The puff adder's venom is cytotoxic. It causes severe swelling and necrosis. Cell destruction. Fatalities are rare, as victims tend to get medical help fast enough."

"Okay so, the snakes are part of the fantasy."

Aidan lifted his tumbler to his lips. "If he wanted to kill them with snakes, the black mamba would've been a better choice. They're found in the northern regions of South Africa and along the east coast. Once you're bitten, you have about thirty minutes left to live. There are no venomous snakes in Chile. In Spain he chose den adders, again not a deadly snake as long as you don't have any other health problems."

"Two victims. A male and a female. Two snakes, and three

leaves. Buried in coffins in shallow graves. Why does it feel like I should know what this means?" Aidan opened his mouth, but I held up my hand. "We're not looking for one killer."

Eleven

Zurich, Switzerland
Monday, 25 January, 6:21 p.m.

None of us spoke while we ate. My mind preoccupied by my stupidity. How didn't I realise sooner that we were looking for more than one killer? An additional question to answer – how many unsubs?

Aidan stepped into the bedroom to take a call, and I cleared the table and pushed the trolley into the hallway. Defeat visible on Aidan's face when he returned. "I'm heading out, going to meet with our operative. Fin, do you want to come with me?"

"No, take Rowan with you. I need to put the skills Eli taught me to use. No point going with you if I can't see the body. Photos will do."

Rowan laughed. "I'll ask reception to send up ice for your knuckles."

I frowned. "Why?"

"If you're going to go ballistic on Liam, you might need to ice your knuckles afterwards." Rowan stood and repositioned the Glock at his back.

"No, I'm going to do my own hacking. While Eli focuses on our unsubs I need to dig into our victims' pasts. How is he/they, finding the victims? We're not talking about prostitutes or people abducted from the street. In one country, or on one continent, it would be much easier. The murders are all over the globe."

"Perhaps you're looking for one killer, but he has help in each country." Liam added.

Plausible, but I didn't think so. If too many people knew, the risk of someone talking would be too big. *Unless they have a reason to keep their mouths shut.*

Aidan pulled me against him and kissed me until I was breathless. "See you later, Wife."

I nodded and slapped his delectable derriere.

"If you left any other woman alone with Liam, I would've told you you're crazy." Rowan shook his head as he followed Aidan.

Liam turned to me as soon as the door closed. A playboy type grin plastered across his face. "We might as well. It's not like we haven't slept together before."

I removed a bottle of water from the minibar and found a stationary pad and pen in the desk's drawer. With my back to the room, I kept my eyes on the paper on the desk, but my focus remained on Liam. He made himself comfortable on the L-shaped couch and switched on the television, keeping the sound low.

"I take it you never told Aidan about our night together," Liam said while flicking through the channels.

"Of course, I told my husband. We don't keep any secrets from each other."

Liam's laughter interrupted by the ringing of his mobile phone. He spoke in German to whoever called him. It was time I learned at least two other languages in order to keep up with the Walkers. They all speak multiple languages. Fluent in each, without even a hint of an accent. Ryan and Heather had prepared their sons from a young age for the roles they would one day play in Fortius. I thought about my precious little girl and wondered what it must be like for Heather to have three of her sons in constant danger. The shape of the danger differed, but its presence constant. It lurks around every corner, and even though we're all trained soldiers, no one is bulletproof. Unless you wear Kevlar, of course, but still.

"Ich bin tot," Liam said.

It took me a few seconds to realise he spoke to me. Tot means dead. Ich bin? I am. Perhaps my German wasn't as bad as I thought. "Das ist gut."

Liam whipped his head in my direction, my back still to him. *Perfect place for a mirror.* In this mirror, or any other, Aidan will always be the most beautiful of all, and then Rowan, except when he wore his hair in a man bun. Liam's lips moved, but I didn't understand a word.

"My German isn't fluent. Learned a few words while Lizzie and I travelled across Europe years ago with my parents. So, how many times have you died?" I asked and turned to face him.

"This is the first time. Ludwig Schneider no longer exists."

"What happened?"

"Rob Granger likes pipe bombs. Rowan's cover is solid, people will be reminded of how dangerous he is on tonight's news. As for me, I'm going to be unemployed as soon as we land in Marcel."

I returned my attention to the note pad on the desk. "No, you won't. We'll create a new cover identity for you, and you will work with Rowan again. This time following his every order. If you as much as huff, or roll your eyes, I'll have you sent to the furthest, most isolated place in the world. Better yet, perhaps you should spend a year on Grey Island."

My parents had a thing for manors, the Walkers have a thing for grey. The island in question is a black site, a tropical prison where our enemies are kept. Mine included.

"Anything to get me as far away from you as possible. You can't deny it, Finley. There's something between us."

I pushed to my feet and sat on the edge of the desk. "Yes, there is. My husband. Stop the crap, Liam. You've known better than to flirt with me since the first day we met. You can throw around the little sleeping together comment as much as you like. Let me tell you something. There's a big difference between having sex with me and sleeping in the same room."

I returned my bum to the chair and refocused on the words scribbled on the A5 size piece of paper. "For the record, if you have sex with me once, no other woman will ever satisfy you." I winked when his big eyes met mine in the mirror. "Thank you again for staying with Ainsley and me the first time Aidan went away for work."

Aidan and I had planned it all out. He had told Liam he didn't want to leave his wife and daughter alone, while I wanted to get to know Liam better. A ruse. An opportunity to bond with Liam and gain his trust. It was time for him to grow up and get over his passive-aggressive hatred towards Rowan. Men in their thirties shouldn't act like children, even less so in our line of work.

"Why is Aidan the only one of us lucky enough to meet the perfect woman and convince her to marry him? Nathan's marriage went up in flames. Rowan avoids relationships. And I'm the family slut."

"Slut? That's the word you want to go with?" Strange how much Liam and I bonded in that one night. The following morning, he had asked Aidan not to spend another night with me and Ainsley; seeing me breastfeed made him uncomfortable. Liam never even saw my breasts; he had closed his eyes and fell asleep on the couch in the bedroom. I suspect him not wanting to spend another night could come down to him realising what domestic life can be like. After returning from an operation in Nigeria, being home with a woman who understood the horrors he had seen, and a beautiful baby girl who reminded him of what we fought for, it might've been too much for a man who has never had a meaningful relationship.

"Well, what would you call me?"

"Lost. With the mother of all chips on your shoulder." I turned to face him. "I would love to delve into your psyche and psychoanalyse every aspect of your personality, and the reasons for all of your various bad decisions. But I have murder victims waiting for me to catch their killer. Or killers."

I took a deep breath and joined him on the couch. "Nevertheless, you're my brother, and I'll always make time for you. Now listen up, buttercup, because this is about to get real. You have meaningless sex because you're afraid of rejection. This doesn't stem from Quinn choosing Rowan when you were young. No, this comes from you concocting a made-up scenario where your mother chose him over you. Have you even considered how hard a decision it must've been for your parents? They already had three sons, you were barely a year old, and then they brought a newborn into the house. Instead of seeing your parents' actions as them rejecting you, consider the remarkable people they are."

Liam stood and made coffee for both of us. "You're wrong."

I laughed, holding onto my stomach. "No, I'm not. This goes way beyond Quinn falling in love with Rowan and not you. You're so self-centred that you never even considered the fact that their pasts forged their bond. They're outsiders. They don't share your blood. Fair enough, Quinn didn't live with you on a full-time basis or have your surname, but she and Rowan are more Walker than you've ever been. Unless you cut your bullshit, grow up, and realise what a remarkable family you have. Think about their pasts. Where they came from. Do you think it's easy for them? They'll forever feel they need to earn the love and respect of this family. That, my dear brother, is why they chose each other. Not everything in this life is about you, Liam Walker. I love you, but if you don't stop playing the victim I will, from this day forward, slap you every time I see you."

I thanked him for the coffee and continued. "Captain Walker, you're a formidable soldier. I saw your records; I know the people you served with. They all speak highly of you, and of your bravery in combat."

Liam opened his mouth, but no words came out. He placed the mug on the coffee table and stared at his hands. "Aidan's the genius, the world-record-holding-sniper, the perfect husband and father. Nathan has a way with people; you can't not love him, and he's very good with numbers. Not as good as Aidan, but still. Rowan's the larger than life, deadly teddy bear, who has no idea of the way women look at him. He has that whole tall, dark, handsome, and dangerous thing about him. I'm just Liam the super soldier."

I wrapped my arms around his neck and hugged him tight. "I get it, more than you can imagine. Do you think it was easy growing up in Lizzie's shadow? She's the epitome of the perfect woman. Intelligent, beautiful, and classy. Well now, not so much when we were students. Every family has a slut; our family had two. Don't tell anyone I said that. Lizzie will try to put me in a choke hold. All of my mother's grey hairs had been my doing. I was the tomboy, the wild child. The one that other children liked, teachers not so much. I broke every rule I could, and then to top it all off, I joined the army. Best decision I ever made. I found myself." *And almost lost my life.*

I took lives and watched my squad get murdered. Perhaps I didn't find myself, but rather lost myself, and morphed into who I became.

Liam increased his hold on me, but remained quiet, so I continued. "We are who we are. As long as our actions don't hurt anyone else, we can continue being us. Your actions are hurting people, and almost got us killed today, but you're hurting yourself the most. When we get back to Marcel, take some time off, go to the house in Wild Bay and breathe. Take time to think about everything and you'll realise your parents bringing Rowan into the family shows their kindness, selflessness, and loving hearts. Consider what I said about Quinn and Rowan's bond. And for the record, it's nothing more than a bond. You know why they ended their short romance. It borders on cousin kissing."

"They did more than just kissing." Liam pulled away and took my hand in his.

I shrugged; I would never break their trust by telling anyone they recently had sex. "It's all in the past. Now, seeing as you called dibs on all the brunettes in the world, find yourself the right one. And please leave the blondes to Rowan. That's your deal, remember?"

"All bets are off. He slept with Anna."

"First, and then you slept with her to prove a point. Stop being childish. Stop thinking with your penis." We both laughed.

I pressed my lips to his cheek and stood. He squeezed my hand. "I love you, Fin. Is this the way sisters talk to their brothers?"

"I don't know, but this is what I would say to Lizzie. I love you too, brother. Now, that will be 5000 euros." I held my palm out to him.

"What?"

"Did you expect therapy to be free?"

Liam laughed and released his death grip on my hand. "I tell you what, Dr Williams-Walker, I'll pay you by not screwing up again. Okay?"

Deep down I knew he would try but doubted this would be the end of Liam's long list of screw-ups. As long as no one gets hurt or killed, his cheek would remain free of my handprint. "Deal."

Liam shook his head. "If I screw up again, you can slap me."

"If anyone in this family or Fortius gets injured or killed because of your recklessness, I will make it my personal mission to destroy you."

Liam grinned. "You can always lock me up next to your ex on Grey Island. Nothing like some white torture to destroy someone."

I returned to the desk and picked up the pen. "He's dead. Chewed his own wrists. At least he saw some colour before death came for him." Gabriel lasted longer than I had expected him to. His death hadn't bothered me one bit, and this was the second time I spoke about it. The first time being when Aidan informed me. My response had been a single word: okay.

Twelve

Zurich, Switzerland
Monday, 25 January, 7:45 p.m.

Aidan found me on the carpet. Pieces of paper formed a half moon around me. He stood behind me and stared down at the pages. "So instead of a murder board, you created a murder floor?"

I giggled, perhaps for the first time in my life. "Yes. Does this make sense to you?"

"It does." Aidan squatted and wrapped his arms around me. "They, are telling us a story."

"I don't follow." I rarely understand the workings of his brilliant mind. As for the workings of his beautiful body, that language I speak without even a hint of an accent.

"Poison from a frog. Organophosphate poison. Buried alive. Exsanguination by severing both hands. Death with no identifiable cause, as if the women simply fell asleep, never to wake up again. Burned alive."

I turned and stared up at him. "I'm dumb remember, spell it out for me, or draw me a picture."

Aidan kissed me hard. "You're not dumb, clever enough to marry me." He drew his bottom lip between his teeth.

"Focus, Commander Walker. Deaths to avenge, killers we need to bring to my justice."

Aidan's left eyebrow raised. "Are you telling me or yourself to focus, Commander Williams-Walker?"

"I'm not commander of anything. Not even of my murder floor."

Aidan pressed his lips to my ear, his voice low and filled with promise. "You command every part of me. Mainly the part which is forcing me to hide behind your back, so as not to give my brothers another reason to be jealous of me."

I laughed and leaned back in his arms. *Do other people talk like this when death surrounds them?*

Rowan stepped closer and held out a white envelope towards me. "Same dress. Golden poison frog toxin."

"The Frog King," Aidan said.

I waited for him to continue. When he didn't, I constructed the most intelligent question I could while a very hard part of him pressed against my back. "The what now?"

"I told you, the murders are telling a story." I gestured with my hands for him to continue. "Look at your notes, you've solved it."

The words scribbled on the pages surrounding us mocked me. I didn't solve diddly squat. When I told Aidan as much, he laughed and pressed his lips to my hair. He stood and pulled me to my feet.

"Dr Williams-Walker, profiler extraordinaire, I need you to push the profiler and mother buttons inside your brain at the same time."

"Huh?" My expression must've matched how dense I felt.

"Fairy tales, my love. The murders are based on fairy tales."

I pursed my lips to stop another *huh* from escaping. Instead, I stared at the pages at my feet. Victims two, eight, and fourteen were all murdered with an organophosphate poison. They died wearing the same dress, their hair black. The bodies of the victims staged in Perspex boxes. *Glass coffins.* "Snow White!"

Perhaps I had been out of the profiling game for too long. I lost my serial killer hunting touch. The entire time, the answers were right in front of me.

Aidan placed his hands on my shoulders. "Don't start shooting stuff. I also didn't realise it until I saw it written out like this."

"Lying to me won't make me feel any less inadequate." A herd of swear words galloped through my mind.

"Okay, I suspected it, and during the ride to meet with the

operative I did some research. Some of the fairy tales he, or they, are recreating aren't in most of the books available today."

I turned and stared up at Aidan. My husband with an IQ of 210, and on a scale of one to ten in the looks department, he also scores at 210. I never felt happier about being good in bed, on a couch, or wherever, even if I have to say so myself. At least Aidan loves me for more reasons than my lower IQ. Whenever I mentioned anything about being dumb, he reminded me I hold a doctoral degree in criminal psychology. Something very few people ever accomplish. He then also reminded me that I had completed my thesis while hunting a serial killer and undergoing fertility treatment. *Why are we always so hard on ourselves?*

The pages at my feet told the stories. Which stories, I didn't know yet. I took Aidan's hands and wrapped his arms around me as I stared down at the riddle, desperate for some of his brilliance to transfer through our clothes. "The Frog King. Snow White. The victims who appear to have died in their sleep, could be Sleeping Beauty. The male and female victims who were burned alive might represent Hansel and Gretel. I'm not familiar with the others."

Aidan pressed his lips to the back of my head. "Sleeping Beauty was originally known as Little Briar Rose. The stories were all written by the Grimm brothers. The three snake-leaves. The girl without hands. Those are the other two fairy tales being recreated."

"I don't recall ever hearing those stories," Rowan said. I forgot he and Liam were in the room with us.

"Long story short – princess dies, wanted her husband to be buried with her, so he gets in the crypt. A snake slithers into the crypt, the prince kills the snake, the snake's mate slithers in and sees the dead snake. The snake leaves and returns with three leaves and places it on the dead snake. Soon thereafter, the snake awakens and both slithers away. The prince then puts the leaves on the princess, she too comes back from the dead—"

"And they lived happily ever after," I finished for Aidan, or so I thought.

"No happy ending for this story. The princess falls in love with another man and tries to kill the prince. Her father finds out, and then the princess and her would-be-lover are executed. Again, this is just the short version."

"Okay, not cool of her considering the poor prince spent time with her corpse and sacrificed himself to die with her."

Aidan opened the bottle of water I had left on the desk and downed the content. "The girl without hands is quite clear. The girl loses her hands, but somehow doesn't bleed to death. Fairy tales aren't very factual. Can you imagine if an author had to write something like this today?"

"Depends on the genre," I said. "Question, what can cause death, but is undetectable?"

Aidan shrugged. "My first guess is insulin. It metabolises fast. Ten units are enough to kill a non-diabetic."

"Please explain to those of us without medical degrees how much that equates to," Rowan said from where he sat on the couch. The closest he had been to Liam since the Anna/Maria fiasco came to light.

Aidan ran his hand up my back and massaged my neck with his thumb and middle finger. I couldn't suppress the whimper. The look on both my brother-in-law's faces told me it might've been more of a moan.

Aidan's fingers stopped their magic. "One unit is 34.7 micrograms of pure crystalline insulin. Times ten and converted to milligram, that's 0.347 milligrams of insulin. Which isn't a lot, or difficult to get your hands on. I need to review the autopsy reports to see whether the pathologists tested the injection sites for insulin. It isn't the perfect murder, but without a standard toxicology screening method it's possible they didn't test for it. Which cities are we talking about?"

I dropped to my knees and picked up the relevant piece of paper. "Hong Kong, London, and of course, Budapest." As I read the names, I realised Aidan tried to make me feel more in control of the investigation. With his eidetic memory, he knew which cities the possible insulin murders occurred in.

We had been partners in everything since we first met but working together might prove tricky. Aidan sees answers long before I even realise there is a question. *How can we work together if I'll end up feeling inadequate?* He never did it on purpose, and for that I loved him even more. But I had to find a way to do what I do best – understand the criminal mind. I've hunted many serial offenders without Aidan's help. With it, we can identify the unsubs much faster. Faster equals less victims.

Somehow, I would get over my own insecurities. Being a full-time mother for the past year left me doubting my own abilities. *Do all mothers experience this when returning to work?* However, I had taken two lives without giving it a second thought. I could do what I do best and harness the super computer that is my husband's brain.

Aidan pressed his lips to my ear. "You're brilliant in your own right. An apex predator. You've been out of the game, but the game hasn't left you. We'll make this working together thing work. I still need to thank you for saving my life."

I hated, and loved, when he knew where my mind wondered off too. "Spank me, is what I said," I whispered.

Aidan huffed a laugh. "We don't do that, my love. Sparring with you is enough of a turn on. Do you want to go a round?"

"I need to dig into our victims' lives, starting with the first victim in Mexico. Somehow, they're finding the victims. This is organised down to the finest detail."

I stepped away from Aidan and spoke to the killers while staring at my reflection in the window. "You're intelligent, cunning, and think yourself above the law. Did you start fantasising when you were young? More than one killer shouldn't share a fantasy this detailed. Unless you're a group, each killing in your own country."

I tapped my palm against my forehead. "Only one gets the tattoos. Are you the ringleader? The author of the fantasy, the rest are your hands and feet where you can't go."

My SIG felt at home gripped in my hand. I sighted down the barrel, pointing it out into the dark Swiss night. "No, that's not you. Control, precision, everything has to be in your hands." I lowered my weapon and turned to Aidan. "One killer, but he has help." My palms itched.

"How did you go from multiple killers to one in a matter of hours?" Rowan asked.

"She understands him." A predatory sneer spread across Aidan's face. It mirrored my own.

"He's still here but won't be for much longer. Someone's helping him. No way one killer can control the male and female victims at the same time. I checked the autopsy reports of the victims who were buried alive, no traces of any tranquilliser in their toxicology reports. One killer, but he has help. He keeps his circle tight and he holds the power. Full control."

I turned to Rowan. "Call Janos, ask him who is the best tattoo artist in Zurich. Then, ask Eli to run background checks for ones with criminal records. We might catch him getting his ink done, if he hasn't already."

"Fin, are you sure we're looking for only one killer?" Liam asked.

Rowan spoke first. "Janos was right from the start. One killer. But the big guy, the one Janos thought is a bodyguard, he's the helper. Janos said they both wore disguises. No way for him to identify them in a line up."

"Because they don't want to be identified." I wanted to scream. I had lost my killer touch. Pun intended. From the beginning, Janos gave us the answers. As much as I wanted to shoot myself in the foot, not in the proverbial way, I reminded myself in a murder investigation nothing is a given. One must consider all possibilities. It's called being a good detective. Sometimes the evidence leads you in the wrong direction, but I realised soon enough that our killer had only one helper.

Whoever the killer was, he hid his face for more than one reason. He was someone recognisable. An actor, a celebrity, an athlete? Someone getting paid a lot of money for not doing much, if you think about it. If that was the case, we had to investigate almost every politician in the world. To be inclusive, of course.

"I need to hunt."

Rowan and Liam left to track down the local tattoo artist. Aidan carried his laptop into the bedroom to read all of the autopsy reports. What did I do? I became a cyber sleuth. At least this time not in the abyss, or as most people know it – the dark web.

Thirteen

Zurich, Switzerland
Monday, 25 January, 9:26 p.m.

Aidan tossed me a Kevlar vest and holstered a SIG on either side of his thighs. I fastened the Kevlar and pulled a long-sleeved shirt over it, while Aidan assembled two HK416 A5 assault rifles. Seconds later he handed me one, and we both covered it with our long coats as we headed out of the hotel. Neither of us said a word until we got into the black Mercedes-Benz GLS, which had been waiting for us at Dübendorf Air Base.

I tossed our coats on the back seat and positioned both rifles between my legs. "Are they still in place?" I asked.

Aidan nodded. "I should've left you at the hotel." The engine roared, as did my hormones. As much as it infuriates me when he dons his protector cap, I love it.

"Commander Walker, may I remind you I've already saved your life once today. Let's try not to make it twice in the same day. I don't care what you say or what orders you give, there's nothing I won't do to keep you safe."

"Keeping you safe would've meant leaving you at the hotel. Ainsley needs one of us to return to her."

I let out a heavy sigh. "Ainsley needs both her parents. Us, hunting together, is the best way to ensure that. You and I both know, as much as your brothers love you, hell will not stand in my way if someone hurts my family. And, you know better than to not let me in on the action."

"If you didn't keep up your training with Eli, I would've. Are you ready?"

"Yes." I placed an earpiece in my right ear, and in Aidan's

as he kept his focus on the road.

Rowan's voice filled my head. "They're leaving. Will pursue."

"We're two minutes out." Aidan dabbed at the onboard navigation system, and I realised this wasn't the version the vehicle had come out with. Four coloured dots appeared on the screen. "Rowan's blue, Liam's green, I'm red, and you're black."

"Well thank you for remembering my favourite colour. Don't start with it not being a true colour. I see it, I like it, I buy it, I wear it."

Aidan laughed. "I know, Mrs Walker."

"Silver Porsche Cayenne. The bigger of the two is driving. Janos didn't mention Ink-boy isn't small himself. Biggie is armed."

Ink-boy? I pursed my lips; my stomach did the laughing. "Biggie being the supposed bodyguard?"

"Yes. If this turns into a hand-to-hand combat situation, Finley, you better leave Biggie to me. Aidan, order her to stay away from him."

"If Fin gets the shot, she's going to take it." Aidan placed his hand on my thigh. "No going after him down a dark alley by yourself. Direct order. You better not defy me this time."

"Yes, sir." Half of me meant it, the other too excited to be this close to the persons responsible for the deaths of twenty-five people.

"License plate comes back as a rental," Liam said. "Eli is running the credit card details now."

Aidan patted my thigh. "Climb on my lap."

In my ear Rowan and Liam both cleared their throats.

As I moved onto Aidan's lap, I glanced down at the speedometer. We were doing 80km/h in a 50km/h zone. If that wasn't reason enough to shoot something, then what is? "Why are you driving so slow, Grandpa?"

Aidan moved out from under me and settled in the passenger seat. We fastened our seatbelts at the same time. "We're already attracting attention. I can't afford an international incident on my watch. We have no jurisdiction, or protection here. You drive. I shoot." Aidan squeezed my thigh. "Urban area. Civilians. And you haven't been in a situation like this in years. When we get home we can run simulations, but right now, it is what it is."

"I get it." I did but didn't like it.

Aidan removed his phone. The light of the screen illuminated his face. "Ainsley is playing on the beach with Mom and Dad."

"We will both return to our daughter. That's a direct order from your wife."

"Yes, ma'am." Aidan pressed his lips to my neck.

On the screen, the dots merged. To my left, a black GLS, my brothers inside. I eased my foot off the accelerator. Adrenaline splashed inside me; goose bumps rippled over my skin. My palms itched. Two cars up ahead – the silver Porsche Cayenne. "What do you need me to do?"

"Stay alive. Rowan will run them off the road." Aidan lowered his window.

I pointed up. "Sunroof."

"Civilians. Not about to blow our cover." Aidan lifted the rifle. "Rowan, just like Baghdad. Finley, speed up."

"Where are they heading?" I asked.

"My guess? Zurich Airport. They killed. He got his ink. No point in sticking around," Rowan said.

"We take them out on the A51, it leads to the airport. Less traffic this time of night; minimal risk of civilian casualties." The authority in Aidan's voice made me even more excited.

"I don't need them alive," I told Aidan.

"Civilians. We can't take unnecessary risks."

As soon as we reached the A51, I pressed my foot down on the accelerator. My heartbeat violent, my breathing no longer controlled.

Aidan positioned the rifle on the dashboard and smiled. "Breathe, Fin."

"In position," Rowan said.

Too many cars on the road. I tried my best to stay focused and follow Aidan's orders.

"Speed up, go past them, and do a handbrake turn." Aidan shifted in his seat.

I didn't know if I could do it, it had been too long since I last had to. Aidan was right, we couldn't risk the lives of civilians and I didn't want their deaths on my conscience. The road slick from an earlier downpour which missed the hotel. "Get in the back. Shoot from there."

"The lady thinks on her feet." Liam's voice filled my right ear.

Aidan moved to the back seat. I pressed the button to lift the passenger side window. The icy wind made my eyes water.

Rapid gunfire didn't fill the silence in the GLS, or the quiet of the night. A rapid succession of popping sounds came from the back seat. I kept my eyes on the road and thanked whoever invented suppressors and silencers.

Aidan cursed. "Bullet-resistant everything. Rowan?"

"On it!"

I glanced in the rear-view mirror and slowed down. Cars honked, I ignored them. The Cayenne swerved and scraped the barrier. Biggie regained control, speeding up and headed straight for us. "Aidan, buckle up. Now!"

At the last second, I changed lanes without using the indicator. The Cayenne crashed into the GLS. The adrenaline pumping through me obliterated the pain shooting up my neck. Aidan fired again. The Cayenne reversed and sped away. My turn to curse as I pushed my foot down to the floorboard. Rowan and Liam raced past us.

"Not your average rental," Liam laughed, then cursed.

Why are we all swearing? Oh, yes, serial killers getting away.

"License plate is a fake," I said instead of the word I wanted to scream. The one starting with an f.

Sirens echoed in the distance.

"Give me your guns." Aidan held out his hand. "Slow down."

I did the best I could with one hand on the steering wheel. Blue lights flashed in the rear-view and side mirrors.

"Pull over. Let me do the talking." Aidan jumped out as soon as I brought the SUV to a stop. He waved his arms, and a police car pulled up behind us.

I remained in the driver's seat but glanced at the back seat. No sign of our SIGs or the HKs. A police officer tapped on the window and gestured for me to get out.

"Thank you, Officer. That vehicle ... came out of nowhere. Look at the back of my SUV." I lifted a trembling hand to my mouth and forced tears into my eyes. I had worn masks before, this time no different, I reminded myself.

Aidan translated, and the officer nodded before taking Aidan's statement. Aidan shook his head, then nodded before the officer returned to his vehicle. He asked me to get into the passenger seat and drove us back to the hotel.

Fourteen

Dübendorf *Air Base, Switzerland*
Monday, 25 January, 11:37 p.m.

The passports Aidan had handed to the police officer weren't under our real names. By now the civilians who witnessed the events on the A51 would've called the police and gave their versions of what they thought to be the truth. We left the SUVs a block away from the Baur au Lac. The local operative had waited there, ready to clean up after us. Which in our world means the SUVs would be taken to an undisclosed location and blown to smithereens. How I wished I could've lit the fuse. It had been a long time since I last played with C-4 playdough or pressed a detonator. Perhaps he would burn the vehicles and have them crushed in a scrap yard. An explosion would be the less boring option of the two.

Rowan returned from his preflight inspection and dragged a big hand down his face. "I believe I know who Biggie is. Not his name, but where we can find him. He'll be heading for Dubai, they never cancel a party. The tattoo on his right hand, I've seen it before."

I leaned forward, resting my elbows on my knees. "Who is he? And what party? Or is this the party you said was a discussion for another day?"

"Yes, but you need to wait. It's time for me to get us in the air. You can rip into me later for losing them."

"I won't, we all know things can go balls up in situations like this. At least, we have a lead on Biggie. And we know he isn't just muscle; he showed some serious evasive driving skills. Perhaps this will slow down the rate of the murders, now that they know someone is on to them."

"I only caught a glimpse of his tattoo, but if it is what I think it is, he's ex-special forces. The kicker is – he shouldn't be alive." He held up both hands. "Let me do some digging first and get my facts straight. Whoever he was with tonight, might not be the person who organises the parties."

"It's as good a place as any to start, Ro. I'm as much to blame for losing him as you are, not that you are. Sorry, I'm tired and I'm crashing now." I leaned back in my seat.

Aidan fastened my seatbelt and pressed his lips to my temple. "I don't think you did too badly for your first time."

"I have to be better." My eyes refused to remain open. Ainsley's face filled my mind. At least both her parents were still alive.

"When is this party?" Aidan asked.

"Wednesday night. I have an open invitation, so whether I show up or not won't alert anyone to anything. Aidan, I'm going to need your wife for the night. We need to get Fin something *appropriate* to wear."

My eyes shot open. "Why?"

"Rowan's going to have sex with you." Liam winked with a smile.

"Okay." I closed my eyes again, waiting for Aidan's response.

"Get us to Dubai and enjoy your penis while it's still attached to your body. No way in hell you're going to have sex with my wife."

Without opening my eyes, I patted Aidan's thigh, dragging my hand up high enough to make him twitch in his seat. "You're a party pooper, Aidan Walker. You never let me do anything fun."

"If you weren't half asleep, we could renew our mile high membership." Aidan leaned his head against mine and intertwined our fingers.

"Do you not even realise I'm sitting right here?" Liam let out a laboured breath.

"We do. Do you see what you're missing out on, *slut*?"

Liam and I both laughed. Aidan asked what he missed.

Liam stood and fetched a bottle of water from the kitchen.

Aidan pressed his lips to my ear. "You're getting through to him."

I yawned. "Yes. I'm stealthy. He doesn't even realise it yet, but his days of sleeping around are over. I'm sorry I screwed up tonight."

"All four of us are alive and wound-free. It's a win."

I snuggled into Aidan's arms as best I could, sitting next to him, realising I no longer dreaded takeoff. Perhaps too tired to care if an engine exploded. "Fair enough, but who says he won't kill again before I can kill him?"

Dubai, United Arab Emirates
Tuesday, 26 January, 11:00 a.m.

I've been to Dubai a couple of times, and from experience I can tell you that you don't want to be there in summer, the heat unlike any other. A dry desert summer isn't something everyone is made for. I guess wherever we are we acclimatise and get on with life.

I stepped out onto the sundeck and stretched my arms above my head, grateful to be here during their supposed winter. Perhaps Rowan could be my personal pilot. Whenever he commanded the aeroplane, I slept.

The sun glistened on the ocean, and I wished we were here for reasons other than murder. Twenty-five murders. I wondered how many more would die before I ended it, by ending him, or them. Whoever helped him can't go unpunished. Someone had supplied them with a bullet-resistant Porsche Cayenne in Zurich. I wondered what kind of help he received in the other countries. Who helped? And who would they help to murder innocent people? And why?

"Everything is set up, and here you don't have to worry about leaving anything behind." Aidan wrapped his arms around me.

"Whose house is this?"

"On paper it belongs to my parents, but it's a Fortius safe house. If you look over there, towards Jumeirah Beach, *we* own the majority share in that hotel." Aidan pointed to our left.

"Fortius or your parents?"

"No, Finley, you and me. I wanted to surprise you, by bringing you and Ainsley here for our first international vacation, and then tell you. Guess the cat is out of the box now."

I didn't miss his subtle Schrödinger reference. "How?" I stared in the direction of the hotel towards which Aidan pointed from where we stood on The Palm.

Aidan pressed his lips to my neck and held me tighter. "Payment for a situation I handled. Remember my first operation away from home after Ainsley's birth?"

I nodded and rested the back of my head against his chest.

"My father has been channelling certain *payments* to all four of us. He calls it preparing for our inheritance, as only so much is in their names. *We* own sixty percent of that hotel. Thirty percent in your name, and thirty in mine."

The correct response failed me. Because of the nature of our work, I never expected to know everything about Fortius' operations, or acquired funds and resources. I could ask Aidan for details, and he would tell me the truth. For the time being I needed to put myself in the shoes, and mind, of a killer I couldn't profile. Nothing he did made sense. Not understanding infuriated me and made me yearn to shoot something. I think all criminal profilers feel this way at some point in the investigation, as do homicide detectives and everyone else involved in solving heinous crimes. Now it was only me, three of the Walker brothers, and Eli.

"Do you think we can go to PF Chang's for Dynamite Shrimp? I don't have time to go shopping for the ridiculous outfit Rowan wants me to wear, but I'll make time for Dynamite Shrimp. Perhaps it will burn my neurons into solving the riddle of our killer's identity."

"You get to work; I'll take care of your outfit."

I turned and stared up at my husband. "What if we don't catch him? What if he isn't even in Dubai? What if Biggie was just his personal bodyguard in Zurich, and seeing as Biggie is hired muscle, there's no other connection between the two?"

Aidan pressed his lips to my forehead but said nothing.

"I can make Biggie talk. He *will* tell me who hired him in Zurich."

"If I'm correct about the tattoo, you might not be able to break him, Fin. No matter what you do." Rowan walked out onto the sundeck and positioned sunglasses over his eyes. "The best of the best trained their unit, similar to the training all our operatives undergo. If Biggie was part of that unit, it means he's around sixty-years-old, if not older. Before we get ahead of ourselves and make assumptions about Biggie, let's focus on the murders."

"The victims. I need to focus on the victims." I kissed Aidan. "Commander, I might need your help. Just give me a few hours to do what I should've been doing during the flight."

"You can't hunt when you're tired, Finley. Even orcas need to sleep, although their sleep pattern is what's known as unihemispheric sleep. Now you have a proper murder board to work on. Liam set everything up for you and I stuck the map against the wall. Go talk to *him*, dig into the victims' backgrounds, and I'll join you in a bit to talk it through."

As I made my way to the office, I Googled unihemispheric sleep and wished I could sleep with one eye closed while the opposite side of my brain rests. I dialled Eli's number, not even bothering to figure out the time in Marcel.

"Fin, I found something. It isn't much, but it's a start. I emailed it to you. Are you behind your laptop?"

I asked him to give me a minute, I first had to take in the room. The windows were darkened. A mobile whiteboard positioned next to a screen the size of the one in Aidan's office. Not one screen but multiple screens which can be viewed separate or as one image. This room another command centre, as I refer to them.

"How was dinner last night with Heather and Ryan? Heather said Ainsley couldn't get enough of you, and you ended up bathing her and putting her to bed."

"Just some quality time with my goddaughter. I love Ains as if she's my own. Lizzie's worried about you, but I talked her out of following you across the world. How are you holding up?"

I swivelled in the chair. "I miss my baby girl, but the sooner I catch this sonofabitch and whoever is helping him, the sooner I can be home." An image filled my laptop's screen as I opened the email Eli had sent.

"Hold on, look at the screens." Eli accessed everything and anything from the comfort of his own command centre at his and Lizzie's house. To live next to your sister isn't the worst thing in the world. After everything we've been through, being neighbours gave us a sense of security.

Eight images of a man filled the screens. Not the same face, but the same build – big.

"I need Rowan to verify this is Biggie." I walked to the door and shouted Rowan's name. He charged into the house, running at full speed through the living area, his Glock in hand.

"At ease, soldier." I laughed and stepped back to let him into the office.

Rowan returned his gun to the holster at his lower back. He placed both hands on top of his head as he stared at the screens. "Biggie? Might be him."

I placed my mobile phone on the desk and pressed the speaker button. Eli's voice filled the room. "I widened the search parameters. All of these weren't taken at ports of entry."

"Where?" I asked.

City names, locations and dates appeared underneath each image. Buenos Aires, Singapore, Perth, London, Paris, Cape Town, Budapest, and Zurich.

"He was in each of the cities at the time of the murders."

I stepped closer to the screens and crossed my arms over my chest. "Biggie can't be our killer, he isn't the one getting the tattoos. The person he works for is our killer."

"Is it possible they're killing together?" Rowan asked.

"They are, but the fantasy is one person's. Biggie might just be the muscle, moving coffins and 200 litre steel drums around. He might even control the male victims. Eli, anything on our other unsub, the one Rowan has dubbed *Ink-boy*?" I still preferred killer, but as we now had at least two unsubs, distinguishing between them became necessary.

"Not at the moment, but I'm not giving up. Do you need help with the victims?"

"If I hit a wall, you'll hear from me." Team serial killers are rare, but not unheard of. I should know, seeing as I had been captured and tortured by a team. *The Scarecrows.* Somehow these murders didn't feel like a two-man fantasy. I took a deep breath, reminding myself that I could trust my instincts, even though it had let me down in the past.

I'm a perfectionist and control freak down to my core. There's nothing I hate more than being wrong. For now, I focused on the victims. How, and where, did their paths cross with the killer's?

Fifteen

Dubai, United Arab Emirates
Tuesday, 26 January, 1:31 p.m.

A pattern emerged. Not a definitive one, but at least I felt closer to understanding how the victims had met their end. They had something in common, without it being a shared interest for all. I wasn't sure yet how this linked back to the killer. I made another note on the murder board and returned to the laptop. Even though some victims had been deceased for more than a year, their free email accounts lived on. The password cracker Eli created made this easier, and faster, than if I tried to do it myself. Technology has never been my friend.

The door opened to my right, but I kept my focus on the first victim's email account. The victims' social media accounts offered me a door into their worlds. An overwhelming sadness filled me as I trespassed in their lives, the ones they had posted for the world to see. Whether it was real, or the fake lives most people post online, I'll never know. The sad reality – it no longer mattered. Nothing mattered except bringing their killer to justice. *Killers?*

I released a virtual worm thingy; another of Eli's brilliant creations. I'll never refer to it as a 'thingy' in front of him, but whenever he starts with his geek talk, a part of my brain shuts down. No option to reboot.

"Take off your clothes."

"Do we need to practise for tomorrow night?" I asked Rowan.

He placed running shoes next to my laptop. "We're going for a run."

"Is this your idea of foreplay? Perhaps I'll tutor you in the art of seduction before you meet the love of your life. To ensure she doesn't run away when you mention getting all sweaty is your idea of getting her in the mood."

Rowan laughed. "I assure you, there's nothing wrong with my skills, technique or the level of guaranteed satisfaction a woman has with me."

"Dude, this is disturbing." I shivered. "You're like a brother to me."

"It's not as if you haven't seen his penis before," Aidan said, leaning against the doorframe.

I turned my chair to face him. "For the record, Husband, I didn't see your brother's pee-pee. His tattoo is spectacular, and I might get a similar one to the other one he has. Seeing as I'm now part of the family business. Perhaps, Commander Walker, you and I can get inked together."

Aidan shook his head, but my eyes focused on the SIGs holstered at his thighs. *Why is it such a turn-on?* "It was stupid of him and Liam to get it, it puts us all at risk."

"Shoot me for trying to bond with the brother who hates me." Rowan shrugged and pointed at the running shoes. "Five minutes, Fin. Clothes off. Clothes on. You and me? We're going to be pounding the tar and sand. Hard."

"As much as I would love to pound stuff with you, I have too much work to do."

Rowan leaned over my shoulder and stared at my laptop's screen. He mumbled something in a language I didn't speak and started typing, his chest pressed to the back of my head. "There, Eli's pet will do the data collection for you. By the time we get back you'll have access to all the victims' emails, text messages and phone calls."

He closed the tab and clicked on another I left open. Rowan rubbed a big hand over my head. "Good girl, I see you're already running a facial recognition detector through their social media accounts. Aidan, I think we might need to keep her. She's a natural."

A grin spread across Aidan's face. "In more ways than one."

My cheeks caught fire, and I pursed my lips. The memory of the first time Aidan and I had showered together pulsed between us. The energy in the room changed. I could only stare at my lover. Despite our current circumstances, I never wanted him more. This seems to be a thing for me. Just when I think I can't be more in love with him, or lust after him, he does something, says something, and then – system failure. An internal error only he can fix. And does the man have his ways. *Murders. Focus woman.*

"Why don't you join us? I bet you can run circles around Rowan, even though you're much older than him." *Six years isn't that much.*

"Sorry, dude, perhaps another time. I'm running an entire organisation. This isn't the only operation that requires my full attention. Rowan, I hope you plan to leave the room before my wife undresses."

"I see her as one of us, one of the men." Rowan stood his ground. "It's not like I haven't seen women naked before." He spared me by not saying he had seen me naked; when he cradled me in his arms and carried me out of that bunker. "I can wait until tomorrow night to see what she keeps hidden underneath all her black clothes."

I rolled the chair back and turned to Rowan. "It's a sex party?"

He nodded.

"There's no way in hell another man, or woman, touches me and doesn't lose a hand. How are we going to blend in if I don't participate in the orgy? I can stand back and watch, not that I want to see you have sex with someone, or other people go at it." I've always preferred one-on-one action.

"No one will touch you. You're Rob Granger's date. Everybody knows not to touch what's mine. Except Liam." Rowan shook his head, and I placed my hand on his arm.

"Will they expect the two of you to join in? Is it like Fin said, an orgy?" Aidan asked.

"Sort of. It's very exclusive, you don't even want to know

what the annual membership fee is. Some couples join in once the performance is over, the rest find a room. They always hold the parties in mansions, castles or penthouse suites in some of the most luxurious hotels in the world."

"Where's the party tomorrow night?" I had an arsenal of other questions. One being why Rowan had an annual membership. For Liam it made sense, but not Rowan.

"A week before the party we're informed of the city, the date, and time. On the day of the event, I receive a text message an hour before it starts with the address."

"It's a security measure," Aidan said and stepped into the room. "How can we keep Finley untouched, if we can't do a recon of the property?"

Rowan laughed, the sound ominous. "First party I ever attended, a fellow member may have flirted with my date. I broke his neck. After that, no one has ever dared to even look at my dates."

"Quinn went as your date, and she flirted on purpose. Rob Granger is feared for a very good reason. Whose neck did you break?" Over the past few days Rowan turned into a bit of an enigma. I had only ever seen his soft side, the typical gentle giant. One most women would kill to get in their bed, even if for just one night. He's my brother-in-law, but a handsome man is still a handsome man.

"CEO of a Fortune 500 company by day, one of the biggest distributors of violent footage of children being raped by night. Kiddie porn is the worst term ever coined." Rowan glanced down at me. "I take the smile on your face as approval."

My head bobbed up and down. "If there's anyone there tomorrow night you want me to take out, just say the word. It's been far too long since I last annihilated a predator." I stared down at the orca tattoo on my left wrist. "Let's go for that run, you need to talk me through what to expect tomorrow night."

"One thing you need to understand going in, the organiser expects everyone to have sex."

Aidan cursed, Rowan and I both turned to him. "Ro, I get

it. The information you gather at these parties is invaluable. Sorry, but there's no way I'll allow the two of you to have sex. Finley is my wife. Not a fellow operative. There are lines we must never cross, and this is as big as they get."

"Perhaps you skipped that part, as your teenage years weren't like ours, dry-humping might do."

I burst out laughing and then got an idea. "Who organises the parties?"

Rowan turned before he reached Aidan. "That, my dear sister, is the million dirham question. No one knows."

Dubai, United Arab Emirates
Tuesday, 26 January, 3:10 p.m.

A ten kilometre run, and a shower with Aidan later, I felt energised enough to see what Eli's thingy uncovered in my absence. Aidan sent Liam to buy groceries and prepare lunch. In part I suspected as punishment for the mess he created in Vienna. Part he was the only one not bringing anything to the table. Not that I brought enough to deserve a pat on the back.

Rowan placed a plate next to my hand and pulled out a chair across the table.

"The parties, were any of them held in the same cities, or around the time of the murders?"

Rowan wiped his mouth and placed the napkin on the table. He turned to the map Aidan had stuck to the wall. Red dots indicated the locations of the murders. "Some of the same countries, but not at the time of the murders."

He walked around the table and stared at my murder board. "For instance, the murders in Paris were last July, they held a party in Marseille in February. The murder in Croatia was in Split last August, but a party was held in Dubrovnik before the first murder in Mexico. Off the top of my head, those are the only connections I can think of. Then again, I've only been a member for two years." Rowan returned to his food.

"Do you think Biggie is involved with the parties and the murders?" I stared at the chicken and salad on the plate next to my hand.

"If he is who I suspect, he's a sixty-something mercenary. Whoever pays his asking price will get his services."

"Would someone that old be capable of moving coffins and steel drums around?" I dug into my food and waited for Rowan to answer.

He laughed and drank a sip of orange juice. "Please ask Dad that. He's sixty-five and I've seen what he is still capable of. He trains with the new recruits, and he often beats the younger ones on the obstacle course."

"Okay, so it's plausible that even though Biggie is older, he's still capable of helping our killer."

We finished the rest of our meal in silence, and when I returned from the kitchen, I dialled Eli's number. He answered before I even heard the ringtone. "Rowan asked me to look for footage of the mystery behemoth in the cities he listed. As soon as I find something concrete, you'll be my first call."

"Thank you, but I need you to verify something for me. Don Peo, the male victim murdered in Santiago, I suspect I found something interesting in his emails. He received an email from a certain Alejandro Sanchez, but the email was deleted from his inbox the day after his murder. Only that email, nothing else. It wasn't in his trash, but that thing you created found it. Why would a choreographer's email be deleted? *After* Don Peo's death? The police found his body on Tuesday, and Wednesday someone accessed his emails and deleted it."

"What did the email say?"

"Just a standard 'You've been selected to audition', with the date and time he had to be at the given location. I checked, and Don Peo's mobile phone was in the vicinity of that building, but at the time it stood vacant. Someone lured him there."

"Alejandro Sanchez is a choreographer. It wouldn't raise any red flags for a dancer to receive an email like this."

"My point exactly, but why delete it? I need to locate Alejandro Sanchez." I leaned back in the chair and closed my eyes.

"Done, he's in Madrid, Spain. Moved there December two years ago."

"Hold on." I started typing close to the speed at which Eli's fingers fly over a keyboard. Rowan came to stand behind me but said nothing. "The female victim in Majorca was also a dancer. I accessed her mobile phone records."

"I will run a search and see if any of the numbers link to a dance studio or dance production company." The familiar sound of Eli pounding away at his keyboard filled the ensuing silence.

I waited. My stomach lodged in my throat. This could be something. Or nothing.

"Well done, Mrs Walker. Alejandro Sanchez owns one of the biggest dance theatres in Spain. The day before Catalina Garcia disappeared, she received a call from Sanchez's office in Madrid."

"He links to two of our victims, on different continents. It's time I chat with Señor Sanchez." I downed the orange juice Rowan had brought me and placed the glass down a bit too hard. "How does Sanchez go from being in Chile, to owning one of the biggest dance production companies in Spain, in a little more than a year?" I pushed my chair back and bumped into Rowan's legs. I apologised and started pacing around the office. The marble tiles cool beneath my feet.

"You have muscle helping you get rid of the bodies and staging them. Are people finding victims for you?" The killer didn't answer, so I continued, "I need to find any other potential links between the victims. Eli, I might need your help on this. We don't know how long before he kills again, he might have his next victim already." I don't like asking for help, but to save lives, I'll swallow my pride and vanquish it to the darkest corners of my soul.

Aidan stormed into the office, excitement visible in his eyes.

"He screwed up. The medical examiner found a used condom inside the Zurich victim's mouth."

I gagged, and then realisation bitch-slapped me so hard I almost lost my footing. "He didn't screw up; it was done on purpose. Why are we only hearing about it now?"

"Seems after news broke of our minor incident on the A51, the detective in charge of the investigation realised there might be more to the murder than just a random act of violence. It appears Hans, our operative in Switzerland, made himself a new friend."

Not a single piece of evidence had been found on any of the previous victims. The original crime scenes never found, except for the murders in Edinburgh, London and Paris. The houses had been scrubbed down. Better than some crime scene cleaning crews can do it. In those three cities our killer hadn't left the victims in parks, or isolated areas. No, he left them in the houses he had rented, with fake credit cards of course. Eli tried to trace their origins, but at that point in time hadn't found a legitimate name, or company, connected to any of the three used. The Perspex boxes which served as glass coffins didn't have as much as a fingerprint smudge on the outside. The 200 litre drums untraceable. The coffins? Standard issue for your larger individuals – big enough for two victims. The fingerprints, hair and DNA found belonged to the victims.

The medical examiners found proof that the female victims had sexual intercourse before death. None showed any of the signs you might expect if the rapes had been violent. Not that it meant the women weren't raped.

None of the victims showed any restraint marks, indicating they weren't tied up at any point. The day after they had last been seen, their bodies were found.

Aidan spoke as I still stared at the murder board. "What is it?"

"The time he spends with them, before killing them, isn't part of the fantasy. It's all about the act of killing, and the staging. Like you said, the story he tells."

I stared at the photos of the victims. Their deaths had been excruciating, except perhaps the ones who might've been killed with insulin. "Aidan, if the killer used insulin, would death be painless? Do the victims fall into a coma and die?"

"Maybe. If the insulin was administered before they went to bed, they might not have woken up when their bodies went into hypoglycaemia. If the victims were awake, they might've experienced confusion, heart palpitations, anxiety, trouble talking, seizures, clumsiness, sweating or shakiness. Only the killer can tell us what happened."

"He watched them die, except the victims who were buried alive."

Aidan told me what happens to the human body when organophosphate poison is ingested. The women had died inside their Perspex coffins. Their handprints the only ones found on the inside of the boxes. I couldn't bring myself to imagine what death must've been like for them. When death comes for me, I hope it will be quick.

"He hacked off the hands of the victim in Edinburgh. How did the forensics team not find a single drop of blood inside the house? Even if the killer used bleach to clean up the blood, luminol would've reacted to the haemoglobin. She didn't die inside that house. The houses form part of the staging. That's why the forensic teams found nothing in the houses in Edinburgh, London or Paris. He didn't sleep there, neither did the victims. This is all one big game."

I hate playing games. Unless I make the rules.

Sixteen

Dubai, United Arab Emirates
Tuesday, 26 January, 5:58 p.m.

Aidan sat down on the sun lounger and rubbed my feet. *Bliss.* "What time do you want to leave for dinner?"

"Why don't the three of you go and bring me back some Dynamite Shrimp? I need to keep working through the autopsy reports." I smiled when Aidan's eyes met mine. "I love you, Mr Walker."

"No, back up. Do you think I missed something in the autopsy reports?" Aidan turned and stared out over the ocean. "I love you more, *Duncan*."

I kicked him in the ribs, not hard enough to leave a bruise. "For that, there won't be a round two of what happened earlier this afternoon. Is it just me or are the days blurring into each other?"

"You've been out of the game for a while. There aren't a lot of profilers who can say they hunted an international serial killer, let alone found themselves in a different city every day. For the past year you were a full-time mom, and you put up with my fears. It's normal to feel out of your depth, give yourself some time."

"I can't help but wonder if us being here is a waste of time. What if the guy Rowan calls Biggie isn't the one from the parties?"

"Our only other option is to go home and wait for the killer to strike again. That could be months from now."

I scooted closer and wrapped my arms around the keeper of my sanity, pressing my cheek to his back. "His cooling-off periods are becoming shorter. At first it was months between kills, except for the three in close succession. He's killing every month now, three people just this month. January isn't over."

"Is this escalation significant?"

I shrugged. "I'm struggling to wrap my head around how he finds the victims, or rather, who helps him find the victims. And this larger-than-life man who was with him when he got the tattoos, in Budapest and Zurich, that we know for certain. The tattoo artist told Hans the same as what Janos told Rowan. They wore disguises. Biggie's handguns were visible, and he did all the talking."

"The killer is someone famous, or infamous. A person who can persuade otherwise law-abiding individuals to find him victims."

"I want Alejandro Sanchez." I pressed my lips to Aidan's back.

He turned and pulled me onto his lap. "How much do you love me, Mrs Walker?"

I rubbed myself against him. "Is that a trick question?"

Aidan moaned as I pushed my lower body down on him. "You need to stop doing that."

I laughed and kissed him hard and fast. "You don't want me to, and whatever my Aidan wants, he gets."

Aidan leaned his forehead against mine and smiled. "It's been a long time since you *interrogated* a suspect. Do you think you still have it in you?"

Butterflies scurried inside me, and I pulled back, keeping my hands on the back of his neck. "What did you do, Commander Walker?"

"Do you want coffee? It's going to be a very late night."

I bit my bottom lip. The flapping of the darkness' wings drowned out the sounds of Rowan and Liam inside the house.

"This face of yours, woman, you drive me crazy."

"What face?" I pushed out my bottom lip and then smiled. I couldn't help it.

"You don't even know what I've done for you. You can feel it, can't you?" Aidan brushed his lips against mine.

I nodded, my lips still against his. "Who am I going to play with?"

"In less than seven hours Alejandro Sanchez will wake up in Dubai." Aidan stood with me in his arms and lowered me until my feet reached the deck. "Come, I need to show you a room my mother designed."

Excitement filled me. Heather Walker and I are alike in many ways. One being we enjoy torture. However, I believe the more appropriate term nowadays is interrogate. It doesn't matter what people want to call it, the way we do it, gets us answers.

If Alejandro Sanchez knew the name of our killer, I would make him tell me. If he didn't, well then, he'll have a crazy story to tell. A story no rational person would ever believe. People don't just fall asleep, get tortured, and then wake up in their own bed again. Who would take him seriously, if he didn't have even the slightest scar or bruise to show?

Aidan sent Liam to buy dinner. Food shouldn't be delivered to a safe house. I ordered two servings of Dynamite Shrimp. There isn't a PF Chang's in Marcel, so whenever possible, I ate enough to last me until the next time. Before Aidan and I returned to the office, I asked him if we could bring Ainsley to Dubai in March. With all the hours Aidan had spent working the past year, the three of us deserved our first family vacation.

Eli's spy thingy found another connection. The victims in London, Edinburgh, and Paris were in contact with the same person. An up-and-coming photographer who had taken up permanent residency in a London cemetery. The date on his death certificate corresponded with the day the victims in Paris had disappeared. A single bullet had ended his life; he died on his way to a photo shoot around 0800 hours.

"Aidan, is this the work of a sniper?" I pointed at the screens, showing the autopsy report and the crime scene photos.

The best sniper in the world intertwined his fingers behind

his neck and stared up at the screens. "Yes, easy kill."

"Easy for you doesn't mean easy for everyone else, military trained or not." I smiled at his back. For more reasons than one, I was grateful my husband played for the good guys' team.

"You could've done it. It isn't hard to shoot someone standing out in the open. The killer squeezed the trigger from the other side of the Thames. The width of the Thames at Woolwich is a mere 448 metres."

I wanted to roll my eyes but didn't. "The report says an eyewitness saw him stop to take a call, while he walked in the direction of the Woolwich foot tunnel. His murderer wanted him in that exact location."

Aidan brought up a map of the area on his laptop and displayed it on the bottom right-hand screen. "It's close to the airport; killer had to get to Paris."

"Why would the killer take him out *if* he placed four victims in the killer's hands?"

Aidan turned to look at me. "Sniping loose ends."

I laughed. Aidan's best jokes are the ones he doesn't realise he made.

"If Biggie has the level of military training that I suspect he has, he could've made that shot." Rowan pulled out a chair and placed a box on the table.

"What's in the box?" I asked.

Aidan's smile turned wicked. "Your outfit for tomorrow night."

The grin on his face said it all. He had chosen a dress for me once before. That night had turned out better than expected once we got home from my bachelorette party. "I'm not going to like it, am I?"

"The theme of the parties is always fantasy. I briefed Aidan on what to get you as he *knows* your sizes."

I'm not the first person to dread opening a box, and this wasn't the first box I didn't want to open. Aidan's naughty smile lingered as he gestured towards the box with his chin. "You'll approve once you see it. This way you won't be unarmed."

"Bad idea, bro. They search everyone on arrival and keep all weapons locked away until you leave." Rowan pushed the box towards me, it glided over the glass surface.

One cut with the Ontario MK 3 Navy knife Aidan had given me for our first Valentine's day and the box opened. I stared into it. My brain didn't want to process what my eyes saw. At least every item appeared to be black.

"You can choose a wig from the ones in the closet." Aidan came to stand beside me and closed the box. "I think it will be best if you tried it on in our room. I don't want to remind Rowan I'll cut off his favourite part if he gets as much as a twitch in his penis while seeing you in this."

Aidan turned to his brother. "It twitches, I cut it off."

Rowan stretched his long arms out above his head. "I've seen her in a bikini, and besides, she's going with me and not Liam. Sister to me, unattainable to him. Big difference."

"I wish she wore a bikini to this party." Aidan shook his head and slumped down in a chair.

My future lack of flesh coverage set aside for the time being, I refocused on the man who had been murdered in London. "Why would you kill him? Four victims in three cities, he could've given you access to many more. Ignas made a name for himself photographing models, actors, and dancers. I looked at his website, none of the victims' photos were part of his portfolio."

It isn't unusual for an artist to go by his first name. What struck me as odd – two years before no one had even heard of Ignas the photographer. Before his death, everyone who is anyone wanted to be on the other side of his camera.

Rowan walked closer to the screens and cursed. "Ignas and Biggie might've known each other."

"Why do you say that?" I asked.

"They were born in the same country."

Seventeen

Dubai, United Arab Emirates
Tuesday, 26 January, 8:09 p.m.

I ate too much Dynamite Shrimp but didn't regret it. I needed the sustenance for when Alejandro Sanchez sat tied to a chair in the room Aidan showed me earlier. In a couple of hours I might learn the name of the man responsible for the deaths of twenty-five people. Eli found proof that Sanchez had been in contact with the female victim in Chile, Don Peo, and the two victims in Majorca. Only two of them dancers, the others he had offered backstage work. Easy money for students.

It was clear the killer preferred younger victims, Franz Brandstätter at twenty-six the oldest of them all. Not the fairest. With the victims' faces lined up next to each other something else became apparent. The female victims were beautiful, not due to camera filters or make-up plastered onto their faces. They had a natural glow. Dare I say hope and ambition were visible in their eyes? Perhaps I wanted to remember they were ripped from this world far too soon. Most people in their early twenties have high hopes and dreams for what their futures might hold.

The men on the other hand weren't remarkable. Not ogre ugly, but also not the type of men who would get a second glance when a woman walked past them on the street. The killer's fantasy never focused on them. The women his darkest desire.

I ignored the voices of the three men sitting in the command centre. Unless they had something to offer, like the killer's name and whereabouts, I didn't want to hear it.

Rowan touched my shoulder. "Fin, can you fake it?"

With my eyes still glued to the victims' faces, I said, "Of course, there isn't a woman in the world who can't fake an orgasm."

"Excuse me?" Aidan's voice much louder than usual.

I turned to my husband and sighed. "You know the female body better than most women know their own. I'll never need to fake it with you because you don't give me a reason to. You're so good, the orgasms catch me off guard. Every. Single. Time. We've been together for years, and not once did I ever wish you would hurry and get it over and done with. I'm not referring to you, *lover*." I walked to where he sat and pressed my lips to his forehead. *Men are so predictable.*

"Liar," Liam said.

"Not lying at all, I had quite a few sexual encounters before I met your brother. I speak from experience when I say that every woman who has ever lived can fake an orgasm. Men in their early twenties don't care what a woman wants or needs. It's all about their own gratification. We might as well be blow up dolls. Certain biological things happen when a woman climaxes, and *that* she can't fake. So, if a man isn't focused on his lover's reactions, and responses, he won't realise she's faking it."

Show me a woman who hasn't faked it because she wanted it to be over, because waxing her own bikini line would be more fun. Or she took pity on the poor guy who tried so hard but didn't have a clue what he was doing. We've all been there. Some of us perhaps even more than once.

"What things?" Liam asked.

I covered my face with my hands and shook my head. With his body count, and not the kill count, he should know the answer. Unless sexually he remained stuck in his early twenties despite being in his thirties. "Liam, I'm sorry to say, but I'm pretty sure most, if not all the continent full of women you've slept with, faked it."

Aidan smiled when our eyes met. The smile turned into a scowl as soon as I asked, "May I teach Liam?"

"No." Aidan lifted the water bottle to his lips.

"Not by having sex with him. I can draw him pictures. The stick figures I'm talented enough to draw will suffice. Whatever I can't draw, I can show him pictures. Not of myself, ones in your medical textbooks. His future wife will thank you, Aidan."

Rowan laughed so hard I wanted to cover my ears. "I'll pay for him to see a sex therapist." He turned to his brother. "Perhaps if you slept with the same woman more than once, you would understand what we're talking about. A one-night stand orgasm is nothing compared to what you have in a committed, caring, relationship." I didn't miss Rowan's use of the word caring instead of loving.

I returned my focus to the victims' faces on the screens. Aidan wouldn't take kindly to me saying one time, with a skilled man, can be better than a year-long relationship. My husband would internalise again, even though what we share doesn't compare to anything either of us had experienced with previous partners. For all his brilliance Aidan has one big flaw. If he considers for one second he made a mistake, or wasn't good enough, he ends up spending hours at the shooting range. Sometimes he ran so far I had to drive to fetch him because he couldn't make it back home. For a trained soldier, avid runner, and the daily workouts of Fortius' operatives, it said a lot as to how far I had to go to pick him up. Both in the literal and figurative sense.

"Finley, I asked whether you can fake a British accent? Well enough to do it for a couple of hours," Rowan said.

"I'm not sure, mate. Perhaps if the queen demands it." I tried.

"Okay, Finley won't be going as a Brit. Perhaps if you drink a bottle of Walker before we go, you might pull it off."

"A bottle of Walker will make me butcher a Scottish accent, I speak from experience."

"Is it necessary for Fin to talk at all?" Aidan asked.

I spun around and stared daggers at him. "Excuse me?

I assure you, Commander Walker, I can get results with or without a fake accent. Besides, Fortius has invisible two-way earpieces, I'm sure you have access to a voice changer that can fake an accent for me." I placed my hands at my sides and breathed hard. "Need I remind you when I hunted predators – on my own – I didn't need a fake accent, or help. I might not have the same level of training as you and the rest of the team, but I'm no less capable of taking care of myself. Or taking down a serial killer."

"Damn, she's sexy when she's angry. No wonder you put a ring on her." Liam slapped his hands together. "I get why you chose *that* outfit for her. Fin's going as *your* fantasy."

Rowan turned his chair to face Aidan. "I gave you clear instructions on what they expect women to wear. If Fin doesn't blend in, she'll draw unnecessary attention."

"My wife wasn't made to blend in or disappear in a crowd. The last thing you want is Finley to dress up like some puffed up, pink, plaything. She'll be as uncomfortable as an orca on land. Fin will wear what I got her. End of discussion. At least wearing that she'll be armed. I'm not sending my wife in anywhere unable to protect herself."

"She's a human weapon, I've seen the way Eli trains her. They don't spar, it's full-on combat." Liam swivelled his chair from side to side.

Rowan placed his hands on the table and pushed to his feet. "She's knocked me on my ass more than once, and she's not going in alone. I'll be with her the entire time. Do you not trust me to keep your wife safe?"

Anger turned into a violent storm inside me, and I marched out of the office. Once I reached our room, I slammed the door shut and emptied the contents of the box out onto the bed. Aidan knew me well. Wearing this I would feel more like myself. Even though I would look similar to what I had when I needed to earn extra money after almost totalling my father's newest muscle car.

I returned to the office dressed in what Aidan had bought.

The black robe slash coat thingy, I didn't tie at my waist only at my neck. The satin drifted behind me reminding me of a superhero's cape.

"This was the last time you will ever talk about me as if I'm not in the room. It's demeaning. I'm far more than Mrs Aidan Walker. I'm more than an ex-soldier and, as you called me, a human weapon. I have instincts, skills, and I can charm the life out of anyone. Weakness isn't part of my DNA. If I have to rip someone's larynx out to get to the person responsible for the murders of twenty-five people, I'll do so and not lose a wink of sleep."

I held up my hand and walked around the table. The knee-high leather boots more comfortable than they looked. "Aidan, don't start with whether that's even possible. I'm making a point."

"That you are. I like the wig."

I let out an exaggerated breath. "Don't try to flatter me. We both knew strawberry blonde will work with my complexion and eyes." I relaxed my arms, satin caressed my skin as the robe slipped down. I tossed it onto the table.

The Ka-Bar TDI pressed against Rowan's throat. If he breathed too deep, he would bleed. Laughter bubbled out of me and suppressed the rage I felt leaving the room earlier. "Boys, let's get one thing straight. I'm part of this team now, and not just Aidan's wife. I can hold my own, as well as any of you. Tomorrow night I'll get close enough to Biggie for us to confirm whether the tattoo on his right hand is what Rowan suspects."

I turned to my husband. "Unless I say a safe word, you *will* let it play out, and trust me to do my job. Understood?"

Aidan nodded.

With a few clicks of the mouse, my military records and the case files the Marcel Police Department compiled on The Hangwoman's victims lit up the screens. "I'm not only a wife, mother, your sister-in-law, or ex-military. This will show you my training, and skills, but it doesn't tell you what I'm capable of when hunting a human predator. Buckle-up boys, you're about to see first-hand why your parents trust me to take over the interrogation reigns from the infamous Heather Walker."

"What's your safe word?" Liam's gaze travelled over my exposed flesh. I considered throwing the Ka-Bar at his face but decided against it.

"I don't have one."

Eighteen

Dubai, United Arab Emirates
Tuesday, 26 January, 11:17 p.m.

Both the female victims in Australia had been models, signed on by the same agency. The day before their murders, someone deleted their photos from the agency's website. Eli found the information; nothing is ever lost. Except the victims. At the time of the murders the agency had been small, since then, it grew into one of the most lucrative in Australia. With offices in Perth and Sydney at the time of the murders, it had since opened offices in Adelaide, Melbourne, and Darwin. Upon further investigation, I discovered the owner's father was a member of parliament.

I answered my phone without looking at the screen, expecting a call from Heather with an update on how my daughter's day was going.

Eli skipped all formalities. "He struck again, in Abu Dhabi—"

So close. "Aidan, do we have someone there who can help?"

"We don't." Aidan pulled out the chair next to mine.

"The woman is alive," Eli said.

I covered my mouth with my hand. First the condom, tied off to keep the semen inside, and now a surviving victim. Someone who perhaps saw our killer's face, and that of his helper. I rubbed my hands together. We were closing in on him.

"Are you sure she's one of his victims? He informs the police of the body and location after they're dead. Where is she?"

"This time he didn't mention a body, but said a victim, and

that the police should hurry and send an ambulance. She's being taken to NMC."

Aidan dragged his hands down his face. "We don't have an operative or contact in Abu Dhabi. Our prisoner arrives in less than two hours. It doesn't give us enough time to travel to Abu Dhabi, speak to the victim, and get back here. Not without a helicopter. The victim might not be conscious, or she might have brain damage depending on the dose he gave her. Organophosphate poison, even though not always lethal, can have lasting effects on a patient. During my time in the ER I saw more than once the damage it's capable of."

"You go to Abu Dhabi, and I'll talk to Sanchez. You're a world-renowned doctor, Aidan, someone there would've heard of you." An invisible fist struck me in the gut as I said the words. I hated reminding Aidan of the life he had left behind, because of the actions of those we never speak about.

Rowan walked into the room with Liam right behind him. "What's going on?"

Aidan told them about the surviving victim. Liam spoke first, "I know a nurse who works at NMC."

"Define *know*?" I asked, despite knowing the answer.

Liam shook his head. "It lasted a week. A holiday fling. She knew it going in. No hearts broken or bad words spoken." He laughed once he realised he'd rhymed.

"Call her, and head to Abu Dhabi. Now. Rowan, go with him. Eli, see what else you can find."

"I can tell you one thing, the voice of the person who called it in isn't the same as with the other murders. For one, it's lower, and this time he again spoke English, but his accent is heavier. Most of the other times he spoke in that country's official language – or tried to at least."

Aidan pushed to his feet. "Arabic is the official language of Abu Dhabi, although English is widely spoken. The helper called it in this time. Why?"

"Perhaps the killer can't even attempt to speak Arabic. Which other countries did he speak English where English isn't either the main language or widely spoken?" I asked.

"Vietnam, Croatia, Greece, and Hungary," Eli said.

Aidan drew a deep breath and walked to the murder board. He picked up a red marker and started writing next to each of the countries I had listed earlier. Spanish next to Mexico, Argentina, Chile, and Spain. English next to Singapore, Hong Kong, Australia, South Africa, Malta, Scotland, and of course England. French next to Paris, France. German next to Austria and Switzerland.

I joined Aidan and watched his beautiful mind and hands at work. "Our killer speaks Spanish, English, French, and various German dialects."

Which made him educated, or one of the Walker brothers. I laughed at the idea, not out loud, and kept my bad humoured joke to myself. For a moment I thought about it. Joke aside, Rowan had said Biggie is his size. Liam's a womaniser. They've both travelled to all of the known murder locations. Between the two of them they spoke multiple languages. Rowan, the only one to have seen the tattoo on Biggie's hand. A tattoo which shouldn't be on someone's hand, according to Rowan. The Cayenne in Zurich could've been occupied by any of Fortius' enemies. A ruse to make me not consider them as suspects? Could they be the killers?

No. They were both in the house with us the entire time in Dubai. Although, Liam left for a couple of hours, longer than needed to pick up dinner. Perhaps the victim survived because the killer didn't waste time waiting for her to die.

Nineteen

Dubai, United Arab Emirates
Wednesday, 27 January, 00:05 a.m.

I focused on the victims who were murdered with an organophosphate poison. Their autopsy reports contained the same note – *damage to the epiglottis and oesophagus.* I researched organophosphate poisons and realised it wasn't something our victims would've consumed without knowing it. It has a chemical smell and a bitter taste. Grateful that the victim in Abu Dhabi survived, I couldn't help to wonder why she still breathed. None of the twenty-five victims before her had evaded death.

"The damage to the victims' epiglottis and oesophagus, what can cause it?" I asked Aidan when he returned to the command centre carrying a mug in each hand.

"Educated guess – the killer pushes a pipe down their throats and uses a funnel to pour the poison into their bodies. He knows the correct dosage for it to be lethal and purchases it in each country. Organophosphate is used in several pesticides, insecticides, nerve agents, and medications. An estimated 200,000 people die from organophosphate poisoning every year. Some ingest it by accident, others commit suicide, and it's used to kill more than just insects." Aidan drank his coffee while staring at my murder board.

"The Perspex boxes, do you think he buys them in country as well?"

Aidan nodded. "He used a thinner variant in Buenos Aires than what he used in Perth. Eli's trying to run down possible suppliers in each of the countries, but I doubt it will lead anywhere. The killer may have paid with a fake credit card and had it delivered to a random address."

"The premeditation with each murder is unlike anything I've ever seen. I wonder how our killer finances this murderous globetrotting of his. And how he's able to convince, or coerce, others into supplying him with victims. Consider Sanchez, after the murders in Santiago he would've known what would happen in Majorca." I placed my hand on Aidan's shoulder and made no attempt to suppress my tears. "Sanchez has to pay for his involvement. You need to leave the room at some point and let me avenge the victims. *Please.*"

Tears spilled down my cheeks. Over the years I saw far too many victims. Every murder, every rape, every photo taken of a child and shared with millions of paedophiles still gets to me. It will never change, and the day it does, I'll be in serious trouble.

The darkness inside me will never let me be free of the lust for vengeance coursing through my veins. I hope it never gives up the fight, and will always remind me that I can, and must do whatever is necessary to avenge the victims.

Aidan turned to face me and dropped his mouth to my forehead. "I'm not leaving you. Whatever you do, you'll do it for the greater good. I love your heart, Finley. Don't ever think the same thoughts, the same lust for vengeance isn't something I feel every day. I'm just less vocal about it than you are. Fortius, this life we chose, I'm doing it to make the world a better and safer place. If breaking Sanchez allows us to stop this killer, then I'm all in. No matter what."

Aidan pulled me closer and held me as I cried for twenty-five human beings. And for a woman lying in a hospital bed in Abu Dhabi.

Safe in my husband's arms, I realised Rowan and Liam weren't murderers. They are like Aidan and me. Warriors. Protectors. "I can't believe Liam's penis might help us catch a serial killer."

Aidan laughed and held me tighter. "To be honest, I never expected it would be of any use to anyone but him. I hope the victim is able to tell them something, but more than anything I hope she doesn't suffer from any long-lasting effects. A person shouldn't survive a serial killer to only suffer for the rest of their lives."

"Why did he kill Ignas? He worked across Europe – he could've supplied an endless amount of victims. Unless Ignas realised that an investigation will lead back to him, making him the prime suspect." I pressed my lips to Aidan's, wiped my face and took a step back. "Perhaps Ignas didn't want to be a part of it anymore. Earlier you said the killer might've seen him as a loose end, or a potential whistle-blower."

Only the killer held the answers to my questions about Ignas' murder. With Alejandro Sanchez arriving in less than an hour, there were things I needed to take care of. But first, I memorised every detail of the four people whose murders he had a hand in. If not for Señor Sanchez's greed, they might not have met death so soon.

Dubai, United Arab Emirates
Wednesday, 27 January, 00:45 a.m.

The two-way earpieces in Rowan and Liam's ears gave Aidan and me full access to whatever they heard while in Abu Dhabi. Through the contact lenses in their eyes, we saw what they did, but on the screen in the command centre.

The nurse wasn't of much help, although she gave Rowan and Liam scrubs to sneak into the victim's room. A police officer stood sentry outside her door; he refused to let either of them in. It had been foolish of me to think anything will be easy with this investigation.

Rowan spoke to the police officer in Arabic, and then he and Liam left. I turned to Aidan and asked what Rowan had said. "He said they understood and will ask a female nurse to attend to the victim."

The nurse stood as Rowan and Liam entered the staff's

break room. "Thank you for trying." Liam pressed his lips to the unnamed nurse's cheek.

"I can go in. What do you need me to do?" she asked. "First, I need you to tell me the truth. I knew you were lying when you told me you're a businessman. Why are you here? Is your name even Logan?"

Liam pulled her down on the couch and held her hands in his. "Yes, Nina, my name is Logan. For the record, I never told you what I do for a living, you drew your own conclusions. The truth is I came here on holiday, and the week we spent together wasn't a lie. As I told you then I wish things were different, and I still do."

Rowan stood by the door. "We need your help. That woman survived being attacked by a serial killer. Somehow, she survived. None of his other twenty-five victims did. That's all I can tell you about this investigation. Logan told me about you, and the time you spent together. The last thing we want is to put you in any danger. If you can take some time off, we can arrange accommodation for you in a hotel in Dubai, under a different name. You'll be safe there."

I turned to Aidan. "Is there a mandatory class called 'Lying 101' all operatives are forced to take?"

"No, they're good at their jobs. If lying to this woman gives you the opportunity to take out a serial killer, then nobody gets hurt."

Through the contact lenses in Liam's eyes, I noticed the confusion and fear in Nurse Nina's eyes. "Tell her you work for Interpol," I instructed Liam.

He did, and Nina let out a deep breath. "Okay, that makes sense. Serial killer? Twenty-five people? Why isn't it being reported in the news? Interpol?"

"He has killed in multiple countries, that's why we're involved."

Nina shook her head. "Why didn't you tell the police officer at her door that you're with Interpol?"

Clever woman. Not clever enough to not have slept with

Liam Walker – or Logan – whoever he had claimed to be. Not that I faulted her for it. He's an attractive and charming man. Maybe we've all met a Liam Walker at some point in our lives, or we were a Liam Walker.

Rowan moved forward. "It's pointless to inform the local police. The killer doesn't stick around and never kills more than once in the same city. Nina, please we need your help. This victim is the best chance we have of identifying the killer and bringing him to justice. I promise, we will keep you safe. No one will ever know you helped us by talking to the victim for us."

"Her name is Alicia Rideout."

I pulled my laptop closer and searched for an Alicia Rideout in Abu Dhabi. Nothing. I expanded my search and found an airline ticket in her name. She had arrived from Ireland the day before. Her passport number made it easier. Miss Rideout was an actress, who performed in historical pieces in castles around Ireland. I relayed the information to Liam and Rowan. Not that it mattered, as they weren't going to talk to the victim. *No, the survivor.*

Nina rose and glanced between the two men she would never know shared the same surname. "What do you need me to ask her? If she's awake. I will not wake her. She needs the rest after what she's been through."

Liam stood and placed his hands on Nina's arms. "How did the killer find her? What does he look like? Is someone helping him? Anything. Thank you, Nina. And as my colleague, Rocco said, your safety is important to us. We won't let the killer get to you."

I tried not to laugh, knowing Rowan would hate anyone thinking his name is Rocco. When Aidan and his brothers were children they had a dog with that name.

"That won't be necessary, my fiancé is a police officer." With that, she left the room.

"Liam, did you know about her engagement?" I asked.

"No. I'm many things, but not a homewrecker. She told

me she had called off her engagement a month before we met. Guess they patched things up. This was six months ago."

Aidan placed his hand on my leg. "Our guest has arrived. Are you ready?"

Twenty

Dubai, United Arab Emirates
Wednesday, 27 January, 1:18 a.m.

Aidan reached for the door and turned to me. "How do you want to do this?"

On the other side of the door, Alejandro Sanchez waited. He didn't know he was in Dubai. I, on the other hand, knew what his future held – pain. "There's no indication that he speaks English. Interrogating him might lose a bit of punch if you have to translate for us. Certain things are universal and won't need any words. Fear and pain. Those two I can translate myself."

Aidan grabbed my hips and pressed me up against the wall. "Right now, I'm not your husband or the father of your child. Do whatever you need to get us answers. As soon as we step through the door, I'm Fortius' second in command, nothing else. Understood?"

"Yes sir." I kissed him hard. Aidan had dished out his own kind of justice when we first met.

He lowered me and pushed my hair behind my ears before covering my face. "Rowan and Liam will update us when they get back to the house. Let's do this, I have a surprise for you. I won't need to translate."

Aidan eased the door open; I kicked it. The door slammed against the wall. Sanchez lifted his head, his eyes wild. He mumbled against the duct tape covering his mouth. His emotions didn't need translating. I took a seat across from him while Aidan yanked the tape from Sanchez's mouth. I laughed when he whimpered; clumps of facial hair stuck to the tape. The stage set. My laughter created the perfect atmosphere.

Without a doubt, Sanchez realised nothing good will happen to him in this darkened room. No windows. No mercy. The instruments for our chat I had selected earlier – well, the day before, as we were well past midnight. It stood against a wall and I turned to look at it. So did Sanchez.

I waited for his eyes to meet mine. "Hola, Alejandro." He didn't respond. "Don Peo. Isidora Diaz. Diego Gonzalez. Catalina Garcia."

Sanchez shook his head despite the recognition flashing in his eyes as I said the names, and an eerie sounding voice translated. I kept my eyes devoid of the shock I felt at the sound of the voice. The voice not one anyone wants to hear when you lay in bed at night or walk down a dark alley.

I leaned forward and removed the Ka-Bar from where I had hidden it underneath my chair. The blade gleamed in the overhead light. The tip cool as I tapped it against my lips. "I hope you don't make this easy for me. I've been waiting a long time to play with you, Alejandro. Please try your hardest to keep your secrets for as long as you can." I pointed to my right, to the instruments which would bring me joy and him pain. "I want to use *all* of those toys."

Sanchez rambled as another voice translated, this one not creepy at all. "I've never met them or even heard their names. Why am I here?"

I glanced up at Aidan, who stood behind our guest. He winked and nodded.

"Who is he?"

Sanchez shook his head. "I don't know what you're talking about."

Handy little thing this translator device. Aidan never ceases to amaze me. I pushed to my feet and plunged the blade into the side of Sanchez's left thigh. If I nicked an artery Aidan could take care of it. Aidan glanced at my handiwork and nodded. *Is it strange to have felt proud of his approval?*

Once Sanchez stopped screaming, I continued. "You received two payments; I can show you the proof. The first payment enough to get you out of Chile and allowed you to land on your feet in Spain. The second as recent as October last year, days before Catalina and Diego went missing. Tell me, Alejandro, how much is a person's life worth to you?"

"I won't tell you." Sanchez stared at the concrete floor between us. In the middle of the room's floor a steel grid; to make cleaning easier.

My handprint would be visible on his face for hours to come. I stared at my red palm and stretched my fingers to ease the burn. "No, you *will* tell me. Thank you for not making this easy." I lifted my eyes to Aidan's and leaned my head to the right. Aidan stepped away.

A single kick to his chair. Sanchez crashed to the floor. I fetched the towel. Aidan grabbed the hose.

As I lowered myself onto Sanchez's chest, I forced a sigh. "Oh, what big eyes you have, Alejandro. Oh, what secrets you keep. Perhaps this will help jog your memory." I covered his face with the towel and held it down. Aidan opened the valve. Sanchez thrashed as water filled his lungs.

He coughed and spat water onto my pants as Aidan lifted the chair until all four feet met concrete.

"Again?" I asked. We already washed his face and lungs five times, I doubted he wanted our help a sixth time.

"No!" I didn't need the translator device for this one.

"Tell me who he is!"

Sanchez coughed and spat out more water, this time on himself. "He never gave me a name. He contacted me *after* he paid the money into my bank account."

"Who deleted your email to Don Peo after his murder? The email which instructed him where to go, the very place the killer waited for him."

The look in Sanchez's eyes told me he didn't do it.

"You helped him to murder Don Peo and Isidora Diaz. Newspapers ran articles on their deaths for a week. You knew!" I slapped him again, harder than before. "You could've gone to the police, but you didn't. You kept the money and left Chile."

The baseball bat stood ready in the corner of the room. I grabbed it and swung through the air to warm up my arms. I'm not as young as I used to be, when I had last swung a bat around.

"I needed the money, for a better life."

I laughed so hard the baseball bat fell from my hands and rolled to a stop at Sanchez's feet. Barbwire kept his arms and legs in place.

Aidan's palm connected with the back of our guest's head. Pain spread across Sanchez's face as Aidan's fingers dug into the back of his neck. "You knew what he was going to do when he made contact again in Spain. There's no excuse for that."

My husband and I reached for the bat at the same time. "Ladies first," Aidan said and turned to Sanchez. His Spanish fluent, yet he spoke in English, perhaps for my benefit. "The Brigada de Homicidios questioned you. You lied to them and said Señor Peo had cancelled his classes with you a month before his death. We have video footage from the ATM across the street from where your studio used to be that proves you lied. Don never missed a single class."

There is an ATM, but no video footage. I enjoyed seeing this side of Aidan. I always wondered what it would be like to interrogate with him. It exceeded my expectations, and so did he, in the days that followed.

Alejandro Sanchez is an acclaimed choreographer, with a successful dance production company in Madrid. There are certain limbs one needs to pursue this passion.

I lifted the bat. Aidan held up a hand. "This might help." He walked to a cabinet and retrieved a syringe and a vial.

Aidan eased Sanchez's sleeve up. "My sincere apologies for what we've done to you, Alejandro. Please understand our frustration as the man who paid you, is using our money to do it. I don't like it when people steal from me, and even less when he has fun without me." Aidan jabbed the needle into Sanchez's shoulder and tossed the syringe aside.

I expected our guest to fall asleep from the prick of the

needle, and from the liquid Aidan injected into him. Instead of closing, his eyes became more alert and I realised I loved Aidan Walker even more.

I counted to thirty, rolling my shoulders. The sound of bones crushing filled the silence, followed by a slew of Spanish swear words. The blasphemous words didn't need translation and fuelled my growing rage. My arms cramped, the bat fell to the floor.

Sanchez kept screaming. The adrenaline coursing through his veins was my friend and not his.

Aidan retrieved another syringe and vial and injected the liquid into our guest's neck. I waited for Sanchez to drift off to dreamland. Before his eyes closed, he sang like a canary.

Twenty-one

Dubai, United Arab Emirates
Wednesday, 27 January, 2:59 a.m.

Rowan waited for us on the sundeck. To my left, the most beautiful view of Dubai. City lights dotted the night sky. To my right, the darkness of the ocean. I stretched my arms and rolled my shoulders.

"I take it you got in some exercise?" Rowan asked, stretching his legs out in front of him on the sun lounger.

I nodded and downed the bottle of water Aidan handed me. Interrogations leave me thirsty. "He didn't give us a name. I don't think he knows. He did however describe Biggie."

"The tattoo on his right hand?" Rowan asked.

"No, said Biggie wore gloves. Described his build, and said his Spanish isn't fluent, but he got the message across." The need for gloves I found strange as that time of year would've been summer in Chile. In Spain, all it had taken to convince Alejandro Sanchez to play a role in murdering two people was a simple phone call. One Eli already traced down the rabbit hole to nowhere. A burner phone. Another dead end.

"Biggie didn't want Sanchez to see his tattoo. An idiotic idea on Biggie's part to get such a recognisable tattoo on his right hand."

Rowan agreed yet reminded me of the ink on my left wrist.

"I covered it with a leather strap, just as our faces were covered the entire time we *chatted* with Alejandro." For more reasons than one, I needed a shower after the time spent in that room, with a man who had travelled all the way from Madrid to Dubai for nothing.

Rowan shifted and lowered his feet to the deck. "I'll take

care of the body."

"What body?" Aidan asked and placed an arm around my chest as he came to stand behind me.

"Sanchez's body." Rowan pointed into the house.

"No, Sanchez is heading back to Madrid. His transfer should arrive any minute." Aidan pressed his lips to the top of my head. "Did you have fun?"

No, I didn't. As much as I love torturing evil people – human predators – it leaves me feeling empty when they don't tell me what I want to know. Unsatisfied. Time wasted. Time I could've spent hunting the killer. This had been necessary as now we knew Sanchez deserved the punishment he would receive. The death penalty. Not this day, but soon enough.

"You're letting him go?"

Aidan laughed. "Pretty much. We'll leave Alejandro in an alley in a bad part of Madrid. It will appear to be a random attack."

"You left marks on him?" Rowan turned to me. "It's never a good idea to leave bruises unless you kill someone. Even more so when the person is, by all accounts, an upstanding citizen. The last thing you want is for someone to believe the ridiculous story he'll now be able to tell anyone. Including the Spanish Police."

For a second, I considered retrieving the bat and using it on my brother-in-law. "Rowan, do not insult my intelligence. I ensured Alejandro won't be able to live out his passion until *I* go to Madrid and put a bullet between his eyes. He doesn't deserve to enjoy the few days he has left on this earth."

I stepped out of Aidan's arms and came to a stop at Rowan's feet. With my hands on my sides, I stared down at him. "There's always method behind my madness, even more so behind your brother's. Let me explain it to you, son. We're sending Sanchez back because we suspect he'll contact the killer. He's more afraid of us than he is of Biggie, seeing as he is now under the impression Biggie works for us. We told him we want our money back because it was stolen from us. He doesn't have much to his name; spent it all to set up his dance company. As soon as Sanchez wakes up, he expects Biggie will pay him a visit. From their previous interactions, he knows Biggie isn't someone anyone should mess with. Sanchez told us it took some persuasion from Biggie's fists to get him to email Peo and place a call to Diaz."

Rowan stared up at me. "I'm sorry, Fin."

"So what if I gauged out his eyes, or shredded his tongue with a fork? My methods shouldn't matter to you. Do you question your mother whenever she does what I just did?"

Rowan shook his head.

"Don't ever second guess me again. I've tortured more people than you ever will. If I decide to let him, or anyone else live, you accept it. Sanchez is our only other living lead. And if I want to send him back alive, without the use of his legs, then it's my prerogative."

I turned to Aidan. "Will he ever walk again?"

"No. He won't get medical attention in time, and you went to town on his legs. I would love to see x-rays to confirm whether the damage is as extensive as I suspect." Aidan yawned. "I counted twenty blows, not including the four to his arms. Your aim worsened towards the end."

"Yes, well, it's not like my training includes swinging a bat around every day." I shrugged and returned to Aidan's arms.

"What information do you bring from Abu Dhabi? Where's Liam?" Aidan asked.

Rowan dragged a hand down his face. "He's taking a shower. Nina confirmed she was in fact single at the time of their fling, so at least there's that."

I tossed the empty water bottle at Rowan's head, his reflexes better than Liam's. He caught it before it connected with his face.

"Alicia Rideout, did she tell Nina anything?"

Rowan nodded and asked us to sit. "Two unsubs. Biggie, and the other one demanded that she call him 'your highness' during sex."

"He sees himself as the prince in this macabre fairy tale he recreates with every kill." I placed my hand in Aidan's.

"His highness had sex with her. Biggie pushed the pipe down her throat, poured the liquid down the tube and then put her in the Perspex box. Once the *prince* left, Biggie opened the lid and injected her with something. That's all she remembers."

Alicia Rideout might not have remembered it, but she put up one hell of a fight. Unlike the other victims, based on the information in their autopsy reports. Her arms were covered in defensive wounds, her left eye was swollen shut, and her knuckles bruised. This woman wanted to live.

"He could've injected her with atropine, pralidoxime, and benzodiazepines. It counteracts the organophosphate. She would've needed adequate oxygenation, depending on the initial dosage of poison given. Until I see a toxicology report, I can't say more. Will Miss Rideout suffer from any long-lasting side effects?" Aidan asked.

"Nina said it doesn't seem like it at the moment, and she promised to keep us up to date with the victim's progress."

"Survivor. Alicia's not only a victim, but a survivor. She *survived* him. Why?" I pinched the bridge of my nose between my thumb and middle finger. "For the record, Rowan, it's rape."

"No, she said she consented. Her agent arranged the meeting, and he was charming, a proper gentleman. Only after they had sex did the bigger guy appear and try to kill her."

"Where did they meet?" Aidan asked.

"A private house. A car picked her up at the hotel and drove her there. She thought it would be for an audition. After she read a few lines, he asked her stay for dinner, and she didn't have reason to suspect she was in any danger."

I will never judge a woman for indulging in her own desires, even if that meant it would be a one-time thing with a man she didn't know. Alicia Rideout wasn't the first, or last, woman to have tried sexing her way into a job. To call it *sleeping* your way to the top doesn't make sense.

Rowan pushed to his feet. "Eli located the car used to pick her up, license plate came back as fake. No footage from the cameras outside the hotel to give as an unobstructed view of the driver's face. He knew the locations of the cameras. With everything we've learned about them so far, we can assume he wore a disguise."

"Could she describe this prince character?" I asked as I stood.

Rowan shook his head. "Blue eyes, dark hair, attractive but nothing to write home about. His brows weren't as dark as his hair, and he had no facial hair. Spoke English with a flawless British accent."

"I need the name of her agent. He knows the killer. I might use the modified electric prodder on him." Waterboarding two people in a row is boring. "Did she see the tattoos on his back?"

Rowan shook his head. "She didn't mention it to Nina, and I didn't want to say anything about it to a nurse who might end up leaking a crucial piece of information to the press."

Twenty-two

Dubai, United Arab Emirates
Wednesday, 27 January, 8:00 a.m.

The things Sanchez had said before drifting off to sleep played through my mind. The request he had received was for any man, as long as the man was desperate for work. Don Peo had fit the requirements, as he carried the financial responsibility of taking care of his ageing parents and nieces and nephew after his brother- and sister-in-law died months apart. Cardiac arrest, and a work-related injury. This had left four children orphaned, and Don Peo desperate. Sanchez had also said what the life of a human being was worth to him – 50 000 euros. Four people murdered for 200 000 euros.

Biggie had identified himself as Claus Rheeder when he first contacted Sanchez. None of the Claus Rheeders I found online matched Biggie in appearance. Even before I started digging, I expected it to be another dead end. Frustration bubbled inside me. For failing to apprehend the killer and put a stop to the murders. Three people were murdered since I learned about this serial killer's existence. Alicia Rideout lay in the ICU. Aidan read her medical reports and said her body would make a full recovery. Her mind and soul? Time would tell. People process trauma in different ways, and I hoped Alicia would survive the aftermath.

Aidan and Rowan walked into the command centre. One placed a plate in front of me, the other a mug of coffee. Perhaps it was time I prepared a meal for them, or at least made them a cup of coffee.

"Why are you searching for a Claus Rheeder?" Rowan asked staring at the screens.

Aidan told him what Sanchez said, while I dug into the spinach and feta omelette. "I've only heard the name once before. Years ago, when Dad mentioned it," Aidan said.

I turned to him. "Context?"

Aidan leaned his hip against the table. "Claus Rheeder was the head of the BSS. One of the best trained black ops teams in the world. They were devoted to their country, and the doctrine of their head of state. The whole king and country thing. Their commander-in-chief made them a hit squad, and they took out anyone—"

"The dragon tattoo. Biggie could be Claus Rheeder, or another member of their team." The white mug dwarfed by Rowan's big hands.

Aidan shook his head and pulled his laptop closer. "Claus Rheeder is dead, dad took the photo."

The buckshot left little in terms of visual confirmation that the disfigured body I stared at belonged to Claus Rheeder. I told Aidan so, he laughed. "Dad pulled the trigger. If he says that's Rheeder, then it is."

"A black ops division who drifted out of white waters and into the black?"

"No, they were never in white waters. The BSS was founded and operatives were trained for a single purpose – to eliminate enemies."

"I know what BS stands for, but what's BSS?" I smiled when Aidan rolled his eyes at me.

"Bergia's Secret Service. Two of their operatives got away; their whereabouts are unknown. Dad tried to hunt them down, but these guys were trained as well as we are."

Aidan turned his focus to Rowan. "The dragon tattoo. They all had it on their right shoulders. Are you sure this is the design you saw on Biggie's hand?"

An intricate black dragon appeared on screen. The ink on a dead man's shoulder.

"The one on his hand is much smaller, it loses some of the detail, but the lines which form the wings caught my attention the first time. Then when he exited the tattoo studio in Zurich, I noticed the tail. The multiple hooks at the tip look more like something Finley used during her Hangwoman days than a dragon's tail."

I walked to the screen and memorised every detail. If we were in luck, I would see it on Biggie's hand at the party. "Cat-o'-nine-tails." My focus on the ink and not what remained of the man's face. "If they were a death squad, this minor detail makes sense."

I had studied the world map for hours on end, staring at the red dots indicating the locations of the murders. For the life of me, I couldn't recall seeing Bergia. Before I reached my laptop, Aidan displayed the world map on another screen and enlarged it.

Bergia lay landlocked between Lithuania to the north, Belarus to the east and south, and Poland their western neighbour. The entire country the size of New York City.

"Four hundred years ago, Bergia occupied a much larger area of that part of Europe. Their original capital was next to the Baltic Sea. Countless wars, and poor money management by generations of rulers forced them to sell off most of the land. Or they lost control of it during the wars." Aidan drank the last of his coffee. "Their current ruler and I met years ago during my second last tour."

I lifted my arm into the air and waved it around.

Aidan laughed. "Yes, Mrs Walker?"

"Fortius took out the BSS; on whose instruction?"

"King Szymon's."

Again, my arm shot up. Aidan crossed his arms over his chest and leaned back in his chair. He nodded, and I asked, "King? Did you meet him during the war?"

"Yes, and yes. Szymon believes a true leader leads from the front, like the kings did throughout the ages. Not the way politicians operate now by sending in troops to get slaughtered while they sit in the safety of their comfortable offices, giving orders when they've never even been in the line of fire."

"I like him already." I've always respected the kings and queens of old. They were on the battlefield, fighting alongside their warriors, dying with them.

"I thought you would. Szymon's grandfather founded the BSS, and like I said, they were nothing but a death squad. Once Szymon sat on the throne, he contacted me and asked for my help with solving his inherited problem. He thought I could take them out one by one from a far. I told him with their training a blitzkrieg was the only option. I asked him to leave it to me, and within twenty-four hours we took down eighteen of their twenty operatives."

"Twenty? That's not much of a secret service." I shrugged and rubbed my hands together. "Guess for a country that small you wouldn't need more than twenty. Did Szymon's father share in the grandfather's doctrine?"

"Szymon I died when Szymon II was twelve-years-old. He was next in line of succession. Women weren't allowed to rule, so none of Szymon the first's sisters could become queen. The second Szymon has since changed that law, and many others."

"Why did Szymon ask you to annihilate them?"

"The citizens feared for their lives with the BSS taking out anyone King Mikolaj suspected of being a threat to his sovereignty. They even eliminated supposed threats in other countries. Szymon wanted his people to know he had no intention of ruling the way his grandfather did, through fear or tyranny. With their training and the little support they had from factions both in Bergia and neighbouring countries, Szymon didn't have a choice but to make such a drastic decision."

I pushed to my feet and paced the length of the floor to ceiling windows. "Biggie might be one of the two who got away. Is it possible that the other is our killer, if we stick to the assumption that Biggie's role is that of a helper and not the actual killer?"

Rowan cleared his throat. "Alicia Rideout didn't mention him being older."

"Not if he wore a disguise. I've seen how Quinn can

transform her face with special effects makeup." I turned to Aidan. "We might've found the two BSS operatives who got away."

Twenty-three

Dubai, United Arab Emirates
Wednesday, 27 January, 10:25 a.m.

Alicia Rideout's agent would suffer an excruciating death. I would see to it myself. He had fled Florida after pleading guilty to procuring a person under eighteen for prostitution, as well as felony solicitation of prostitution. Max Jefferson hadn't been considered a flight risk, yet he obtained a fake passport and fled to Russia. With no extradition treaties between the two countries, he started a new life. Jefferson's new life ended that of at least four others.

I stared at Max Jefferson's new name – Oleg Petrov – his face had changed little since he fled the United States seven years earlier. This made finding him through the facial recognition software much easier.

"Who do we have in Moscow?" I asked Aidan.

"Depends. What do you need them to do?"

An image played in my mind. The perfect death for a paedophile. I regretted not trying it at least once during my Hangwoman days, perhaps I soon would. "Anyone who knows how to perform a blood eagle? I don't want him to die, so whoever does it needs to know how to keep him alive until I get there. Will they need to administer antibiotics? How much time will I have to get to Moscow before he dies?"

Aidan pressed his palms to his eyes and chuckled. "Every morning I wake up and wonder what will come out of your mouth today. I'm so glad I married you."

"Yes, yes, I'm in love with you too. Who do we have in Russia?"

"Someone with the stomach to carry out your request."

"Who?" Excitement pulsed through me, tinged with a hint of regret that I wouldn't be the one performing the blood eagle. It's not necessary for a medical professional to do it. Anyone can cut open a paedophile's back, crack his or her ribs and pull out the lungs of a sexual predator. *Easy-peasy.*

"Quinn's there, but she doesn't have a lot of free time as she's working." Aidan shook his head and covered his eyes with one hand. "She'll enjoy it too."

"There's a very good reason Quinn and I are best friends. Don't tell me you haven't wondered whether it's possible."

"There's enough research to stand for both sides of the argument, by all counts it will be an excruciating death. Who do you want to kill this time, my darling wife?"

"Max Jefferson, aka, Oleg Petrov." I shared with Aidan what I learned.

Aidan stood and walked to the window. "He rapes a child and with those charges it would've been a slap on the hand. Sounds more like someone wanted to give him a high-five for destroying a child's life. He has connections to someone high up, or someone screwed up the investigation."

"It doesn't matter. A child learned the dark truth that sometimes evil prevails, despite the fact that she had the guts to come forward. She's nineteen now."

"How does this piece of excrement connect to our investigation?" Aidan feels the same way I do about paedophiles. A dead one can't reoffend. They always do, after the pitiful prison sentences they receive. The judicial systems of most countries are a joke.

I opened the browser and showed Aidan what I found on Max Jefferson. A former movie producer who had reinvented himself as an agent to hopeful actors and actresses. "Alicia Rideout. Vesta Merwe, the victim found on Petra beach in Patmos. Both the victims in Cape Town. They were all his clients."

"After the party tonight, we'll head to Moscow and have a chat with Jefferson. Similar to the one we had with Sanchez.

I'll instruct the operative in Moscow to get eyes and ears on Jefferson. Quinn won't have the time to do surveillance. And if you're honest, you want to blood eagle him yourself."

I nodded as fast as my neck allowed, still a little stiff from the collision in Zurich. Before murder occupied my mind again, I grabbed my phone and dialled Heather's number.

"Hello, my girl."

"Good morning, Mom. How is Ainsley doing?" I pressed the speaker button for Aidan to hear.

Heather laughed and didn't stop. After she had returned from Columbia, I wondered whether she would ever laugh again. Ainsley's babbling became more distinct. I pursed my lips and shut my eyes. My daughter was safe, and by the sound of it having fun. Her grandmother found her own healing in the time they spent together. Everyone had what they needed. The ache in my heart intensified; in silence, I prayed our hunt would end soon. I wanted to be home with my daughter. More than anything, I wanted to inform the parents of twenty-five people that the person responsible for the deaths of their children met a gruesome end. Not giving them specifics, just a nudge towards closure. What I intended to do to the killer and his not so little helper, I couldn't voice to anyone but Aidan.

"Mama." A single word spoken by my precious child filled my heart and calmed the raging darkness within me.

"Hey, baby bear. Mommy loves you."

Aidan wiped my face and pressed his lips to my temple. "Daddy loves you too, Ains. Mom, Dad, if she starts walking while we're away, please don't tell us."

It hit me then. Being away from her was just as hard on Aidan. I wrapped my arms around his waist.

Silence. Ainsley started making noises again, and I heard the truth in Heather's veiled reply. "Of course, you'll see her take her first steps."

Aidan looked as miserable as I felt. "Thanks for lying, Mother. We've had other firsts with her, and there are many more to come."

"I'm glad you and Dad were there to see it." Yes, I lied. I wanted to be there, not halfway across the world tracking a killer who I began to doubt I could stop, despite all the leads we had. Parents who work outside the home miss out on so many little things, which are in fact the big things. It's part of the sacrifices we make. At least Ainsley's grandparents were there for one of her biggest milestones.

"How are things on your end?" Ryan asked.

Aidan looked at me, mischief played in his eyes. "Finley got to waterboard someone, swing a baseball bat around until her arms cramped, and she's going to blood eagle a paedophile in Moscow. Tonight, she's attending a sex party. She has slapped Liam, and schooled Rowan, Liam, and myself. None of us will ever forget who she is or what she's capable of. The Ka-Bar TDI she pressed against Rowan's neck while seducing Liam by walking around in nothing but a few strategically placed latex straps, got the point across."

"Just another day at the Fortius office, and in the Walker family, then." Ryan laughed.

"Pretty much."

My eyes narrowed as I stared at my husband. For this he would pay, not that he had said anything I wouldn't have told Ryan myself. Parents have only so much alone time to do what they can't when there is a baby who might cry at any moment. Our baby cared for and loved. I wanted to be taken care of, the Aidan way.

"Dad, I need information on the two BSS operatives who disappeared."

"Why?"

"They might be the killers we're hunting now."

Ryan sighed. "I don't think they are who you're looking for."

"Why not?" I asked.

"The two surviving BSS operatives – a man, the other a woman. She's the lone wolf type. An assassin responsible for most of the hits carried out by the BSS. I've gone over the case file. None of the murders fit her MO. The reason she was their top assassin – she walked in, killed and left. No mess, no fuss. In and out. Fair enough, she didn't just walk in, she was also a world class gymnast and an avid rock climber. Ivana made the right decision and used her skills as a cat burglar. There isn't a place she can't get in or out of."

"Wait a minute, old man, you know where she is?" I stared at my phone's screen.

"Of course. She's even stolen some things for us over the years."

"You turned her?" Aidan asked.

"Not me, your mother. Trust me, after three days in a room with Heather Walker, there isn't a person in the world who won't agree to anything just to get out. We aren't careless so we keep tabs on her; she's been in the Maldives for the past month."

Tabs meaning they had inserted a tracker thingy before they let her leave wherever Heather kept her company. Better the enemy you know, I guess.

"That leaves us with the man. What can you tell us about him?"

"The BSS's explosives expert. Ivar has spent the last ten years in Orenburg, Russia."

"Did you turn him as well?" I asked.

"No, he's in Black Dolphin. I need to go, it's time for Ainsley's breakfast and she loves the aeroplane noises I make. She does it as well while she tries to feed me. I'll talk to you later."

Black Dolphin Prison. What did Ivar do to get himself locked up with serial killers, paedophiles, terrorists and cannibals? It couldn't have been a mundane crime. Black Dolphin is one of those places no one ever wants to find themselves in. Perhaps if more prisons operated the same way, there would be less reoffending. Then again, no one sent to Black Dolphin ever leaves. Once a prisoner walks through the gates, they're there for life.

Ivana sunbathed in the Maldives, and Ivar sat in hell. As for us? Nowhere close to identifying the killer.

Twenty-four

Dubai, United Arab Emirates
Wednesday, 27 January, 2:30 p.m.

Under no circumstance were we allowed to have sex, dry-hump, or let our lips touch. Not even if our lives depended on it. Rowan and I glanced at each other and tried our best not to laugh as Aidan lay down the not-going-to-happen fornication laws.

"Understood?" Aidan stopped pacing and turned to look at us.

I felt like a teenager going on her first date. Not that my father had ever told me not to dry-hump anyone. That would've been awkward.

"Yes sir, Commander Walker, sir. May I request permission to dry-hump you when we get back?" I asked. Next to me Rowan burst out laughing.

"I'm glad you find this amusing. We're hunting a serial killer, and his accomplice might be at the party. You'll be in danger the entire time you're there."

I stuck my arm in the air. Aidan placed his hands behind his back and nodded. "Yes sir, I will be. However, you're forgetting one thing – as long as I'm there they'll be in danger too."

Rowan giggled, a strange thing for such a big man to do. "Stop poking the Aidan bomb," he whispered.

I swung my chair to face him. "I enjoy poking the Aidan. Even more so when the Aidan pokes me."

Aidan covered his face with both hands. "You two are acting like children. Tonight, you'll play your parts. But I'm serious, unless it's a matter of life or death I do not want any of your parts to touch."

"Define parts? Are you referring to our cover identities, or sexy parts?" I pursed my lips, desperate not to laugh.

Aidan took a deep breath and mumbled in a language I didn't understand.

Rowan reached for the sky with his left hand. "Commander Walker, sir, may I hold my date's hand? Perhaps place my hand at the hollow of her back, or wrap my arm around her? You need to keep in mind, if we don't create the illusion that she's there as Rob Granger's date, and therefore off limits to anyone and everyone, someone will try to get it on with your wife."

"Fair enough." Aidan crossed his arms over his chest.

"You're regretting the outfit you chose for me, aren't you?" I stood and walked to my boss, standing so close to him, my breasts pressed against his upper abs. "Rowan and I know what we need to do tonight. You're being a little dramatic with all these ridiculous coitus restrictions you're imposing on us. My love, Rowan and I love each other very much, as brother and sister. Believe me, if we tried anything we'll either gag, or laugh, and nothing sexy will happen. Climb off your little husband horsey and focus on the mission."

"Yes ma'am." Aidan grabbed my bum and lifted me up. I wrapped my legs around his waist and crashed my mouth to his.

"Excuse me, the sex party is tonight, not here. Disgusting much?" Liam's voice forced my lips from my boss'.

Aidan lowered me until my feet touched the cool tiles. I glared at Liam. "You're just jealous because you can't go. Question time, Rowan, how were you able to take Liam with?"

Rowan leaned back in his chair and gripped the armrests. "Unlike other people, I tend not to engage in sexual relations with civilians—"

"Because of your cover as Rob Granger?"

Rowan nodded. "Whenever a party is held in a city where I don't have a contact who can escort me, I take Liam along. He has no trouble finding a woman willing to go with. The parties aren't dangerous. People are there for sex, and the odd chance of making a business connection, like Rob and Theo did. Thanks again for screwing that up, Liam."

Liam pulled out a chair and sat down hard. "Blame me as much as you want. Maria needed my help. As for Anna, she wanted to experience what it is to be satisfied by a Walker."

My nostrils flared as my breathing increased. "Focus! I need to get back to working on the links between the victims and the killer. I don't have time for the two of you going another round. Liam, you screwed up, own up to it and move on. Rowan, what's done is done. I swear if I didn't have use for the two of you, I would send you both packing."

"Sorry, Finley," they both said.

Rowan cleared his throat. "Rob's a tier one guest, which means I can attend any parties I want, and take along as many guests as I like. Rumour is Rob gets off watching his right-hand men with other women. Which I, Rowan, don't. So, whenever Liam, or one of the other operatives, went along, I listened to music in the en suite bathroom while they got it on with the women."

A sadness filled me for Rowan. Underneath all of his strength and teasing, he remained a lost little boy who wanted acceptance and love. Not at the expense of his own moral code. This meant he preferred the company of women who understood his line of work and the danger being associated with him puts them in. I understood why Anna Wagner sleeping with his brother hurt him so much. Rowan had cared for her, but I knew he never loved her.

Liam rested his elbows on the table. "The outfit Aidan chose for you; they'll know something is up if you walk in their looking like a dominatrix who didn't have enough money for the full outfit."

A grin spread across my face. I had been working on something else earlier, with the help of Eli and Quinn. "Boys, meet Kelly. No last name. As you'll see on the screen to your left, that list of names are all unsolved murders linked to an unidentified female assassin. For the fun of it, I chose the Kelly cover. Kelly means war. And that's what I'll bring to the killer, and everyone connected to him."

"Fin, we choose names starting with the same letter as our own." Liam rested his chin on his arms.

"Good for you, Liam. I've gone by many names in the past, including Cerberus. It won't be an issue to be *Kelly* for one night. Now, as for my outfit, it's perfect. The sooner I can get us visual confirmation of the tattoo on Biggie's hand, the better. Neither of you noticed the alterations Aidan made to it. A lot of rumours are going around in the underworld about Kelly The Assassin. We have Quinn to thank for that. You would be wise to listen when she talks. She's been at this since she was eighteen, much longer than any of us."

I smiled up at Aidan. He touched his fingers to my lips. "I can see the darkness playing in your eyes. Good. One glance at the death and destruction raging in them, and Biggie will keep his hands off of you."

I pouted. "Oh, but Commander Walker, I want him to touch me. How else are we going to get his fingerprints?"

Rowan and Liam cursed at the same time. "You're going to kill him," Rowan said first.

"Not tonight, but yes, I am. Biggie, the serial killer and every other person involved in the murders." I crossed my arms over my chest. The darkness no longer hid in the shadows of my being. She had returned with a vengeance. Unleashing her was the only way to get justice for the victims.

When I held my daughter in my arms again, I might cry, because Ainsley's mother is a warm-blooded killer. I don't take lives because I enjoy it. But if I don't, who will?

Who will stand for the victims when everyone else fails them, including whoever had helped a child rapist escape to Russia? Who will bring closure to the families of twenty-five people who didn't deserve to die to fulfil someone's morbid fantasy?

The deaths of the innocent haunt my sleep; knowing

a predator has taken his or her last breath is like a shot of melatonin.

I walked to the whiteboard and flipped the screen over. This was the first time since university I used a mind map; who could've thought something so simple will prove so useful.

"Rowan, you said they check the ID's or passports of everyone who attends, apart from taking away their mobile phones and weapons. When they run a background check on Kelly, they'll see her record is clean – too clean. It will raise enough flags with Biggie if he's black ops trained. He won't deny Rob and his date entry, but if he knows what's good for him, he'll keep an eye on me."

"You're okay with her using herself as bait?" he asked Aidan.

Aidan scratched the back of his head. "No, but I trust Finley. As I trust you to keep her safe."

"What's with the mind map?" Liam lifted his legs onto the table and crossed his ankles.

The circle in the middle reserved for 'Killer and Biggie'. The lines moving out of the main circle ended with the people who placed the victims in the killer's hands. Sanchez. Max/Oleg. Ignas. The fourth the daughter of a member of Australia's parliament. From each of these circles I had made more lines and wrote the victims' names and the countries in which they were murdered.

"Eli found someone else we need to investigate – Luciana Hernandez. She's an agent for musicians. The victims in Mexico and Argentina were both singers. Eli discovered deleted text messages sent between Hernandez and the two victims."

"This leaves us with the victims in Malta, Budapest, Vienna, Zurich, Hong Kong, Singapore and Da Nang." Aidan inspected my mind map. I wondered if this is how his brain processes information; with invisible lines connecting crucial elements and bypassing irrelevant points. "The victims in Hong Kong, Singapore, and Da Nang are all artists. Sculptor, painter and a land artist. We could be looking for a curator or a collector."

I grabbed my phone. "Eli, can you please run a detailed search for anyone who was in Hong Kong, Singapore, and Da Nang up to say, six months, before the victims in those cities were murdered? Narrow it down to someone who might be an artist, a curator or a collector."

Eli laughed. "You love making life difficult for me, don't you?"

"No, I don't, except when we spar. The thing is, you're the master hacker, and I'm your mere student. I can only aspire to your greatness, oh powerful master of the keyboard and hidden world of ones and zeros."

"Hong Kong and Singapore are major cities; their airports are both important hubs with Hong Kong's the world's busiest for cargo. What you're asking is going to take me some time."

"I know, but I've gone through the victims' social media accounts, emails, mobile phone records, text messages, there's nothing there to indicate how the killer got to them. We've established various people are supplying our killer with victims." I stepped back and stared at the mind map. "It's a spider web."

"What are you talking about?" Eli asked.

"The killer is in the middle waiting to devour his prey. People are placing the victims in his web. Why do they help him? And what's Biggie's role in this?"

I turned to Aidan. "Are you sure I can't torture him? We know he isn't a former BSS operative. I bet I can break him."

Aidan shook his head. "He can lead us to the killer. He's our best chance of identifying the killer."

I thanked Eli, ended the call, and answered an incoming call at the same time. "Miss me?"

"Never. I'm on my way back to Marcel, but our Moscow operative has sent a very interesting photo to you and Aidan. You owe me big time for allowing you to be Kelly. Believe me, you don't want to know how many people I had to kill to make that name feared in the underworld."

I rolled my eyes at my new best friend. "As if the people

you killed were law-abiding citizens. You're like me, Quinn. We don't lose sleep or blacken our souls when we eliminate a criminal. The reason you're forcing emotion into your voice – you regret not being the one to blood eagle a paedophile. I'll send you a video, okay?"

"I hate you, Finley." If I had a diamond for every time she had said that since we first met, I would've been able to bedazzle my entire G-Class, inside and out. *Gross.*

"Whatever, Quinn, you love me. Thank you for the Kelly cover, and the photo I'm looking at. You've just added another name to my hit list, and I suspect we've found the person responsible for Max Jefferson's Oleg Petrov identity."

Quinn ended the call after I badgered her into admitting she loves me. *Isn't that what best friends do?*

I turned to Aidan. Anger etched into his face. "He's a Lieutenant General in the Moscow Police."

I closed the distance between us and placed my hands on his neck. My thumbs brushed over the stubble framing his jaw. "For now. He'll be dead soon."

"You can't just go around killing people," Liam said. "You're a mother now."

I didn't look at him, instead I kept my eyes on my husband's. "Yes, I am. All the more reason to eliminate anyone who touches a child or protects those who do."

"We're protected in Russia. Finley can do whatever she wants, to whoever she wants." Aidan's smile reached his eyes.

I wrapped my arms around Aidan's waist and turned my focus to Liam. "I will find every last one of them and rip them from this world, leaving nothing but carcasses in my wake. If you don't have the stomach for it, leave now. Tomorrow morning, we head to Moscow."

Twenty-five

Dubai, United Arab Emirates
Wednesday, 27 January, 5:25 p.m.

Lieutenant General Volkov had been photographed entering the property owned by Oleg Petrov. Two hours later, he left. Aidan had given explicit instructions – everywhere that Volkov went, an operative was sure to go. Another kept surveillance on Max, Oleg, soon to be blood eagled man. In my gut, I knew he didn't give up his destruction of children. *Once a predator, always a predator.*

I spent hours combing through the missing children reports for the Moscow area. The information posted on the website of a local volunteer group, and not an official government funded site. I closed the command centre's door and cried for a man sentenced to eight years in prison for beating a convicted paedophile to death, after saving a child from said predator.

This is the world we live in. Heroes are sent to prison, yet paedophiles get a slap on the wrist and returned to society to continue destroying the lives of even more children.

On one hand, a law-abiding citizen had protected a child and would spend eight years of his life in prison. On the other, a convicted sex offender had been sentenced for thirteen months and allowed to leave prison to work. Six days of the week. It didn't matter that this played out on different continents, or a few years apart. The fact remains – evil prevails.

A question kept mulling inside my head. Why would governments not do everything possible to protect their children? If they're opposed to the death penalty, life in prison will suffice.

I fell to my knees and prayed for this man who will spend

eight years in a Russian prison. I begged God to keep him safe, and for his early release. He didn't deserve this. Neither did his family. Or the young boys he had saved, who learned the law isn't always on the victim's side.

Aidan walked in and sat with me on the floor. He didn't say a word. He understood. My heart will always be with the victims, and this time a man who was a victim of his country's legislation.

"Fin, we need to get ready," Rowan said from the door.

I wiped my eyes and savoured the warmth of Aidan's lips against my forehead. "I can't take them all out. There are millions of them."

The true pandemic of our time – human predators preying on children.

"One by one, my love. There are more people like us out there, and we must never lose sight of the end of this war. One day it will end." Aidan stood and helped me to my feet. He wrapped his arms around me and held me tight. "For now, keep your focus on hunting this serial killer. Getting to Biggie is the biggest step we've taken so far. Sanchez tried to get hold of him but said something about 'the phone being switched off'. His speech was a bit slurred from what I assume are the painkillers he received before being discharged. The cameras inside his apartment are handy."

"Promise me you'll let me do whatever I need to do tonight. If the darkness takes over, then and only then, may you order me to stop."

"I promise. Liam and I are heading out there with you. I'll be overwatch."

"Where's the party being held?" I asked and buried my face in his chest, drawing as deep a breath as my aching soul allowed.

"In the desert," Rowan said, still standing in the doorway. "Fin, are you okay?"

I shook my head; tears threatened to fill my eyes again.

"Do you want to slap Liam until you feel better?"

I laughed. "Great brother you are, Ro. I'll be fine. Don't worry about me. I'll get my head in the game and complete the mission. Tonight, a serial killer's helper. Tomorrow a paedophile."

"Channel your rage, Fin. Harness it and let it ground you. Soon we'll know what the hell is going on, the names of everyone involved, and then we'll hunt them down."

"Yes sir." I straightened my spine. Perhaps we could break into a Russian prison and set an innocent captive free, seeing as we were going to be in Moscow. "How can they organise an orgy in the desert, in a country where premarital and extramarital sex is illegal?"

Rowan shrugged. "I suspect they'll have people positioned at a distance to alert them if the police or any locals head towards where we'll be. Do you need help getting dressed?"

I smiled at my brother-in-law and closed the distance between us. Lifting onto my toes, I wrapped my arms around his neck. "Thank you. Now, Rob, let's get dressed. I've got a date with a big man, one who will fall hard for his role in the deaths of twenty-five people. I hope Eli doesn't call soon to inform us of another body."

I turned to Aidan. "Any news on Alicia Rideout?"

"She's stable and will make a full recovery. Liam asked Nina to speak to her again. Miss Rideout remembers nothing else. For the time being I think we leave her be. We also don't want to put her in more danger than she already might be. It's best if the killer believes she's dead."

Twenty-six

Exact location: Classified, United Arab Emirates
Wednesday, 27 January, 7:55 p.m.

Rowan wasn't my favourite brother-in-law anymore. He refused to let me drive. Instead, he took it upon himself to see if he could roll the Toyota Land Cruiser. Failing that, Rowan tried to make me scream with what I believe was his idea of dune bashing. Even as a teenager, I had been better at it than him. One of the many things my father had taught me. We shared a love for speed. And nothing beats the adrenaline rush of not knowing what the other side of a dune looks like.

A small part of me also didn't like my husband very much, but then again, he didn't know the location of the party when he chose the little I wore. At least the sun had retreated for the night, or I would've ended up with the worst tan lines imaginable. Before we left the house I had grabbed my combat boots, not trusting my ability to walk in knee high leather boots across the Arabian sand.

"You can't wear that." Rowan glanced down at my military issued shoes.

I clicked the boots together but remained in the Land Cruiser. "If we need to run, I don't want to struggle in the sand with heels."

"Why will we need to run, Finley?"

"Who is Finley?" I checked my makeup in the sun visor mirror. A stranger stared back at me.

Rowan placed his hand on my exposed thigh. I stared at his hand on my leg, forgetting it was too dark inside the SUV's cabin for Aidan to see his brother poke the Aidan bomb. I removed Rowan's hand and returned it to the steering wheel.

“Four guards. Positioned 500 metres away from the camp to the north, east, south and west,” Liam said. A military grade drone gave us the layout of the camp erected in the middle of the desert.

“We’ll take up position to the west, I’ll have the best vantage point from there. Are you ready, Mrs Walker?”

“Who is Mrs Walker?” I asked Aidan. “My name’s Kelly, and tonight I’m going to make Rob Granger the luckiest man in the world.”

“I’m going to dust my wife’s entire body for fingerprints as soon we get back to the house.”

I sighed as we drove past a guard. “You forget one thing, Commander Walker. I need to remove these latex straps, and panties before we head back if you want any usable prints. Wait, before you jump on the husband horsey, I packed something else to wear for the return trip. I’m pretty sure Rowan can keep a lookout while I strip down naked in the desert and take my time to get dressed. Sir, I’ll let you watch through your scope and won’t tell the boss that you did.”

Aidan laughed. “I am the boss.”

“Not of Kelly, you’re not. I’m a lone wolf; an assassin for hire. I take out bad guys and receive payment from other bad guys for doing it. Man, Quinn has an exciting life.”

She didn’t. The same loneliness festered inside her which lived in Rowan. Quinn had lost herself in undercover work; it allowed her to hide from herself and the questions about her past. I may have gotten her a bit drunk on margaritas one night and probed a little. I’m not proud of doing it, but it was for the greater good. Understanding her insecurities, allowed me to help her address them. Help she had asked for and remembered doing so the following morning. We were making ground, and nothing was more important than seeing my new best friend happy. And for Quinn to make peace with the fact that some of her questions might never be answered. Ashley, my other best friend, helped too, in her own, more subtle ways.

“I tell you what, Commander, I’ll get Biggie to touch my

butt. It's the part of me with the most coverage. Then when we get back to the house, you can help me forget about the horrible man who touched your wife."

"Guys, come on. Quinn warned us it's like constant verbal foreplay working with the two of you. I'm surprised there's no sibling for Ainsley on the way yet." Liam's voice filled my ear and pushed a dagger into my heart. Ainsley will never have a brother or a sister. Ever. Aidan and I hadn't told the family yet. The only person who knew – Lizzie. I tell my sister everything.

Aidan exhaled slowly; the sound sent shivers down my spine. "We're in position, can see you pulling up."

Rowan brought the Land Cruiser to a stop, pushed his fingers through his long hair, and turned to me. "Are you sure you don't want a safe word?"

I touched my palm to his cheek and smiled. We were being watched, not by Aidan and Liam. "I don't need a safe word. You might not be armed, but I am." I wrapped the leather straps around my forearms and ensured it covered the ink.

Rowan touched the back of his fingers to my face and brushed his thumb across my bottom lip. "I won't let anything happen to you."

"I've got your back too, bro. Let's do this, Rob." I pushed his hair away from his neck and leaned forward until my mouth pressed against his ear. "I love you, Commander Walker. No safe word. You'll know if I need help."

"Breach," Liam said.

Rowan and I laughed, staring at each other the way people about to have sex do. It freaked me out but being this close to the person linked to the serial killer I wanted to annihilate, trumped everything. Biggie had kept his eyes on us since Rowan switched off the ignition. His face obscured by a mask, but his hands weren't covered.

Rowan positioned his mask over his face, I didn't need one. Quinn had shown me how to apply special effects makeup over a Skype call. If things didn't work out for me at Fortius, I might make a career as a makeup artist. Who would've guessed

I have a knack for this type of makeup? Perhaps Quinn was just a good instructor.

I slid out of the Land Cruiser and focused on the surrounding darkness. Somewhere the best sniper in the world watched me through the scope of his McMillan Tac-50. Rowan slammed my door shut and pressed my back against the vehicle. He towered over me, and I wondered if it was a mistake not to wear heels. Then again, dynamite comes in small packages, and the C-4 strips hidden in the soles of my shoes held the punch.

Rob Granger's long hair played in the wind; his face illuminated by the lamps positioned around the camp. Once we stepped past Biggie, Rowan and I were on our own. Aidan could still see what we saw, as Rowan and I wore contact lenses with embedded microscopic cameras. Invisible two-way earpieces in both of our ears.

It's time. Kelly pushed onto her toes, wrapping her arms around Rob's neck. Biggie's gaze remained on us. *Perhaps he has a thing for Rob Granger.* "I waited a long time to play with you. For the record, I like when things go south. That's where all the action is," I spoke loud enough for Biggie to hear.

Rowan's eyes laughed but his Rob face remained intense. He grabbed my thighs and pushed me up against the passenger side window. "I know you're going to be trouble, Kelly. Tonight, you're mine. If you as much as look at another man, I will drag you out of here. We've been heading towards me being inside you for a long time. I won't let you screw this up, not before I make you scream my name."

I wrapped my arms around his neck and pulled my bottom lip between my teeth. "What are you waiting for? Take me. Now. Right here." Deep inside Kelly, I laughed.

This was weird and disgusting, but the most fun I had since chasing the Cayenne in Zurich. As good as we faked it, the sexual chemistry between Rob and Kelly didn't compare to when Aidan and I are simply in the same room.

I adore Rowan, which made this easier. It also helped that

he's one of the most handsome men I've ever seen. The second most handsome to ever push me up against a vehicle, but he's my brother. His safety as important as getting back to Ainsley and taking down this serial killer. Once the killer's forehead had a permanent hole, I would hunt down every person who helped him.

Rob lowered Kelly until her combat boots pressed into the sand. "No." Rob covered her throat with his hand, almost wrapping it around her neck. "You and I have ourselves a problem, Missy. You're used to being in control, but babe, so am I. It will be worth the wait."

I laughed and realised I needed to improvise. *Crap.* "I bet you can't make me scream your name more than once tonight."

"Challenge accepted." Rob took Kelly's hand and led her to the entrance. Biggie waited; his hands remained behind his back.

"Sorry, dude. Your brother and your wife are going to get freaky tonight," Liam said to Aidan in my ear.

"That's the plan. Enjoy yourself, Fin. You deserve a night of doing whatever you want." Aidan ordered.

Twenty-seven

Exact location: Classified, United Arab Emirates
Wednesday, 27 January, 8:16 p.m.

Biggie checked our passports to verify our identities, and spoke to someone over a two-way radio. He glanced down at Kelly's passport and back up at me. Awareness flashed in his eyes. He took our mobile phones and searched us for weapons. First, he patted down Rob Granger, and then stepped in front of me. I opened the black cape.

"Your date isn't wearing what we expect." He stared at Rowan, meeting him eye to eye.

In my ear Aidan said, "His accent is Polish. Call him a *chuj*."

I tilted my head to the right and placed my hands on my hips. The cape remained opened, and I almost smiled when Biggie's eyes followed the rhythmic rise and fall of my breasts. A strip of latex covered my nipples. The girls didn't have any other cover. "Hey *chuj*, you don't talk to him, you talk to me. Dabrowski, did you hear about him?"

Biggie said nothing. He didn't have to. His eyes answered for him.

"I slit his throat in Gdansk while he took a leak." I stepped forward and placed my hand on Biggie's chest. "You don't tell me what to do. Neither does Rob. Rozumieć?"

Aidan had told me what to say and I hoped my pronunciation was good enough.

Biggie nodded. "The boss won't be happy."

I patted Biggie's cheek, instead of plunging one of the knives hidden in my boots into his eye. *Play with your prey.* "Then your boss can say it to my face. *If* he has the balls. Call him, perhaps it will be good for him to hear a few months back I turned down an offer to pay him a visit. I'm not here to kill. I'm here to *pierdolić*."

Rowan placed his arm around my shoulder. "Do we have a problem?"

"No, just keep your woman in line." Biggie stepped back, allowing Rob and Kelly to enter the Bedouin camp.

Persian carpets covered most of the sand. All around were what I assumed would be private, or not so private sex areas, depending on whether people closed the chiffon curtains. A raised platform stood in the middle of the camp, surrounded by oversized cushions.

"You won't use the word dick, but you instruct Finley to call the helper of a serial killer one." Liam laughed in my ear.

Aidan didn't have to tell me the meaning of *pierdolić*. In context, it was self-explanatory. "You're good at this, Fin. Now, stay alive." Aidan took a deep breath. "Rowan, stop looking at my wife's butt. I see everything you do, remember?"

I glanced around the camp, unable to see anyone's faces. Mine the only one not covered by an easy to remove mask. Where or how could I get a glimpse of Biggie's tattoo? He had kept his hand out of sight during our conversation.

Rowan led me into a sex cubicle and pulled me down onto the cushions.

"You promised me dinner and a show before we have fun." I kept my eyes on his, but my focus on the other people. In here Aidan couldn't see me through the rifle's scope, but Liam could, as the drone kept circling high above us.

"You made him hard." Rowan pushed the fake red hair behind my ear and placed his hand against the side of my neck.

This is weird. "Rob or Aidan?"

"Biggie."

I smiled, laid on my back and stretched my arms out above my head. "Good. Will make it much easier to get him alone. I just need to figure out when and where." I thought about it, and then recalled smelling something very distinct and delicious, when I placed my hand against Biggie's chest. "He smokes, I'll bum one from him. Might even adjust this little strap, a bit of a nip-slip might do the trick." My two sides were at war: the darkness and the light. When it comes to hunting human predators, one will always be victorious. The darkness trembled with excitement; goose bumps rippled across my skin.

"Eyes on my wife's face, Rowan."

"Kelly, don't make me spank you. Every man and woman here knows not to touch what's mine." Rob growled. *Why the hell would Detective Wagner lose this man for one time with Liam?*

"Sorry, Granger, I'm not into spanking. If you're a good date tonight, I might show you what turns me on."

I pushed up onto my elbows and locked gazes with Biggie. I opened my legs wide enough to keep his attention and swallowed hard as bile rose in my throat. The faces of twenty-six people flashed through my mind. The man staring at what belonged to Aidan had played a part in their murders, and the attempted murder of Alicia Rideout.

A primal drum beat echoed in the voids of my soul as the darkness flapped her wings. Empty places created by the death and destruction I saw over the years. "Game time." I pushed to my feet, not taking my eyes off Biggie.

"Stand down," Aidan ordered.

I stepped over Rowan where he lay on the plush cushions and pulled the cape's strings. It fell behind me and I bent down until my nose touched Rowan's. *Thank you, Pilates sessions.* "I'm not going to stay here and watch other people have sex. No matter how good you say the food is. I can eat later. All I need is visual confirmation of the tattoo, and his hand on my ass. The very thing he's staring at right now."

"You're playing a dangerous game, Fin." Aidan breathed hard.

"Tonight, you're my commanding officer, not my husband. Focus, Walker." I lowered myself onto Rowan's legs, and kept my eyes on his, but saw Aidan's in my mind. "The objective of my mission is clear. How long before the decryption-thingy gathers the information from everyone's mobile phones?"

"It takes about fifteen minutes, depending on the mumber of phones and data." Rowan stared past me. "Everyone seems to be here, let's say you have fifteen minutes. Wait until the show starts and then you can go for a smoke break."

"Is the boss here yet?"

"No, he always wears the same mask. You'll know when he gets here; people need to bow before him."

I suppressed my laughter. "You bow?"

Rowan shook his head. Neither would I. Ever.

"He's here. Eli's running the license plate for us," Liam said.

I climbed off my brother-in-law and came to my full length. Biggie was making this easy for me. Too easy. Something wasn't right, I felt it in my gut.

Rowan stood, placing his arm around my shoulder. "I'm not liking this, something is wrong," he whispered.

"Leave. Now," Aidan ordered.

I wrapped my arms around Rob Granger's waist as a man-lion, or a lion-man, walked into the camp. My palms itched. A telltale sign whenever a psychopath or violent criminal comes close to me. It might be my inner darkness reacting to theirs. Every person has a dark side, some of us acknowledge it and know how to control it.

"I believe the man behind the lion mask is our killer. If not, he needs to be on our hit list for another reason."

Twenty-eight

Exact location: Classified, United Arab Emirates
Wednesday, 27 January, 9:07 p.m.

Neither Rowan nor I bowed when lion-man made his way around the camp to greet guests. The man behind the mask said nothing but kept his eyes on me throughout dinner. Perhaps it wasn't the best idea to lie about Kelly being hired to take him out. Or refusing to wear a mask like theirs. *I'm a rebel.*

Dinner was delicious. Rowan and I tried our best to appear in lust. Biggie remained at the entrance, from where he kept watching us.

The other women looked like porn star princesses, puffed up with colourful frills galore. I forced myself not to gag. So much colour hurts my eyes.

I climbed onto Rowan's lap and pushed my fingers through his hair. Leaning forward, I whispered, "It's time. I need a cigarette."

Rowan rested his forehead against mine, his hands moving up and down my back. We were careful not to let certain parts touch, yet still appear to be on the verge of ripping each other's clothes off. "Five minutes." His palm connected with my bum.

"Enjoy the show." I turned towards the stage. Two masked women started doing various things to each other on the very platform which had served as our dinner table. At least they wore less than I did. Their nether regions didn't stay covered for long.

Biggie's hands remained behind his back as I approached. Adrenaline pulsed through my veins. The three Walker brothers wouldn't let anything happen to me, but a lot could happen in the time it took them to come to my rescue. *You're not a damsel, you're a weapon.*

"May I please bum a cigarette from you?" I attempted my most innocent smile. "Stop looking so worried, I'm not here for anything other than to have some fun tonight."

Biggie reached into the front pocket of his black pants and pulled out a packet of cigarettes.

"Not here. Rob hates it when I smoke." I motioned with my head towards the vehicles. From there, Aidan would have a clear shot.

He glanced towards his boss, and then down at my breasts as I took another deep breath.

"Your boss won't even notice you're gone. His focus is on the women in front of him." The things they were doing to each other told me they had done this before, but I wondered whether they were here because they wanted to be. Some guests decided to either join them or start their own side shows. Rob Granger sat unmoving.

"He's going to taste the cigarette on your lips."

"Oh sweetie, that's not the lips he'll be tasting." I winked and walked to the Land Cruiser.

Biggie shook a cigarette out for me, and as I placed it in my mouth, he lifted a Zippo to the tip. I thanked him, and tried to remember when last I inhaled nicotine, firsthand.

"What's the deal with you and Granger?" Biggie lit his own and took a deep drag.

I shrugged and leaned back against the SUV, ensuring to arch my back just enough, and kept my legs apart.

"Dammit, woman, you're turning me on," Aidan mumbled.

"I'm going to do some work for him, and I like to get to *know* my clients first. Of course, it depends on the client. Rumour has it Granger's *chuj* is magnificent. You can't fault a lady for getting more than money for the jobs I do."

He stepped closer, and I reminded myself I needed information from him before I end his life.

"What's your name?" I took a deep drag, lifted my head to the sky and exhaled as slow as my lungs allowed without coughing. An aeroplane flew over and headed towards the lights on the horizon.

"Names are not important here." His eyes fixed on mine as I lowered my head.

"I guess not. Rob will appreciate it if I'm already wet when I go back to him. Do you mind helping me with that?" I dropped the cigarette butt and stepped on it, opening my legs a bit more.

He shook his head but moved closer after dropping his own cigarette to the sand. He squatted, picked up his and mine, and pushed it into his pocket. As he came to his full length, he dragged his fingers along my inner thighs, stopping short of brushing against what only Aidan may touch. If he didn't, I would've punched him in the throat. It isn't easy seducing a serial killer's assistant.

I placed my palms against his hard chest. "I have two rules. One – a man doesn't touch me until I've seen his hands. I have a hand fetish. Two – I never suck a man's *chuj* unless I've seen his face. If you want to be inside my mouth, take off the mask."

He did, letting it fall to the sand. I grinned and kept my eyes wide open.

"Pretty, pretty, pretty." I grabbed his hands and stared down at the black dragon with its distinctive tail. In one swift move Biggie's hands were on my bum, my legs wrapped around his waist. He pushed my back against the SUV and rubbed himself against me.

"Rowan, move," Aidan said in my ear. I stared into the darkness, feeling my husband's eyes on me.

While Biggie dry-humped me, I removed the earpiece in my left ear and placed it on my tongue. His earlobe tasted salty, but the faces of twenty-six people flashed through my mind. Rage coiled, ready to strike, as he kept thrusting against me. Every fake moan I made, a desperate attempt to remain in control of the darkness. She was desperate to play, and it took every bit of self-control I could muster not to break Biggie's neck.

Rowan swore to my right, and I almost kissed him when

he pulled Biggie away from me. He rambled on in Polish and the expression on Biggie's face translated Rob Granger's every word.

I turned to Granger. "You don't own me. I didn't even have time to play with him." I pushed out my bottom lip and turned to Biggie. "I'm sorry, *Piotr.* We'll see each other again soon. And I promise when we do, I'll play with you for as long as I want."

Rob Granger yanked open the passenger side door and pushed his date into the Land Cruiser. The lion-man watched. *Soon I'll see your face, and then you'll die.*

Piotr, or Biggie as we had referred to him, shook his head. I blew him a kiss as Rowan reversed the Land Cruiser and we headed into the darkness.

"Damn, Eli's facial recognition programme works fast." Aidan had relayed the name when I placed the listening device behind Piotr's ear. Now we could hear whatever he did, until he showered, if he scrubbed behind his ears like a good serial killer's helper should.

Rowan kept his eyes on the dark desert as I shimmied out of the latex panties and pulled on a pair of jeans and a black tank top. Aidan could help me later to remove the few straps covering my torso. "Fin, are you okay?"

"Dandy, why?"

"You were violated by a killer."

I hadn't thought about it like that. Instead I kept my focus on the victims, and the reason I needed him that close to me. I reached into my right combat boot and pulled out two cigarette butts. In the glove box I found a plastic bag and sealed it. Piotr's DNA lay in my palm. The closest his will ever come to mine. Until the day comes when his blood drips from my hands. "For now, I'll bury it. When I plunge a blade into his kidney, I'll remember how it felt."

"If no one else will say it, I will. You were amazing, Fin."

"Thank you, Liam. Aidan, are you okay?"

Silence. I tried again. "Aidan?"

"Commander Walker approves, your husband doesn't. I'm going to kill Piotr with my bare hands."

"You can't blame the guy, any man in his position would've had Fin up against a vehicle like that."

I heard a fist connect with muscle, and then Liam apologised. Rowan and I laughed.

"I'm sorry, my love, but I've got his fingerprints and his DNA."

Aidan cursed. "That sonofabitch ejaculated on you?"

I gagged and swallowed dinner for a second time. "No, gross. I picked his pocket. Took the cigarette butt he had the foresight to pick up and drop in his pocket."

"Did you pick up yours?" Liam asked.

"Piotr picked up Fin's."

The men stopped talking. Silence. Darkness surrounded us except for the sand illuminated by the Land Cruiser's headlights.

"What's going on?" I asked.

"Lion-man is pissed because Aidan shot out his back tyre," Liam chuckled.

"It was either the tyre or the back of Piotr's head, and that would've put Finley at risk. It's going to take a lot to forget seeing another man grind himself against you like that. Might've been less disturbing to see Rowan do it."

Rowan and I both shook our heads. No way Aidan would've been less disturbed by that. I asked, "Commander Walker, sir, where are you?"

"Two klicks behind you."

"Sir, when we get back to the house, I request you place me in a shower and scrub me down. I think a decontamination chamber might be an even better idea." I hadn't felt that dirty in years. Memories threatened to surface; I forced them back by focusing on the victims.

"I have every intention of washing every part of you."

"Aidan, distance from your rifle to the tyre?" I asked.

"One kilometre."

"Damn, babe, that's hot."

Aidan laughed; the sound chased away the feeling of Piotr between my thighs. "Babe?"

"My bad, boss, sir, Aidan. But it's hot, very sexy."

Rowan exhaled hard. "I'm going to pull over, then Fin can get in the G-Class with you and Liam can drive back with me. Then the two of you can find yourselves a dune and go at it like rabbits. Quinn was right."

"No can do, Ro. You're being followed, remember?"

"What? Who is following us?" I couldn't hear the information being relayed from the earpiece I had stuck behind Biggie's ear, but they could.

"A guard; you never thought to take your phones before you left."

I turned to Rowan. "I can't believe I forgot about the phones."

Rowan placed his hand on my forearm. "It doesn't matter. Eli already has all the information the *decryption-thingy* downloaded. Burner phones, so it doesn't matter if we don't get them back."

"We can't let that technology fall into the wrong hands. Fin's device is imbedded in her shoe, Eli cloned Piotr's phone. Brilliant move wrapping your legs around his waist, Fin." Aidan sounded too calm, but I appreciated his approval of my methods.

"Why isn't anyone freaking out about the fact that we're being followed?"

Rowan squeezed my arm and then instructed me to lift the back seat. I did and discovered an arsenal. I asked him what he needed and removed two HK416 A5 assault rifles, two Kevlar vests, his Glock, and my SIG.

I strapped the Kevlar to my chest and held the steering wheel as Rowan pulled his own over his head and fastened the straps.

"Aidan, plan?" Rowan asked.

"Baghdad won't work in the desert. Remember Somalia?"

Again, Rowan placed his hand on my arm. "I need you to get on my lap. I'll move out from under you, like you and Aidan did it."

"Okay." It proved a tad more difficult to do with Rowan being taller than Aidan, and us still trying to avoid certain body parts from coming into contact.

Rowan squeezed through the driver and passenger seats to the back seat. He asked me to slow down. I did. "Keep driving. We'll meet up at the house."

"Oh, hell no. You three will not have fun without me. After having a serial killer's helper, who has probably killed numerous people in his line of work, rub himself against me, I will shoot something or someone. I have my own strategy."

I told them my plan, they liked it.

We waited. Headlights became visible and disappeared as the vehicle made its way across the desert. The dunes provided us with cover. Rowan bumped his shoulder against mine. "I think tonight might just be the best night I've ever had at one of these parties."

"Some of the other times you at least had sex. Tonight, you're on your own, buddy."

Rowan grunted a laugh. We lowered the night vision goggles. The vehicle approached. The night remained quiet, thanks to the silencers attached to the rifles. One bullet struck the back tyre; it took me two shots to take out the front. It had been a while since I last fired at a moving vehicle, doing 80km/h over desert terrain. At night, nonetheless. Sand filled the air as the vehicle came to a stop.

Rowan and I moved as one, heading down the dune. The butt of the rifle snug against my right shoulder.

I yanked open the driver's door, the guard's eyes big, his hands raised. "You forgot your phones."

"Who sent you?" I growled.

"The boss."

I motioned for him to step out and turn around. Rowan patted him down, finding only the mobile phones in his pants pocket. I glanced into the Pathfinder. A Caracal EF lay on the passenger seat.

I instructed the guard to turn around and lowered my rifle. Rowan kept his pointed at the guard's chest. "What's the boss' name?"

"I don't know," the guard said and pointed at his chest. I nodded, and he lifted his shirt. The boss was listening.

"You better call your boss and have someone come fetch you. Tell him, I don't take kindly to the help assaulting me. If I ever see his man again, the one with the dragon tattoo on his right hand, I'm going to cut his throat. Ear to ear."

The guard nodded.

Rowan pushed the rifle against the guard's chest, his finger not on the trigger. "Tell your boss I'm done with his ridiculous parties. It's boring, and not worth the money I've been paying. Whoever took a shot at Kelly and hit your boss' vehicle's tyre can expect a visit from me soon."

We left the guard and headed back towards the Land Cruiser where it stood on the other side of the dune. My breaths didn't come out hard because scaling a sand dune is much harder than it looks. The night's events had put a big target on Kelly and Rob Granger's backs. *Perfect.* We needed to get out of Dubai. Fast.

Twenty-nine

Fortius' Boeing 787 9 Dreamliner VIP
Destination: Moscow, Russia
Thursday, 28 January, 00:28 a.m.

Aidan pushed me into the onboard bathroom and helped me undress. He didn't say a word, not until he erased the memory of another man touching what is his.

"You were amazing tonight." Aidan pressed his lips to mine, his mouth not as hungry as before, or desperate to reclaim me.

"Thank you, I did what I had to."

Aidan held me close, and towel dried my hair while I rubbed a towel up and down his chiselled body. "I need to tell you something."

With everything going on, I didn't know what to expect. The last thing I wanted to hear was that the killer struck again. Or that we were wrong about the man behind the lion mask being a killer. I hate being wrong. "Okay, let me hear it."

"As your commanding officer, it's in Fortius' best interest if you continue working in the field." Aidan lowered himself onto the bed and pulled me onto his lap. "As the man who loves you, and Ainsley's father, I can't approve it. You left a trail of breadcrumbs for them to follow, and Fin, they'll be coming after you and Rob Granger. Quinn doesn't have any *Kelly* work lined up and won't take on any jobs for a while, so she'll be safe."

I dropped my forehead to his. "I want to go home, Aidan. The sooner I put a bullet between the killer's eyes, the sooner we can go home. Sometimes it's best to lure your prey and not keep chasing them across the world. I have a gut feeling the man behind the lion mask is the killer, and Piotr is his accomplice. I'm not sure how their dynamic works. I stand by what I said; the fairy tale murders is one man's fantasy. It's too detailed, and personal."

Aidan reached for his laptop and switched it on. We listened to the conversation recorded between Piotr and his boss. The conversation had taken place seconds after Rowan and I drove off into the desert. A translator app translated from Polish to English.

"Have you no honour? The guests are off limits to you. Find yourself a whore, not a woman who claims she turned down money to assassinate me. Who would order a hit on *me*?"

"If you think about it, the list of people is as long as my leg. They all have very different reasons for wanting to see you dead." I recognised Piotr's voice.

"If I didn't need you, I would order one of the guards to shoot you."

Piotr laughed; the sound made me shiver. Aidan placed his arms around me, and I buried my face in his neck.

"I'm not dumb. If I die, the world will know what you are; and I'm not referring to your perverted parties. You're a disgrace to your family."

"Soon it won't matter. And if you step out of line you'll find yourself out of work, if not in a grave."

Again, Piotr laughed. I considered taking another shower. "You're incapable without me. It will be wise to remember who holds the power. For the first time in your life, it isn't you. Maybe I should leave, see if you can find someone else to help."

"No one is irreplaceable."

"Correct. Neither are you. The thing you want most will be taken from you if people were to learn what you are."

"Keep on making your threats. The day will come when I won't need you anymore. Until then, stop rubbing yourself against the guests. The last thing you want is Granger coming after you. He has a thing for pipe bombs; you won't know when, or where, and then one day – boom."

"Kelly wasn't here tonight as Granger's date. She came as a warning to you. Rumour is she always meets with her marks before she takes them out. She enjoys playing with her victims."

"She enjoyed playing with you."

"Perhaps once she has slit your throat, I will play with her again. For now, I'm going home."

"You're not going anywhere. I'm not done yet."

"After what happened in Zurich, you need to lay low for a while. You're too arrogant to accept it, but the fact is, someone's coming for you. You're not us untouchable as you think."

"No one can touch me, and none of it can be traced back to me."

Piotr laughed. The sound familiar. I laugh the same way when I hold a predator's fate in my hands. "I'm going home. In a couple of months, we can continue your little game."

The conversation ended after that. Interesting thing, the decryption-thingy we hid in my boot cloned data from two mobile phones Piotr had on him. Both burners. One with a Dubai SIM card, the other used to communicate with one other number, also a burner phone. Eli traced its most recent location – Bergia.

A knock on the door made me realise Aidan's bare skin still warmed mine. I asked whoever interrupted us to give us a minute. The discussion about my role in Fortius' operations wasn't over, but a part of me agreed. Life wasn't just about Aidan and me anymore; we have a daughter. The child we had prayed for. The one we had almost lost on the day of her birth.

Rowan grinned when I opened the door. I pulled my hair from my face and tied it in a messy bun. He, too, had tied his hair in a messy bun. As soon as Aidan stepped out of the room, Rowan spoke. "Liam sent the processed DNA to Eli. We got a match."

I threw my hands in the air. "When did you process the cigarette butt?"

"I ran it before we showered." Aidan shrugged and wrapped

his arms around me.

"There's a forensic laboratory on this aircraft?"

Aidan pressed his lips to my damp hair. "No, compact versions of what we need while in the field. We verify all findings once we get back to Marcel, at Fortius' lab."

"How do I not know about any of this?"

Rowan rolled his eyes. "Because it will take Aidan a month to tell you everything about our past operations, our current ops, and how we operate. You'll learn on the job. Most of us hit the ground running, just like you."

Reality struck me out of nowhere. *I haven't seen Ainsley since Sunday.* "How has so much happened in four days?"

"Welcome to Fortius, Sis." Liam joined us. "The days blur into each other. You never know where you'll be within the next hour. And the biggest mystery – whether you'll be standing or breathing at the end of a mission."

"Liam, stop drinking and go to bed." Aidan used his authoritarian voice.

Liam lifted the bottle of vodka to his mouth. "If I sleep in the bed, where are you going to make Fin forget about what happened earlier?" The grin on his face made me want to slap him.

"Your brother has already wiped my memory. Twice. Go to bed, Liam, before I smack you up the side of your head. When we land in Moscow, you need to bring your A-game. It's about time I see the infamous Captain Walker in action."

Liam lifted his right hand to his brow and marched into the bedroom. I made a mental note to ask Rowan and Aidan about the frequency and volume of Liam's alcohol consumption once we returned to Marcel. Perhaps he was preparing himself for the cold weather awaiting us in Moscow.

"What match did you find with Piotr's DNA?" I asked, trying to diffuse the building tension. Liam needed more than just my help.

"His mother is in the Maldives," Rowan said and lowered himself onto a seat.

"Ivana is his mother?" Rowan nodded. *Heather.* "When your mother spent three days *chatting* with her, she made Ivana bleed and kept a DNA sample."

"You're even more intelligent than you are sexy. Dammit, Fin. After seeing you dressed like that tonight, the things you said, how am I ever going to find a wife? No one will ever compare to you."

Aidan patted his brother's shoulder. "Thank you for keeping my wife safe. Is your Granger cover still solid? It's taken a couple of hits over the past few days."

Rowan nodded. "Better than ever. I've been looking for a reason to stop going to the parties, and Finley, or rather Kelly, gave me an out. If lion-man is the killer, the parties will be over."

My head spun from all the information, the events of the evening, and fatigue. The worst thing, and I would never say it out loud, I wasn't as young as I used to be. Closer to forty than thirty, but I wanted to feel twenty again. I lay down on a seat as the events of the past few days played in my mind. Aidan covered me with a blanket and took a seat next to my head. He lifted my head and lowered it onto his leg.

"I want that," Rowan said.

"You will, but you'll need to give up Granger for good. You always said you won't marry someone in our line of work, and you can't get involved with a civilian while you're Granger. It's too dangerous, and a liability for all of us." Aidan's fingers glided over my hair.

Piotr is Ivana's son. Did he grow up in Bergia, or did she hide him? Were BSS operatives allowed to have children? From everything I read about King Mikolaj, he didn't strike me as the paternal type. Or employer of the year. Without opening my eyes, I asked, "I need to see everything you have on Piotr. Ivana being his mother explains the tattoo, and his training, *if* she trained him. Who is his father? Where is his father? How did he meet the man behind the lion mask? Why did he want to get it on with an assassin?"

Aidan brushed his fingers against my cheek. "You're spiralling. Sleep now, and in a few hours, I'll brief you. I'll also update you on a few other things, but first, sleep. You need your strength if you're going to blood eagle someone in a matter of hours."

"No *if* about it, and not *someone.* Max Jefferson. If you're just going to stand there, watching over my shoulder and tell me I'm cutting him wrong, you might as well do it."

Aidan pressed a finger to my nose. "I'll do the incision; you can crack his ribs and pull it open. That part is going to be the most fun. We've never done surgery together before."

I smiled, my eyes still closed. "Surgery sounds so clinical. Rather say we've never butchered a monster together before." As I drifted off to sleep, I could already hear Jefferson scream for mercy. Joke's on him, I don't have any for paedophiles.

Thirty

Moscow, Russia
Thursday, 28 January, 7:03 a.m.

A local operative met us at Sheremetyevo Airport. He had coffee and food waiting for us as we got into the Dartz Black Stallion Type-C. The vehicle didn't disappoint inside or out, and I wondered about the price tag, as it comes standard with bulletproof opulence.

"What is this?" I asked staring at the food in my hands.

"Pirozkhi," Aidan said. "You'll love it. It's like bread stuffed with a delicious savoury filling. Pirozkhi is considered a comfort food in Russian culture."

"I'm not even going to try to pronounce it." Aidan finished his breakfast as he sat to my right, Liam to my left, and Rowan riding shotgun. "Can you buy me a Dartz? We haven't discussed my fee for this job."

Aidan choked; me being a good wife, I patted his back. "It's going to take more than one job for you to earn this."

"If you were a loving husband, you would've bought me one instead of altering my new G-Class. A military grade civilian vehicle with this interior? Dude, do you not love me?" I downed my coffee, knowing I sounded like a brat.

Aidan patted my knee, wiped his mouth and drank his coffee. "We operate behind the scenes. A G-Class won't draw too much attention to you, whereas something like this, will. There aren't any in Marcel, or on our continent. I love you enough to make you appear normal when you're anything but."

I turned to face him as much as possible, pressing my back against Liam's shoulder. Liam didn't say a word. "Who are you to say what is or isn't normal? The concept of normality isn't measurable."

"Calm down, Miss Doctorates-In-Criminal-Psychology. I meant it as a compliment. If this is how you want to play, Williams-Walker, then let's do it. Is it, in your professional opinion, *normal* to look forward to torturing someone? Is it normal to not have stopped smiling since you opened your eyes? The first words you spoke were, and I quote, 'I'm going to do a blood eagle today'."

I felt my back against the ropes and remembered it was just Liam. If anyone can take on Aidan, it's me. "Is it normal to have shot a vehicle's tyre because you couldn't take the sight of your wife gathering valuable information? Will you consider it an everyday occurrence watching your wife flay the back of a paedophile? When I hold his lungs in my hands, will that be normal? And the best part is – I don't know who will enjoy it more, you or me. I saw you check the vials of adrenaline and whatnot in your backpack."

Aidan opened his mouth, but Rowan spoke first. "Bro, let it go. She's going to keep on schooling you, and it's no mystery why we all love Fin as much as we do. She's a mixture of a bloodthirsty beauty, filled with vengeance, and she has bigger balls than most of the men we've served with."

I grabbed the driver and passenger seats and lifted my bum into the air. Rowan turned to look at me and I planted a big kiss on his mouth. "I love you too." I fell back in the seat and patted Aidan's leg. "How far to Grandpa Jefferson's house?"

"Forty-five minutes," the local operative said. His name? Dmitry.

I glanced at the temperature display – minus twelve degrees Celsius. This, by far the coldest weather I've ever experienced, but also the most beautiful, especially as we drove out of the city centre. "Do you have enough adrenaline to shoot both of us up? And Jefferson? I think performing a blood eagle in the snow will be spectacular. Imagine the steam rising from his body as I slice him open. Blood droplets freezing even before it hits the snow-covered ground." I pictured it. *Bliss.*

Dmitry cleared his throat. "You're the one taking over from Heather?"

"Da. Why?" It surprised me how many basic words I knew in different languages. I even learned a few Polish words the night before. Ones I hoped to never use again. It would remind me of Piotr thrusting against me. Nausea threatened to overwhelm me, so I took a deep breath and focused on the snow-covered-everything outside the vehicle.

"Ryan warned me to never get on your bad side and instructed me to have food and coffee waiting when you arrive."

I laughed and patted Dmitry's shoulder. "Thank you again for breakfast and caffeine. Hangry and tired me isn't anyone's friend. Not that I'm feeling friendly today."

"You sound happy to me."

Rowan glanced at me over his shoulder. "Torture excites her. Aidan married his mother."

I punched his shoulder but took it as a compliment to be compared to the great Heather Walker. Ainsley couldn't be in better hands until Aidan and I returned to her.

Today I would avenge all the children who were preyed upon by the monster who hid behind the name Oleg Petrov. How long before Jefferson squealed? How much pain would it take before he told me how he had met Cora Fontanilla? The woman connected to the victims in Singapore, Hong Kong, and Da Nang. An art collector, philanthropist, and one of the wealthiest women in the world thanks to her late husband's estate. They never had children of their own.

Fontanilla's husband was pictured with Jefferson a few months before the latter's arrest in the USA. Cora had visited Moscow in December, a few days before Christmas. Eli found a photo of her and Oleg Petrov on her private Mybook social media account. Nothing is private, and people who think it is, are idiots.

A triangle formed. Cora Fontanilla's husband had been accused of molesting several children at an orphanage they built in Thailand. Bill Fontanilla and Max Jefferson were far more than mere acquaintances. They shared the same depravity. The same evil festered in both of them.

Bill had stopped breathing days after the authorities dropped their case against him. The police report states Cora found him hanging from a necktie, tied to the bathroom door's handle in the Bangkok hotel they had stayed in. A man his height couldn't have hung himself from a door handle or broken nine of his ribs in the process. Aidan had read the autopsy report and confirmed my suspicion. The medical examiner may have ruled it a suicide, but we knew better.

Perhaps Jefferson had made a run for it before he suffered Fontanilla's fate. Bill got off easy compared to what I planned for Jefferson. *I will huff, I will puff, and I will blow them up.* The C-4 loaded in the back of the vehicle would help with the blowing up part. My lungs ached after the previous night's cigarette.

"Control your breathing, Fin. Where did your mind go?" Aidan took both my hands in his and pressed his lips to my temple.

"It's a spider web. They're all connected. If not directly, there's a thin thread linking them. What if we can find evidence proving more of them are paedophiles? Destroyers of children who hand over victims to our killer, because our killer knows what they are." I shook my head. "Ivana gave birth to Piotr while she served in the BSS. The birth record Eli found has his place of birth as Poland. Who is his father? Why did Ivana train him? Or did his father train him?"

I wanted to scream. I needed to get out of the vehicle and shoot something, anything. The darkness flapped her wings with so much force, my thoughts were nothing more than leaves in an EF5 tornado.

Aidan glanced down at his mobile phone. "The question as to who Piotr's father is, is no longer a mystery. He's here, in Russia, staying at the Black Dolphin."

"Ivar?" Rowan asked. "Makes sense they would hide him since they weren't allowed to get married or have children.

Who raised him then?"

"Eli is still digging. I told him to ask someone in his department to help. This is turning into much more than a serial killer who murders across borders, continents, and time zones."

"How did our killer find out they're paedophiles? I doubt he is a friend of theirs." I leaned my head against Aidan's shoulder and waited for his presence to calm the destructive storm raging inside me. We still didn't know how the killer got his hands on the victims in Malta, Budapest, Vienna, or Zurich.

I grabbed my phone and searched on the internet for Luciana Hernandez. The woman linked to the victims in Mexico and Argentina. "Something else is at play here. Luciana Hernandez's husband died a week after Jefferson disappeared."

Aidan removed his laptop from the backpack at his feet and handed it to me. I did what Eli does best. Five minutes later, more questions plagued me.

I stared at the autopsy report, shaking my head. A week after Jefferson disappeared, his criminal defence attorney died. The police investigated and compiled a list of potential suspects, only to delete it later from the case file. It's standard practise that all suspicious deaths are investigated, but why delete the information after the medical examiner had ruled it a suicide? A better question – why did the medical examiner rule it a suicide when Hernandez was a lefty and the gun had lain in his right hand?

I called Eli; I needed his help. He had taught me well, but I wasn't close to being at his level. In the time it would take me to slice, dice, and crack Jefferson, Eli could find the answers. For the time being, I didn't voice my suspicions.

The spider web kept getting bigger.

Thirty-one

Moscow, Russia
Thursday, 28 January, 8:23 a.m.

If I knew any Russian swear words, I might've used a couple to describe the cold. Next to a tree, I hunched down, watching Oleg Petrov's house through the binoculars. For the first time since I started choosing my own clothes, I wore nothing but white, although my underwear was black. White offers the best camouflage in the harsh Russian winter. Aidan sat with his back against a boulder and stared at his mobile phone; he monitored Petrov's movement inside the house. The previous day Dmitry installed cameras in every room when Petrov had gone in to town.

Who would I punish first, Max Jefferson, or Oleg Petrov? Countless children had disappeared since Petrov took up residence in this part of the world. I stared at the snow-covered ground and wondered what secrets lay buried beneath our feet. The closest neighbours too far away to hear screams.

"Aidan, once the snow and ground thaws, we need to dig up this place. I can feel them, they're here, screaming from the graves he put them in." I pressed my gloves to my eyes – before the tears froze on my face – and lowered my sunglasses.

Aidan stared up at me. "Are you sure, or do you just want more reason to hurt him?"

A crushing sadness had filled me as I walked from the Dartz to where I took up position next to the tree. Death and destruction hung heavy in the frigid air. "It sounds crazy, but I feel them. Not their spirits, ghosts, or whatever you want to call it. I sense pain, and fear. Soul crushing fear, but not mine."

Months later, my intuition proved correct. The bodies of

forty-six children were returned to their families, not all of them Russian. Those the local authorities couldn't identify received a pauper's burial. We kept records of everything, hoping to one day answer the mystery surrounding their identities and how they ended up in Jefferson's vile clutches.

Aidan dropped his mobile phone into his pants pocket as he pushed to his feet. Rowan jogged past me. "Are you ready?"

I nodded, despite the unknown fear lodging in my throat. It made way for excitement when Aidan said, "It's time."

Oleg Petrov climbed out of the shower and seized his vocal assault on my ears. He couldn't hold a note to save his life. Without making a sound, I laughed. His life couldn't be saved. It lay at my feet, and I would crush him for the cockroach he is. That's not a fair comparison, cockroaches are remarkable creatures who can survive a nuclear bomb.

I sat on the carpet next to Petrov's bed, waiting. My SIG rested on my lap, my finger not on the trigger.

Petrov strode in, reached into his cupboard, and removed what he thought would be his clothes for the day. The jersey, shirt, and vest wouldn't cover his back for long. As he bent forward to pull on his underwear, I wanted to pour drain cleaner into my eyes. The years hadn't been kind to his body. I saw more of Petrov than I've ever seen of my husband.

My finger moved to the trigger. I waited.

Petrov started singing again, and I snapped. *He* was going to get tortured today, *not* my ears. "Hello, Max."

He spun around, lost his footing, and fell backwards against the cupboard. I laughed, anyone in my position would've; the look on his face comical.

It's a glorious sight, the moment a predator realises they are now the prey.

Jefferson spoke in Russian, I shrugged. "Max, there's no need for the charade."

He spun around and dug through his underwear.

Laughter bubbled out of the darkened corners of my battle-scarred soul. "Looking for this?" I lifted his Makarov pistol, which lay on the floor next to me.

Jefferson moved forward but stopped as I shot to my feet. The barrel of my gun pointed at his chest. "Don't do anything stupid, Max. You and I are going to have some fun first. Well, *I* am. You'll learn what true fear is. When someone else holds all the power. Just as you did to countless children."

"I don't know what you're talking about." *Why do they always say that?*

I holstered the SIG at my right thigh and crossed my arms over my chest. It flashed in his eyes. It always does. A split second when they think they stand a chance of surviving.

He lunged forward. I sidestepped, grabbed the back of his neck, and smashed his face into the wall. Jefferson sank to his knees. For good measure, I kicked him in the ribs with my steel point boot.

"Come on, Max, I expected better from you. Get up!"

He did; blood streamed from his broken nose. Aidan emerged from behind the bedroom door, picked up the towel and tossed it at Jefferson's face.

"Downstairs, Jefferson. Now." I motioned with my head towards the door.

Jefferson pushed the towel to his nose and mumbled in Russian.

I kicked his left shin. Blasphemous words spilled out of his mouth. My fist connected with his left eye. "I will not tolerate blasphemy. Understood?"

He nodded, and as he made his way out of the bedroom, I stretched my fingers behind my back. The human skull is hard, and some people's are thick.

We reached the open plan dining room. "Chair. Sit." He did. "No. Other way around."

Rowan bent down and secured my prisoner's hands and feet to the back legs of the wooden chair. In this position Max Jefferson will atone for the things he did, the lives he destroyed.

En route from the airport, I had reminded the Walker brothers I would do whatever it takes, and if they didn't have the stomach for it they could wait in the woods. All three of them stood in the room, waiting for me to release the darkness I held caged for far too long.

I walked to the kettle and made myself a cup of coffee. None of the men wanted one; neither did the predator who sat tied to the chair. The dining room table offered the perfect place to sit while I drank my coffee. Aidan's backpack lay next to me, holding all the toys I needed for my playtime with Jefferson.

"I have friends in high places," said the man tied to a chair.

"Good for you." Aidan joined me where I sat sipping the vile coffee.

I threw the mug into the sink, it shattered sending coffee onto the curtain and floor. I swung my legs back and forth.

Jefferson stared up at Aidan. "The Lieutenant General of the Moscow Police will be here any minute, we're going ice fishing. He's going to rape her in front of you, cut her into pieces, and then he'll cut your heart out. Maybe I'll ask him to do the same to the two idiots standing behind me and save you for last."

Aidan and I turned to each other, and I gestured for Commander Walker to go ahead. "I see your Lieutenant General and raise you one Bratva, and one president."

Jefferson sat motionless, except for the blood trickling from his nose.

"Don't worry, Maxi, your friend Volkov will be here soon enough. Didn't your parents ever tell you to make friends with the intelligent children? Volkov isn't very clever, no sir, he isn't. Kept his stash of footage of children being raped on hard drives in his home safe. By the looks of it, footage recorded in this very house."

The darkness paced; she doesn't take kindly to threats of rape. Her every move made my muscles twitch. I'm grateful she lives inside me, otherwise I wouldn't be able to do what I do.

From outside came the sound of a car door slamming shut. Jefferson, the idiot, smiled, thinking his friend arrived to save him from big bad me.

The front door opened, sending in a burst of cold air. A local Fortius operative walked in carrying a plastic bag. Marika reached into the bag and threw the content on the floor. It rolled and rolled. It stopped in front of Jefferson's chair.

"You were right, Volkov was on his way here. The polite thing to do is to say hello to your friend, Max."

Jefferson stared down at his friend's decapitated head. The saying 'heads will roll' came to mind as Volkov's head had come barrelling across the wooden floor. It's funny, so I laughed. Aidan didn't look at me, neither did Liam or Rowan. The anger of four Walkers converged in that room. We share the same hatred towards those who hurt children, those who should die excruciating deaths for the destruction they cause.

Thirty-two

Moscow, Russia
Thursday, 28 January, 9:21 a.m.

The scissors made light work of removing Jefferson's jersey, shirt, and vest. Volkov's head bumped against my shoe as I stepped around the chair, cutting and pulling material away from my prey's body. I stood back and stared at Jefferson's white skin; it hadn't seen the sun in a long time.

Again, Volkov's head was in the way, so I kicked it as hard as I could. "She shoots, she scores!" I pushed my arms into the air.

Rowan and Liam laughed; the corners of Aidan's mouth lifted.

The head ended in the sitting room close to the fireplace. Jefferson stared after it. "You killed the Lieutenant General of the Moscow Police; they'll bring their full force down on you. There isn't a place in Russia you can hide."

Aidan placed his hand on my lower back. I moved away and out of the splash zone. Aidan's fist connected with Jefferson's jaw. Blood and spit sprayed onto the floor. "You're all the same. You think you're untouchable, yet your buddy's head is laying over there. The president of this great nation has launched a full-scale investigation into Volkov and all the other high-ranking officials who were part of what you did here."

With his hands behind his back, Aidan stared down at our prey. "The ones who flee Russia, Bratva will hunt them down. They owe me a favour. Sorry, Max, but you picked the wrong country to flee to."

I listed the victims' names, the people this despicable thing had placed in the hands of a serial killer.

"You can't touch him." Jefferson sniffed hard and coughed as blood lodged in his throat. I gagged.

With my right hand extended towards the head in the living room, I said, "Like we couldn't touch Volkov, or little old you? Who ordered the hit on Hernandez?"

Jefferson shook his head and stared at the spot where Volkov's head come to a stop before I kicked it. "You can't make me talk."

"I tell you what, Maxi, I'll make you a deal. If you don't talk after I've done this to you, you can keep all your secrets. Okay?" I pulled my phone out of the pocket next to my right knee and showed him a picture.

Jefferson spat on my phone. I slapped him harder than I have ever slapped anyone, and I've slapped quite a few people over the years. Men who had groped me in bars, paedophiles, rapists, and murderers in my wine cellar. The list is rather extensive, and with a predator to torture, I didn't want to waste time trying to remember them all.

Once I washed my phone in the sink with dishwashing soap, I returned to Jefferson. *I love Fortius' toys.* Aidan reached into his backpack and placed the items on the table. None of us wore gloves. By the time we left, the house would burn.

However, when performing surgery it's best to wear gloves. I double gloved, as Aidan instructed, and picked up the scalpel. The blade glistened in the morning sun streaming in through the windows. A serene winter wonderland lay on the other side of the glass.

"Commander, if you would be so kind as to make the incision." I placed the scalpel in Aidan's hand.

"Thank you. But first, I need to give the patient something to numb the incision area." Aidan dropped the scalpel; I picked it up and nicked Jefferson's forehead as I came to my full length. The cut bled like a faucet.

"Oops, sorry, Maxi. I didn't realise how sharp this thing is. My bad." I shrugged and started carving a picture into the wooden table.

"You're making the blade dull." Aidan shook his head.

I sighed as loud as a teenager. "You never let me have any fun. I'm carving this picture for you, my love."

Aidan stared at the stick figure. "Where's the head?"

"In front of the hearth." We both laughed. Laughter is a key element in any marriage.

As Aidan pushed the needle into the vial, I wondered how many other couples are like us; those who torture together, but for good. *I hope a lot.*

Aidan jabbed the needle into Jefferson's arm. "You won't feel a thing."

I glanced at Rowan and Liam. Rowan rested his arm on the butt of the HK416 A5 hanging across his shoulder. Liam didn't appear fazed either. They both smiled when our eyes met. Dmitry and Marika stood outside the house. I didn't want them to see this side of their future boss or his wife. The less they knew the better, and we needed eyes and ears outside. You never know when things will go south. In a bad way.

Commander Walker picked up the scalpel and moved behind Jefferson. I lifted myself onto the dining table, needing to see Jefferson's face when he realised what Aidan had injected him with wasn't for pain.

"I'm going to make an incision from your lower back up to your neck. L5 to C7. This will all be over in a matter of seconds and you won't feel a thing."

I pursed my lips, desperate not to laugh. Aidan enjoyed this as much as I did. The paedophile screamed as Aidan cut into him. The scalpel too blunt for a single controlled cut. Aidan sliced and sliced.

"Max? Max? Max?" I sang, waiting for his eyes to meet mine. "Are you ready to tell me?"

He shook his head. We were cutting him open, yet he remained more afraid of someone else. Impossible. *Oh well, we'll see how long that lasts.*

I jumped off the table and grabbed the rib shear. If my hands got tired there were six other hands waiting to help.

"Who helped you escape from the USA?"

"Hernandez." Jefferson breathed hard, the adrenaline keeping him conscious.

"Why was Hernandez killed? It wasn't to protect you." I tapped the shear to his forehead. "Come on, Max. I won't tell anyone you told me; I'm good at keeping secrets."

"Get it over with. I won't tell you shit. It doesn't matter anymore."

I thought about it – still tapping the shear on Jefferson's forehead – Hernandez and Fontanilla were both dead. Their wives helped a serial killer find victims. Hernandez had been much more than just a despicable criminal defence attorney.

While I had waited in the snow for the perfect time to enter the house, Eli told me who most of Hernandez's clients were: paedophiles, rapists, and murderers. Not uncommon for a criminal defence attorney to have such predators pay him, but the fact that seventy-five percent of them were on trial for crimes involving children was.

Fontanilla had been accused of molesting numerous children at one specific orphanage. I wondered what happened at other orphanages he and his wife had founded in the years before his staged suicide.

"Hernandez is waiting for you in hell. He's in the same fiery pit as the one you'll be cast into. Right next to him is your other buddy, Bill Fontanilla."

The expression on Jefferson's face told me I was right. "It doesn't matter anymore. They're all dead."

Not a web. A ring. It consisted of high-profile men and perhaps their wives. No, not perhaps; their wives were in on it. What other reason did they have to help a serial killer? How did a serial killer learn about this sick circle of paedophiles? None of his victims were younger than twenty. "Who is he?"

"For the last time, it doesn't matter. Everyone is dead."

Those words were the final straw, I motioned with my head for Aidan to get out of the way. One by one I cracked Jefferson's ribs. His screams louder than the sound of bone snapping under the pressure of the shear.

One side done, I asked again, "Who is blackmailing you into handing him victims to kill? A serial killer too pathetic to hunt his own prey. Then again, you destroyed countless children. You're as big a coward as he is." I continued with my work.

The rage I felt every day since the Saturday night fuelled me. I continued. Rib for rib. I pushed my hands in and pulled his ribs apart. The movement of his lungs told me he still breathed. For now.

I stepped back, studying the human anatomy. It was the first time I saw lungs, ribs, and the vertebrae of a spine. Still, Jefferson refused to give me a name.

Not even when I bent down in front of him, far enough away in case he tried to spit again. "You're going to die. It won't be quick. I'm going to pull out your lungs and give you wings. Max Jefferson, I hereby sentence you to death." I pushed to my feet and slapped my palm on the table, seeing as I didn't think to pack a gavel. "Isn't this much better than going to prison? On your way to hell, you'll see the children's faces, this time their fear won't give you pleasure. No, you'll understand it, because that awaits you. Tell me his name, and I'll pardon you. I'll call an ambulance. If they get here in time, you'll spend the rest of your days in Black Dolphin. Save yourself; give me his name."

"All roads lead to Bergia." Those were the last words Max Jefferson, and Oleg Petrov, uttered.

While I stared into his soulless eyes, Aidan pulled out Jefferson's lungs. He didn't look like an angel, or any other winged creature. His face remained that of the monster he had been to countless children. The adrenaline did a magnificent job.

I sat on the wooden floor, crossed my legs, and watched a destroyer of children die. Every second of his last moments I savoured, not because of my need for vengeance, but for every child this monster ever touched. Raped. Murdered.

When he no longer breathed, I stood and placed a brick of C-4 in the cavity his lungs once filled. I'm not sure who did the rest. I ran out of the house and left my breakfast next to a tree. Little did I know how many innocent bodies lay beneath my feet.

Months later, when I learned the exact number of children they had raped and murdered, I wanted to kill Jefferson and Volkov again. This time, even slower.

Thirty-three

Moscow, Russia
Thursday, 28 January, 1:45 p.m.

This didn't change the fact that we were hunting a serial killer. The man behind the lion mask. The predator responsible for the deaths of twenty-five people, and the attempted murder of Alicia Rideout. Before we blew Jefferson's house to hell, we had ransacked the place and took any items which might prove valuable in our search for the killer. As well as everyone else involved in the paedophile ring. I stared at the screens in the safe house, my murder board now digital. Soon we would leave Moscow, but we weren't heading home.

Aidan wrapped his arms around me and I leaned back against him, drawing a deep breath. His scent calmed the violent storm raging inside me. "People in power, covering for each other, murdering each other. Anything as long as the world never learns about their disgusting secrets. Apparent suicides when anyone with two brain cells can see it's a cover-up. Money given to organisations to protect children and the most vulnerable, when those who give the money are the very ones children need protection from."

"They can't hide from us. I'll pull the trigger myself. One thing I can't stomach – when people in positions of power choose to do harm and not use their positions for good. Once we've identified the killer, I'm taking you home, giving my daughter a kiss, and then I'll hunt every last one of them down."

I turned, cupping his face in my palms. "Aidan Walker, you will not have fun without me." I dropped my forehead to his chest. "It isn't fun. What we did to Jefferson didn't bring me joy; because none of it can undo what he did. What does is knowing a dead paedophile, rapist, murderer, whatever, can't hurt another person again."

"I know, my love." Aidan pressed his lips to my hair and hugged me to him. "You can't deny you enjoyed the medical aspect of what we did to him."

I couldn't. I'm curious by nature, and now I knew a blood eagle was in fact possible. "Do you ever think of going back?"

"No. This, what we do as part of Fortius, is much more important. Anyone can become a doctor; not everyone has it in them to do what we do. It's my duty to fight against the evil people of this world, like the ones who've now stepped into our crosshairs. The elite. The one percent. Their crimes won't go unpunished. For far too long they hid their depravity behind their wealth, connections, and public images. It ends now."

I pushed onto my toes and wrapped my arms around the neck of the most magnificent man in the world. His heart, bravery and devotion are but three of the countless things I love about Aidan Walker. "I'm so grateful our paths crossed, and that you and I are alike in as many ways as we are different. I hope Ainsley chooses a life far away from this. I don't want her to carry the darkness we live with every day. If she does, we'll be right beside her to guide her along whichever path she chooses. Can we pray she stays a baby forever?"

Aidan laughed and pressed his lips to my neck. "We can, but she'll still grow up, just as we did. Ainsley will be better protected, and prepared, for the world than most children."

I pulled back and stared up at him. "Do you think we should one day discuss the possibility of adoption? There are so many children in need of loving homes, a home we can give them."

Aidan nodded. "I've been waiting for you to bring it up first. I'm open to the idea. Although in our line of work, it's going to be a tremendous responsibility to care for more than one child. We're already worried about being involved enough in Ainsley's life. Let's shelve this conversation for now, and once we've killed the killer we can circle back. Okay?"

I pressed my lips to his, savouring the warmth, the familiarity in the movement of his mouth and hands. This moment gave me unfathomable peace despite the darkness surrounding us. Happiness is found in the little things, a smile, a kiss, the sound of your child laughing.

"Guys, we need to discuss our next move. Fin, you said we're racing against time, as we can't anticipate when, or where, he'll strike next." Rowan's voice ripped me out of the moment and threw me back into turmoil.

"Okay, let's do this. Where's Liam?" I asked as Aidan and I both turned to stare at the murder board, and the new name added to it. Not the name of a victim, but of a possible link in a perverted chain. A name we found on Jefferson's laptop.

"He's busy saying goodbye to Marika. Liam-style." Rowan opened a bottle of water and lifted it to his lips. None of us were hungry after leaving the property registered to Oleg Petrov.

I had pressed the detonator and sent that place to hell. We didn't find any evidence of any children being in the house, except for the video footage. I couldn't watch all of it; I don't think I ever will. They hadn't stopped the camera after the rapes; Petrov, and Volkov recorded the murders as well. There are things you can never unsee – something I've said countless times – and it remains true. I didn't know who would watch the hours and hours of torture those two men had inflicted on children in order to identify the victims and bring closure to their families. I prayed for the person, for his or her sanity. When confronted with such evil you lose a part of yourself every day. A part of you dies whenever you hear a child scream in fear, in pain. Their pleading words require no translation. Horror is a universal language.

"Who is Günter Kuhn?" I asked, reminding myself there were more people I needed to blood eagle. Although, after doing it I don't think it's a cruel enough death.

Rowan typed away at my laptop. An obscured face filled

the screen. "This is the only known photo of him. Günter Kuhn is an enigma. For years his name has been whispered in the underworld, but no one knows anything concrete about him. All I've been able to piece together is he's a concierge of sorts. Whatever you want, he's the guy to go to. I first heard his name five years ago, when Rob Granger stepped into the underworld. I'm not even sure that he is the 'GK' Jefferson emailed. Rumour is he's based in Berlin but operates throughout Europe."

"Why didn't they use the dark web to communicate? Instead of sending emails when we can trace IP addresses."

Aidan placed his arm around me, his right hand resting on my side. "Günter uses spoofing, so his emails aren't that easy to trace. Jefferson, on the other hand, thought he was protected seeing as his friend was a Lieutenant General. Eli found a voice note he sent to a burner phone saying the best person for the job would be Günter Kuhn. Jefferson gave a date, place, and time for the meeting. Eli is sending us video footage of the meeting now."

An image filled the screen – three men at a train station in Munich. One bigger than the other two. "Can you zoom in on the big guy's right hand?"

Rowan did. "I might be reaching here, but what if that's Piotr and the killer meeting with this Günter character? If he can find anything for anyone, then he might have his hands in the human trafficking pie. It will be easy for him to find the victims our killer prefers – individuals not considered high risk. He chooses people with families, friends, students, or ones with professions outside of their artistic endeavours. People who will be reported missing, even if he didn't place the calls to the police. There's a reason he chooses these people as victims – he knows he'll get away with murder."

I stepped closer to the screen. "Whoever the man behind the lion mask is, he's in the same class – for a lack of a better word – as the individuals linked to the paedophile ring. The only two who don't fit this are Sanchez and Ignas. I think there's a different link to Sanchez, and Ignas was born in Bergia. Jefferson was right – all roads lead to Bergia."

Rowan placed his hands on my shoulders. "Then that's where we will go."

A sound came from my laptop, and I turned to it. I shook my head and patted the custom-made grip of my SIG. "I've been running facial recognition on Piotr, trying to see if his face has popped up anywhere. Here he is."

I stepped back and waited for Aidan to say it. "He's Princess Ylva's bodyguard."

Social media makes it easier for predators to find prey, but it also makes it easier for us to hunt them.

"I need to contact Szymon." Aidan reached for his mobile phone.

I closed my laptop. "No, don't give him a heads up. Tell him you'll be in the area, and if he has time to spare, you want to pay him a visit. Seeing as the two of you are old friends."

"He can't be involved in this, dammit. We fought right alongside each other." Aidan dragged his hands down his face.

"Until you know otherwise, you can't rule him out as a suspect. If the past few years taught us anything, it's that sometimes the people closest to us are the most evil. There's a reason Jefferson refused to give us a name. A king is as powerful as they come, on paper, nowadays. You said it yourself, Szymon leads from the front. And I don't need to tell you lions are associated with power and royalty."

Why lions are called 'the king of the jungle' has always baffled me. They don't live in jungles; they prefer open plains and savannahs.

Aidan let out a long breath. "Okay, valid point. However, we can't go after the King of Bergia on half-ass information, or because we're desperate to end the murders and bring the paedophiles to our type of justice."

I palmed Aidan's perfect derriere. "I'll ensure all our corpses are in one grave before I become a king slayer."

Aidan grabbed my shoulders and spun me around; his

mouth crashed down on mine. "I love your strange and unique sayings, Mrs Walker."

I smiled up at him and patted his left cheek. "It won't be Mrs Walker much longer. Soon you'll bow before me and call me Lady King Slayer."

"I have no issue being on my knees in front of you, just as I'm the only man you'll ever get down on your knees for." Aidan pushed his fingers through my hair and pulled my body against his. The object he would use to knight me pressed against my stomach. *Wow.*

"Please stop," Rowan said. "Do you not realise I'm standing right here? Hello, I take up a quarter of the room."

"Yes, Rowan, you're big. But where it matters the most, Aidan will always be the biggest." I smiled, staring up at my husband, and realised we were weird. From torture, to suspecting a king of being a serial killer, to foreplay. *I love our relationship.*

"Keep it in your pants or you'll be flying economy class to Bergia." Rowan retied his hair at the back of his head.

"I have no problem flying cattle class. I don't like not knowing the pilot or his capabilities should there be a problem like the wings coming off." Rowan smiled and shook his head but didn't interrupt me. "We're not going to Bergia. We're going to Krakow."

"Why Poland?" Aidan asked.

I realised then I hadn't shared with them what Eli uncovered while we played with C-4 playdough at Petrov's house. "Piotr told lion-man he was heading home. Guess who landed in Krakow this morning?"

"Piotr?" Rowan asked.

I shook my head. "Her name isn't on his birth certificate but she gave birth to him."

Thirty-four

Krakow, Poland
Thursday, 28 January, 5:00 p.m.

The tracking device imbedded in Ivana's arm made it easier to decide which hotel to book our rooms at. We would stay in Krakow for at least one night. I found it strange that she didn't stay with Piotr but then again, I doubted he had a permanent residence anywhere; not in his line of work. Liam booked us two suites at Hotel Stary during the flight from Moscow, and I had even spent time in the cockpit with Rowan. Perhaps I did overcome my aviophobia.

The hotel itself is best seen in person. I added it to my bucket list of places to one day visit when murder wasn't my reason for travelling. If everything went according to plan, there wouldn't be time to enjoy the spa. Or the indoor pool with its exposed brick walls, which look more like an old bunker or wine cellar.

A knock on the suite's door reminded me why we were here and not home with Ainsley. Liam opened the door, his SIG in hand.

She looked young enough to be my older sister, older than Lizzie, but not old enough to be a grandmother depending on whether Piotr protected his wild oats.

"Your mother said you want to see me." Ivana took a seat in the sitting area.

I joined her on the other loose standing chair, Aidan sat on the chair at the desk, while Rowan and Liam stood with their weapons in hand.

"Please put away your weapons. Ivana is here as our guest." I turned to her, offering my most sincere I'm-not-going-to-kill-your-son smile. "Can we get you anything? Coffee, room service? You must be exhausted after all the connecting flights to get here from the Maldives. I promise not to keep you long."

Ivana studied my face. "I never knew Heather has a daughter. You don't look like her."

"I'm not her daughter."

Ivana laughed, by the sound of it when she wasn't assassinating people or stealing stuff, she filled her lungs with nicotine. "You play her games. Even though you don't have her brown eyes, the same emotion swirls in yours. What do you want? I don't know what to call you, and I know you won't give me your real names. Even though we technically work for the same organisation." She crossed her legs and placed her hands on her lap.

"You can call me Kelly; it's the name I gave your son."

If I hadn't studied her every move I would've missed it. Ivana brushed her thumb against her stomach, but said, "I don't have a son. Or a daughter."

I showed her my teeth and placed my hand on her forearm. "You do. And for future reference, don't touch your stomach when people mention your son. It's something a woman will notice, especially one you suspect is Heather's daughter. It's an instinctive gesture because of all the times you touched your stomach while pregnant with him. You chose the name *Piotr* for him, didn't you? Or did Ivar name his son?"

Ivana smiled, shaking her head. Her eyes not filled with kindness. "You're good, I'll give you that, but you're also very wrong. I never had a child."

I stood and retrieved a still taken from the video footage recorded of Piotr's face when he had removed his mask, thinking he would get more from me than a bullet in his head. Ivana stared at it. Emotion played in her blue eyes.

"We can do this the long way or the short way. Heather might have the patience to sit with you for three days; for me, three hours will push it. So, let's do this from the beginning. You had sex with Ivar, got pregnant, gave birth to a son here in Poland, and called him Piotr. A friend of yours adopted him and raised him, but you and Ivar played an important enough role in his life that he got the BSS dragon tattoo."

I held up another photo for her; one of Piotr's right hand. "Perhaps you should've told him not to get something this recognisable on his hand." If not for a sleeve covering my tattoo, I wouldn't have been so cocky.

"I don't understand what you're trying to get at. The man in the photo isn't my son." Ivana rested her elbows on the chair's leather armrests. Forced boredom visible on her face, but I saw beyond the mask.

Aidan handed her the DNA results. He told her about the cigarette butt and the DNA Heather had collected from her during their three days together. Ivana stared at it and shrugged. "So, what? I gave birth."

"Woman, do you want to see my patience level when we get to three hours?"

She didn't respond to my threat but turned to Aidan when he spoke. "We've linked Piotr to twenty-five murders and one attempted murder. As the murders were committed in various countries, I will see to it myself that he receives the death penalty. Kelly, how are you going to kill him?"

"Blood eagle. The one we did in Moscow this morning was fun." I showed her photos of Jefferson's body before the explosion, but after Aidan and I had performed surgery on him. With a forced grin on my face, I returned my mobile phone to the pocket at my right knee. Why women bother with handbags is beyond me; cargo pants are much more convenient.

A tear slipped down her cheek and Rowan placed a tissue in her hand. She thanked him without looking at him. I waited. She remained silent.

"I'm hungry, let's order room service. Ivana, what can we get you? Seeing as we're going to be here a while we might as well eat, before I slap an old lady. My parents raised me better than that. Don't get me wrong, I might not slap you but I will shoot you. Think about Piotr and the grandchildren he might give you one day. I don't need to cut him open, or crack his ribs and pull out his lungs. Answer all my questions and it won't come to that. But first, we eat."

I ordered room service and left Piotr's photo next to Ivana. She didn't move but glanced at it while we waited in silence for our food. My stomach growling through an interrogation would've come across as amateurish. That's one thing I'm not.

Thirty-five

Krakow, Poland
Thursday, 28 January, 6:21 p.m.

I pushed the dinner trolley out of the suite and locked the door. With my back against the door, I studied Ivana and wondered how she ended up in the BSS. "Aren't you tired of all the faces you see every time you close your eyes?"

"Your tricks won't work on me. Do what you want; blood eagle me if you wish, but I won't help you kill my son."

I made myself comfortable on the coffee table in front of her and placed my hands on hers. Part comforting gesture, part because I knew how lethal her hands are. "I don't think Piotr is killing these people because he wants to. He's working for someone and that's the person I want."

Ivana didn't remove her hands from mine, neither did she lunge at me. I took this as a good sign. *She's tired.* I felt her exhaustion, the weight of what she had carried for far too long. I wondered if she ever admitted to anyone else that she had a son. The woman in front of me wasn't a ruthless assassin, a black ops operative, or a soldier. This was a mother desperate to keep her son safe. There's nothing in this world I won't do to protect my daughter, even if it means going as far as my mother had to protect Lizzie and me. Even though she couldn't have known how futile her sacrifice would be in the long run. *Don't go back there.*

"If you tell me the truth, you have my word I won't take Piotr's life. Have you ever told anyone? Or did you push it into the darkest corner of your soul, convincing yourself whatever you did is for the greater good? Even if it meant someone else, strangers, raised your son?"

Ivana pulled her hands from mine and covered her face. "Why do you think Piotr's involved with an assassin?"

"Serial killer, not assassin." Aidan remained in the desk chair, his right ankle resting on his left knee.

A deep line formed between her eyes. "Piotr won't help a serial killer. He's a good man. A better person than Ivar and I ever dreamed he would be."

"Why did you train him? The years he spent in Wojska Specjalne couldn't have taught him everything he knows. No, both you and Ivar trained Piotr. Why?" The answer was in front of me but for the life of me I couldn't grab it by the neck.

"Years spent in what?" Ivana asked.

Aidan smiled. "Please excuse Kelly, her Polish isn't fluent. She knows a few swear words. He spent twelve years in the Polish Armed Forces, of which ten was in Wojska Specjalne."

The years Ivana and Ivar had spent training Piotr made him stand out from the other soldiers, and this led to his quick transfer to the Polish Special Forces. We had learned enough about Piotr during the flight from Moscow to realise taking him out wouldn't be easy for any of us. Not in close combat. He was as much a human weapon as anyone working for Fortius.

"He's here now. It won't be difficult to locate him and put a bullet in his pretty face. I don't want to kill your son, Ivana. I will. If it puts me closer to the serial killer we're hunting."

Not a single word formed on her lips or came from her mouth.

"Max Jefferson, aka Oleg Petrov, said all roads lead to Bergia. Piotr has been photographed with Princess Ylva."

When I said Jefferson's name, Ivana's eyes lifted to mine. With nothing to lose, I followed my gut instinct. "Lieutenant General Volkov. Bill and Cora Fontanilla. Carlos and Luciana Hernandez. Isaac Johnson. Who am I missing?"

Isaac Johnson being the father of the woman who owned the modelling agency in Australia, and a member of their parliament. No concrete evidence linked him to the paedophile ring, but worth a shot throwing his name out there to see if

Ivana knew more than we did.

Ivana took a deep breath and stood. She walked to the window and stared out over Krakow. Not her place of birth, but Piotr's. "I have your word no harm will come to Piotr?"

"Yes, we'll spare his life." I joined her, placing my hand on her shoulder.

She snorted a laugh. "You're clever with your words, but you forget I've been in this game much longer than you. I want your word that my son will remain free. To tell me he will live is one thing, I don't want him to spend the rest of his days locked in a cage like Ivar. Not when all Piotr has done is for the greater good of our people."

Aidan spoke before I could. He was, after all, the commanding officer. "It depends on what you tell us. As the acting head of Fortius you have my word that Piotr won't be harmed, and left to live his life. As long as he stays within the confines of *our* laws."

Ivana turned to Aidan. "You are your father's son, Aidan Walker. Your wife isn't too bad herself. What I want is a position for Piotr in the organisation as an ally; he'll be a valuable asset to you in the future. Either you bring him onboard, or I won't say a single word. With your help, this can be much easier and faster than if he keeps going at it alone."

Aidan picked up his mobile phone and switched on the speaker. He relayed Ivana's request to Ryan.

"Ivana, as Aidan said, it all comes down to what you tell them. We will take Piotr in if he passes all the required physical and psychological assessments. The same ones you had to go through. Do we have a deal?"

Before Ivana could answer, Heather's voice came loud through the speaker. "My dear friend, aren't you tired of all the lies you kept for most of your life? Let's end this here and now. You can retire and know that Piotr is protected by us, the same way you've been for many years."

"Why is Ivar in prison?" I asked.

Ivana turned towards the window. "He failed his mission."

I lifted my arms, palms facing the ceiling. "Which was?"

"Assassinating Lieutenant General Volkov. The man responsible for the disappearances of countless Russian children."

I showed her a photo of Volkov's decapitated head. Tears streamed down her face. "The children will be safe. Until the next one takes Volkov's place."

"I need blueprints of Black Dolphin and everything and anything we'll need to ensure our mission doesn't fail."

Aidan stepped forward and placed his hands on my shoulders. "You want to break him out of prison? It's one of the most secure prisons in the world. It's impossible."

"Challenge accepted. I won't stand by and allow another man to suffer in that hell for a crime he didn't commit."

An emotion filled Ivana's face, one I doubted she had experienced in years. Hope. "I like this one. If Piotr wasn't already in love, I would've liked to have you as a daughter-in-law. You're just the right amount of crazy."

He didn't seem in love when he rubbed himself against me. "I'm not crazy, and I'm married. Your son is rather handsome, but very easy. Not my type. I prefer my men a little more dangerous."

"You reached your quota on verbal foreplay for the day," Rowan said, waving his finger at me. "I like the idea of breaking into Black Dolphin. What's the plan?"

"Blueprints, and everything else, then I'll tell you my plan. Aidan can run the variables, probabilities, the other whatnots and thingies for us. Then he'll tell me it can't be done, and I'll remind him – where there's a will, there's a way."

Aidan shook his head and crossed his arms over his chest. "I'm not even going to explain it to you – again – if you're just going to keep calling it *whatnots* and *thingies.* It's a good thing you're so damn sexy, lethal, and I happen to like your crazy ideas. You keep me on my toes and challenge me. You're a valuable asset to this organisation."

Ivana studied both of us with a sly grin on her face. "I bet she's even better in bed; but *that* you learned later. It's not the reason you fell for her; like Ivar and I saw something else in each other. The same fire burns between the two of you, feeding off each other as an energy source." She made us sound like fire vampires.

I turned to Ivana. "Your son will live and your lover will return to you. Whatever you tell us better be worth the risks we'll be taking."

Ivana wrapped her arms around me and whispered, "The tale I'm about to tell you is as dark and unsuitable for the ears of children as they come."

"Oh, like most original fairy tales then?"

"No, my dear. This one is worse than anything ever written. For it is written with the blood of innocent children. The author's blood is blue."

Thirty-six

Krakow, Poland
Thursday, 28 January, 7:55 p.m.

One word came to mind – not one suitable for children's ears. How I wished what Ivana told us was a fictional story, the evidence indisputable. *Truer than most news reports.* I stared at Aidan. Torment, anger and self-loathing filled his handsome face. Commander Walker didn't need me, but my husband did. I marched to him and wrapped my arms around his neck, holding him so close that if he were a lesser man, I might've broken his neck. "This morning I told you, sometimes we can't see the evil in those closest to us."

"I refuse to believe he is a paedophile!" Aidan tried to push me away. I clung to him like a weighted blanket, knowing this was the best way to calm him as we weren't alone in the suite. Ivana and his brothers didn't need to witness how I calm him when we're alone.

"There's no indication he ever laid a hand on a child, but he lied to you in order to get you to execute the very people who knew the truth about his grandfather." I turned to Ivana. "Why did Queen Katja help you?"

Ivana wiped her eyes. "She realised I was pregnant, and she knew what Mikolaj would've forced me to do. His rules were simple. He didn't tolerate weakness in any of us and to him, a pregnant operative was a liability. An Achilles heel. A problem with only one solution."

Queen Katja had taken Ivana under her wing and requested that Ivana be appointed as the head of security for her worldwide tour. Bergia's relations at the time had been strained, because of Mikolaj's lust for power and him annihilating anyone who he deemed standing in his way. Mikolaj had used the BSS for much more than what forms part of most secret service agents' job description. Operatives received kill orders on anyone Mikolaj even suspected knew the truth about his depravity. He considered Max Jefferson, and the other individuals who formed part of the circle, as some of his closest friends. Numerous photos of them surfaced once we started investigating. When you know what to look for it's much easier to find it.

"Katja sent her daughters and granddaughters to boarding schools across Europe as soon as they were old enough to start school. The people of Bergia thought her cruel, but she did it to protect them. Mikolaj wouldn't have thought twice about giving his own blood to his so-called friends." I expected Ivana to spit on the carpet, but she didn't.

Aidan dragged his hands down his face. "Szymon asked me to assassinate all the BSS operatives, claiming he feared for his and his family's safety. We were nothing more than a cleaning crew to bury his grandfather's sins. I'm sorry, Ivana."

She stood and placed her hands on his cheeks. "You didn't know; no one did except the twenty of us. I've long suspected Katja didn't die from a heart attack, and it won't surprise me if Szymon had a hand in Mikolaj's death. Princess Ylva is the first daughter who didn't attend boarding school. Her mother refused. Katja cried when she told me how she had pleaded with Astrid. If Mikolaj touched Ylva, or gave her to one of his friends, Szymon would've had enough reason to kill his grandfather."

"I need to speak to Szymon. Tonight." Aidan came to his full length but didn't take a step forward. "First, we need to get Ivar out of Black Dolphin."

Again, Ivana placed a hand against his cheek. "Ivar is a strong man, and he won't forgive me if we put him above the answers you seek. Piotr won't help a paedophile, but he's close to the family. Maybe he can answer some of your questions."

"Piotr needs to meet with us somewhere discreet. I think

his boss is keeping him on a tight leash, one he started pulling against if their conversation in Dubai is anything to go on."

"He told me about the device you put behind his ear." Ivana crossed her arms over her chest. "With a woman like you by his side, Piotr can do much more with his life than the direction he's willing to take now."

"You trained him well; perhaps it's the only reason he's still alive. However, the fact remains, your son's complicit in the murders of twenty-five people and the attempted murder of another. I might spare his life, and we might employ him, but somehow he must carry the consequences of his actions."

Sorrow filled Ivana's eyes. "He's already paying the price for the decision he made. Piotr might be able to lie to himself and the rest of the world, but a mother sees the truth." She smiled, it seemed miserable on her face. "If I didn't understand his heart, I would've concluded he's a psychopath."

I didn't look at Aidan when I asked, "When are you meeting with Szymon?"

"Saturday. He and Queen Astrid are still in the UAE on an official state visit. They've been there since Tuesday."

The implication struck Aidan the hardest. King Mikolaj had been a paedophile, a warmonger, a tyrant. Could King Szymon be a serial killer? *Stranger things have happened.*

"Okay people, focus. If we need to be in Bergia on Saturday, it gives us a couple of hours to get to Orenburg, break Ivar and the other man out of Black Dolphin, and get to Bergia."

Rowan cleared his throat and stared down at his mobile phone. "Ivar can wait." He shrugged. "Sorry, Ivana, but you said so yourself. Kelly and Rob have a meeting with one Günter Kuhn, who happens to be here in Krakow. On our way back we can pick up Piotr. It's time for him to tell us what the hell is going on."

"Leave Piotr in the field. I'll contact him and ensure he's wherever you'll meet with Szymon. He's much more than Ylva's bodyguard."

I paced the length of the sitting area; everyone stepped

back to give me room. The Walkers knew this is how I do my best thinking. *Formulate a strategy to get Ivar and Vladimir out of Black Dolphin. Meet with Günter Kuhn.* "What time are we meeting Kuhn?"

"2200 hours, at a bar not far from here." Rowan leaned his shoulder against the wall.

Closing my eyes, I took a deep breath and tried to do the calculations. "I'm going to need at least thirty minutes to put the Kelly face on. That leaves us with forty-five minutes to come up with an extraction plan. Rowan and Liam, I want you both in the bedroom. Now."

Liam grinned. "Yes, ma'am. I waited a long time for this. Just never thought Rowan would be watching. Can you wear the outfit you did in Dubai? I've been having dreams about you in it."

I closed the distance between us. My fist connected with his jaw. The alcohol on his breath smacked me in the face. Liam never drank much; something wasn't right. My heart told me to ask what happened but my head and gut demanded I stay focused on the operation. Lives were at stake. "Your conduct is unbecoming of an operative, and even more so in front of our guest. I don't need you on this operation. This would've been your chance to redeem yourself, but I won't tolerate your behaviour another second. Head back to HQ. Now."

Liam looked at his eldest brother; Commander Walker crossed his arms over his chest.

"I out rank you, *Sergeant.* But then again, I'm not the one sleeping with the boss." Liam's right eyebrow raised. So did my temper.

My nails dug into my palms. I had dealt with this sexist crap during my years in the military. I wasn't about to take it from my family. Liam might be the super soldier, but serial killers and criminals are my field of expertise. Rowan stepped in front of me and covered my fist with his hand. He shook his head, hard.

Ivana pushed to her feet. "If I may?" she asked Aidan. He

nodded. "You're a family, a unit unlike any in the world. It has been an honour being a part of Fortius and I will die protecting what you stand for. It's not about rank, it's about who brings the most to the table for a specific operation. That's the only good thing about the time I served in the BSS. We all had our strengths, and instead of undermining each other we used our collective abilities for what we believed were for the greater good of our country."

Ivana walked to the suite's door and turned to us. "I've tried to keep tabs on how Fortius operates since I joined, for I refuse to ever be in the same position Mikolaj put me in. Your parents have sacrificed more than you ever will, and they would be ashamed of you, Liam. You might not realise it, but women need to work much harder at being taken seriously in any line of work. The way you spoke to your sister-in-law is despicable."

She reached for the door handle. "Aidan, I'm going to go freshen up. I promise not to contact Piotr until you order me to." Ivana stared at Liam, her eyes cold. "The lives of innocent children are on the line, and I won't do anything to jeopardise it. The mission *always* comes first."

My fist wasn't the only one to connect with Liam's face. So did Aidan's – after Ivana left.

Aidan pushed Liam down in the desk chair and towered over him. Rowan and I stood next to each other, bracing for the blow even though we weren't on the receiving end.

Fury erupted from Aidan's mouth but his calm, calculated word choice made the impact devastating. "Twenty-five people are dead. Alicia Rideout is still in ICU. An international paedophile ring has been operating for decades. This is the reality of what we face at the moment. We might not be in a war zone, dodging bullets or laying down fire every minute of every day, but make no mistake Liam, this is *war.* One I refuse to lose. Countless children were brutalised for the sheer pleasure of despicable people hiding in the open behind their money and positions. I will bring the full force of this organisation down on them and anyone else whose name pops up during this investigation."

Commander Walker's voice remained low. "Liam Walker, you're relieved of your position in this organisation. Finley's request to speak to you and Rowan in private wasn't the time for your crude remarks." He held up a hand. "None of us have time for your juvenile comments, not when the lives of children are at stake and a serial killer remains free to kill again any minute."

Aidan stepped backwards and crossed his arms over his chest. "You won't work in the field again, or be considered part of this organisation until you undergo a psych evaluation and basic training. You're dismissed."

Without saying a word, Liam stood and headed for the door.

"I have a better idea." Liam stopped walking but didn't turn to look at me. "We need someone in Russia to oversee whatever strategy we decide on. Someone with extensive combat experience *if* things go south. You'll wear lenses in both eyes, and earpieces at all times. You'll follow Aidan's every instruction. This is your last chance with me Liam – as a fellow operative and as your friend. If you fail this mission, or lose focus for even a split second, I'll ensure you never work with Fortius again. I will voice my concerns about your lack of professionalism to your parents as they are still in charge. For now. Commander Walker?" I turned to Aidan.

He turned towards the window and took a deep breath. "Fin is right, we need someone with your experience on the ground. Marika and Dmitry are brilliant covert operatives, but they'll need backup."

I checked the time on my mobile phone's screen and realised we were yet again wasting time because of Liam. Every minute added to the time Aidan and I weren't home with our daughter, but my heart kept screaming Liam's name. "I want to speak to Liam. Alone."

"I'll get started on the blueprints for Black Dolphin, and we need to prepare for the meeting with Kuhn. I never go in blind." Rowan slapped a hand on Aidan's shoulder and together they left.

"In case you haven't realised it yet, I'm the closest thing you have to a friend at the moment." I retrieved a can of Coke from the mini bar and held it out to Liam and called reception. "While we wait for the ice, put the can against your eye, and tell me what happened. I've never seen you have more than two drinks, the odd chance that you do drink. Now you're drinking every day – and on an operation like *this*."

Liam pressed the can to his eye. "I'll head back to Marcel; get out of everyone's way. I'm not made for this."

Frustration swirled inside me. I didn't have time for another pity party. "I want to tell you I'm done with you and that you should leave. However, I can't turn my back on someone who needs a friend, and that's what I'm trying to be. If you walk out that door, I won't try to convince Aidan or your father to keep you on. Why can't you get it through your thick skull that we need you? Dammit, Liam. You bring so much to the table, yet you focus on what everyone else offers and forget you're a valuable member of this team. I love you like a brother, you insufferable man."

Liam sank down onto the floor, his back pressed against the wall, his head resting on his arms. "What's the point of surviving war just to be killed at home?"

I sat down next to him and placed my arm around his shoulder. "Who, Liam?"

Liam shook his head, his body trembling.

"It's just us. You're safe with me."

The turmoil pouring out of him reminded me of a time when I had cried similar tears. A time when I too had been powerless to protect or save. I waited and offered him no comfort other than my arms wrapped around him. His tears soaked my shirt down to my skin.

Liam wiped his eyes with the back of his hand and stared straight ahead. "We enlisted at the same time, went through training together, fought alongside each other." He tried to smile. “We even saved each other’s lives.” Liam lifted his shirt and showed me the scar on the left side of his stomach. *IED.*

The scar on my right side mirrored Liam’s. A keepsake from the night my squad had been ambushed and taken hostage.

“After the war, Daniel joined the police; said he wasn’t done protecting the innocent. He died trying to do just that. Ironic, isn’t it? He survived war, and gets killed while serving an arrest warrant, as well as his partner, Laura.”

I shifted until I faced him, took his hands in mine, and waited for Liam to meet my stare. “What are you going to do about it?”

“He’s dead. Nothing to do about it.”

A grin spread across my face; the darkness paced. A constant reminder of the thousands of wars being waged across the world. “Right now you can do something. Go to Russia and free two men who shouldn’t be in prison. They protected the innocent and they don’t deserve their punishment. Then you focus on the next war, and then the next. You’re a warrior, Captain Walker, you always will be. Use your talents and abilities, and for as long as there is breath in your lungs, you keep fighting. You didn’t join the military because you didn’t have other options. Daniel died a soldier in a different war. The media and people in general just don’t call it that.”

I pushed to my feet and held my hand out to him. “Stop drinking and get your head in the game. Aidan’s right, we might not be dodging bullets or laying down fire, but this is a war we will keep on waging. One battle at a time. The enemy’s face might change, but what we do isn’t any less important. The victims need us. Fortius needs you. Our name means *stronger*, and that’s what we must be in every war. Our strength is in our collective vision to better the world, for as long as there is fight left in us.”

Thirty-seven

Krakow, Poland
Thursday, 28 January, 10:00 p.m.

With Kelly's face covering mine, and wearing one of Ivana's dresses and boots, I sat across from Rowan in a booth towards the back of the bar. The dress and high heel boots part of my Kelly identity. The liquid Walker burned its way down my throat as we waited for Kuhn to arrive. Behind my back the bar teemed with people, Rowan kept a watchful eye. I hated not having a view of the room.

"Are you still upset because Aidan didn't agree to your extraction plan?" Rowan asked, his face devoid of the laughter visible in his eyes.

"No. Liam can do it the boring way. If I went, it would've been much more fun. Like I said, we can shoot the guards with tranquillisers, but no." I exaggerated *no* for as long as I could but needed to take a breath.

Rowan tilted his head to the right and studied the Kelly face. "It's remarkable how well you and Quinn can pull off that face. She just doesn't fidget when wearing a dress."

Over the course of the preceding days, I had come to the realisation that my normal black cargo pants, dark jeans, and black shirts, or tops wouldn't cut it doing undercover work. As I waited for my brain to construct a clever reply, I wondered if Aidan would allow the mother of his child to continue working in the field. Most of Fortius' operations didn't involve serial killers or paedophile rings. The latter would be something I put more focus on. Without red tape, we can hunt them down much faster than through official channels.

"Are you sure Liam will be okay?" Rowan asked before I

could ask him when last he and Quinn had 'bumped uglies', as my sister had called it when we were much younger. It had been the only question or attempt at a comeback I could think of, and I'm glad I didn't ask. The killer still breathed. *For now.*

"Yes, he and I had a heart to whatever pumps my blood. His head is in the war now, and I'm excited to see him execute Aidan's plan." I drained the rest of the liquid Walker and placed the tumbler on the coaster. "Admit it, Aidan's plan is boring."

Rowan laughed. "Yes, it is, but it's by far the safest option with the least probable chance of casualties on either end. The guards aren't our enemy."

I rolled my eyes at Rowan. In my ear, Aidan cleared his throat. "I hate it when you do that."

"Can we at least do something fun before I return to being a full-time mother?"

"We will discuss your working hours and the operations I'll allow you to work on, once we get back to HQ."

Again, I rolled my eyes. This time Aidan laughed. "Our home is HQ. Come on, Walker, I want to do something fun. You can't deny my extraction plan will be the most fun thing we've done so far?"

"If not for the roof over their caged in exercise area, I might've considered it. I tell you what, next time we need to break someone out of prison we'll give your strategy a go."

Rowan reached across the table and covered my hand with his. "Game time. You should consider making this your permanent hair colour."

I forced a laugh and added what I thought would make it sound seductive. "Darling, blondes have the most fun."

Rowan stood and held out his hand to a middle-aged bald guy. Günter Kuhn looked like anyone's dad – or accountant. Which might explain how he had stayed in the shadows until now. "Granger, Rob Granger."

Kuhn shook the wanna-be spy's hand and said, "You can call me, K."

I took a deep breath, desperate not to laugh. In this little scenario, who would I be? Just another woman who ends up in the spy's bed? Uhm, no. Correction – hell no. To be polite, I offered my hand as Kuhn sat down next to me, perhaps thinking he was safer next to a woman. Can't say I blamed him. I looked feminine, not lethal. Little did he know of the dangers hidden underneath the dress.

Kuhn ordered a Scotch from the waitress and turned to me. "I didn't catch your name."

I smiled the way I thought a red-headed woman would, not that smiles can differ, but this undercover work thing was new to me. "Kelly. No last name."

Even in the dim lighting, the recognition in Kuhn's eyes was unmistakable.

"I take it you've heard of me?" Quinn sure had a strange life, with all of her undercover assignments. I wondered how many people she killed for the name *Kelly* to be this recognisable.

Kuhn nodded and turned to Rob Granger, whose hair hung past his shoulders. "You brought an assassin to our first meeting?"

I patted Kuhn's scrawny thigh. "Sweetie, I'm his lover. Besides, Rob doesn't need me to clean up for him. He has a thing for explosives, I prefer adding a dash and a splash of femininity to my kills." A needle pierced through his pants and into the muscle. I kept my eyes on his as I pressed the syringe down.

Kuhn cursed in German and tried to get out of the booth.

I grabbed his arm. "Sit, sweetie, the poison will spread slower if you don't move."

His breathing increased and I patted his back. Anything not to laugh. I don't know why it delights me so much to play with the human monsters of this world, perhaps because their demise won't be a terrible thing. The world will be a better and safer place without them in it. Kuhn just didn't realise yet, but what coursed through his veins couldn't kill anything.

Rob Granger rested his arms on the table and leaned forward. Not a speck of Rowan remained in the man sitting across from Kuhn. "She'll give you the antidote if you answer my questions."

I nodded and winked when Kuhn glanced at me.

"You led me here thinking we would discuss business now that Theo's no longer trying to take over the market in Hungary. Instead, you're killing me?"

"Sweetie, we don't *want* to kill you. Just be a good boy and answer Robbie's questions."

Rob Granger glared at me. "What did I tell you about calling me *Robbie*?"

"Not to do it outside the bedroom." I forced out my bottom lip. "You can remind me about the rules later, Robster. For now, we need to hurry if you want dead-man-sitting to answer your questions before the poison eats away chunks of his brain."

"That's not how poisons work," Aidan said in my ear.

Kuhn worked the top button of his shirt loose. "How long do I have?"

"Sweetie, there are so many variables to consider. Things like your health, when last you ate, any underlying heart conditions, your erectile functioning. I'm no expert, but I guess fifteen minutes, at most." I threw my head back and laughed. "Oh, silly me, I *am* an expert in death. We've been talking about nothing for quite some time now, so let's say you have five minutes left."

I grabbed Kuhn's face with both hands and attempted my best puppy eyes. "You don't want to spend the rest of your life confined to a bed, consuming every meal through a tube inserted into your stomach. Answer Rob's questions and I'll give you the antidote. Don't do anything stupid." I glanced down at my bare wrist. "Oops, I guess we better hurry."

Rowan listed the names of the victims in Malta, Budapest, Vienna, and Zurich. Kuhn dropped his head forward and didn't even thank the waitress when she placed the Scotch down in front of him. He drank it in one big gulp and met Granger's stare. "I will rather die than give you his name."

"You knew what he planned to do to them?" Granger leaned further forward across the table.

Kuhn moved back as far as the back rest allowed. "No, but even if I had known, I would've done it."

The pressure of the Ka-Bar TDI's blade pressing against his manhood yanked his focus to me. "You're one of them, aren't you? The elite little club of predators who prey on children. I tell you what, sweetie, I'll give you the antidote. And then, I'm going to make you *suffer*."

"I've never laid a hand on a child." He glanced down at the knife between his legs. "I swear."

"You're the go-to guy, the concierge for whatever anyone desires. How many children did you deliver to them?"

Kuhn closed his eyes. "One. Just once."

"Who contacted you? Where did you deliver the child to? But the most important question – what's the child's name?" The tip of the blade twisted against him.

"A man who called himself Volkov contacted me, gave me the child's name and address, and told me to deliver the child to a location in Bergia."

I grabbed the back of his neck and slammed his face against the table. Other patrons turned to us. Rowan spoke in Polish, and I guess he told them our friend had a bit too much to drink, as they nodded, smiled, and continued their festivities.

"Günter, the child's name?" The hair on the back of my neck stirred. Something about this didn't feel right. All children are precious, but why this specific one?

"Abigail Davis." Kuhn used his sleeve to wipe the blood from his nose. "I did the job they paid me for and that's it."

"No, it wasn't, because someone else either blackmailed you in to supplying the victims, or you're part of their sick circle." I wished I had injected more than vitamin B into his blood.

Aidan relayed information regarding the circumstances of Abigail Davis' abduction, and her father's employer to Rowan and me. I closed my eyes, listening to Aidan's every word. Kuhn wouldn't die from the injection but this would be his last night alive.

Rowan rolled his shoulders. A predatory sneer consumed his face, and I saw first-hand why people feared Rob Granger. “Were you aware her father worked for Interpol? The day after Abigail’s disappearance he committed suicide, according to his death certificate. A murder-suicide according to the official police report, but we both know he didn’t kill his wife. Or himself. *They* killed him because he was closing in on them. Abigail paid the price for her father’s work, his dedication to rid the world of the very people who raped and murdered his daughter and sent him a video of it. Get up. Now!”

Kuhn got to his feet. Rowan steered him through the crowd and into the dark alley next to the bar. It smelled of stale beer, urine, and Kuhn’s fear.

Rage coiled inside me. I wanted to rip Kuhn to pieces with my bare hands. “You knew what they were going to do to Abigail. She was fourteen-years-old, and you took money for it.” My fists continued talking for me because words failed me.

Rowan pulled me off Kuhn and held me against his chest until my breathing calmed. “You in control again?” he asked.

I nodded. Rowan turned his focus on Kuhn but kept his hand on my shoulder. “Günter, we know who the paedophiles are. Who is the man responsible for the deaths of five people?”

“I’m already dying, I won’t give you his name. Don’t you get it? If he knows about Abigail, what is there he doesn’t? You have no idea how powerful he is. You’re in over your head, Granger.” Kuhn used the wall to ease himself back up to his feet.

I hoped Ivana didn’t mind that I tore her dress. “You have two options, Herr Kuhn. One, give us his name and you’ll die a quick, and painless death. Two, I will do *this* to you, and I promise you, by the time I get to the fourth rib you’ll talk.” I held out my mobile phone towards him and flicked through the photos. “You might not recognise them; the head is Lieutenant General Volkov and the man whose lungs you saw is Max Jefferson, aka Oleg Petrov.”

Kuhn licked at the blood coming from the cut on his bottom lip. "You're lying. They're untouchable."

Laughter bellowed out of the tar-stained pits of my soul. "No one is untouchable. Soon they'll all end up like their friends did. In case you haven't figured it out yet, your fear of him, is nothing compared to the horror I will inflict on you. You claim you *only* handed Abigail to them; I don't believe you."

"I swear." Kuhn wiped the blood from his nose and mouth with his sleeve.

"Sweetie, before the reaper comes for you, I'll make you pay for every sin you ever committed. It won't be fast; it won't be pain free. For Abigail's rape and murder, I'll make you suffer until you beg for mercy. Spoiler alert! I don't have any for paedophiles or traffickers."

A van came to a stop at the alley's entrance. Rowan grabbed Kuhn by the back of his coat and threw him inside.

Thirty-eight

Krakow, Poland
Thursday, 28 January, 11:48 p.m.

Not even Aidan could get Kuhn to give us a name. Instead, he had repeated Jefferson's words: 'All roads lead to Bergia'. Kuhn hadn't lasted long. The icy water of the Vistula River had washed his lungs in a similar way we had cleansed Sanchez's airways. We dried the concierge of the underworld with a blanket. No one heard him scream, as I had gagged him with his own tie. Ethanol and a single flame from a lighter took Kuhn to meet the reaper. It didn't bring back Abigail Davis or her parents.

This killer was the master of all manipulators; unlike any I've ever come across. Psychopath, sociopath, or narcissist? I wasn't sure. An undeniable fact: people feared him enough to take his name to their graves. Nothing we did persuaded them to fear us more. Sanchez remained bound to his apartment in Madrid. Neither he nor the killer had made contact with each other.

Aidan asked Ivana to contact Piotr and set up a meeting.

"He left for Toro about an hour ago. It's important he maintains his cover." Ivana leaned against the door of her hotel room.

"There's no cover. He's helping Szymon murder innocent people and blackmailing paedophiles into helping them find victims." I glanced down at the blood spattered and torn dress. "I'll buy you a new one."

She shook her head. "It's old, don't bother replacing it. I can't contact Piotr. She surprised him here. And she's not aware of my existence beyond what she might've heard about the BSS." Ivana shrugged and yawned at the same time.

"Are you talking about Ylva?" Aidan asked, sounding almost as tired as I felt.

"She's in love with him. If he doesn't ask her soon, I'm pretty sure she's going to propose to him." Ivana's face hardened. "I don't blame her for her grandfather's sins, but I won't allow Piotr to marry anyone if not for love."

"Were you and Ivar married?" I asked, placing my hand in Aidan's.

"Not on paper, but in our hearts."

Aidan stepped forward and covered her shoulder with his free hand. "He'll be safe soon. Wherever you want to go, which ever names you want to take, I'll make it happen."

She smiled up at him. "Thank you, but let's get him out of Russia first and then we can discuss the possibility of our future."

We said goodnight and as Aidan and I stepped into the suite, I turned to him. "Vladimir's family; we need to get them out of Russia too. They'll need new identities and a future."

Aidan pulled me against him and held me tight. "Always thinking about everyone else. How are you holding up? You've allowed the darkness to come out to play a lot over the last few days."

"A long time ago a brilliant and gorgeous, man told me in order to do my job, and be his wife, I need to compartmentalise. He said I need to see an invisible line and not let one persona into the other's world. I will carry his wisdom with me into my new role with Fortius. When I'm home, I'll be Mrs Aidan Walker, and Ainsley's mommy. Out in the field, or in the command centre which doubles as your office, I'll be Finley Williams-Walker."

"Sounds like this man knows what he's talking about. Fin, I'm worried about the toll this is going to take on you in the long run. We fight daily to not get sucked back into the darkness; Ainsley needs us to stay focused."

"Are you talking to me or yourself?" I drew a deep breath

and pressed my ear against his chest. "We're all surrounded by darkness every day. The difference is, we see it and we fight back. We can't change who we are, Aidan. If I don't work for Fortius, I'll find another way to fight the evil in this world. At least as part of this organisation, and family, we can keep an eye on each other and do whatever it takes to avoid letting anyone slip into the abyss."

Aidan pressed his lips to my hair and without letting me go, steered me to the bathroom. We duck walked, and for a few precious seconds I forgot evil circled us. Mikolaj had gone after the daughter of an Interpol agent and destroyed Abigail. I didn't need the bodies exhumed. I knew the agent didn't kill his wife or commit suicide.

"When are your parents going to tell your brothers and the other operatives?" I asked as Aidan and I stepped into the shower. Neither of us had the energy or desire to do anything more than wash the day off of each other. The smell of Kuhn's burning flesh clung to us.

"As soon as we get back."

Thirty-nine

Krakow, Poland
Friday, 29 January, 9:00 a.m.

My daughter's beautiful face filled my mobile phone's screen. She couldn't care less about my face or Aidan's as he stared at her over my shoulder. Ainsley babbled in her delightful way, and then she did it – she walked. Tears welled up in my eyes, gratitude for the miracle child who had grown in my womb, and that she didn't realise her parents were facing evil and war. For as long as we can, we'll shield her from the realities of this world. Not a day goes by that I don't pray for her safety, as well as that of the millions of other children in the world.

Forever my biggest fear will be that she might, one day, need to survive all the things I have. Nothing changes you more than pain, humiliation, and grief does. It affects you in such profound ways you wonder if it altered your DNA. There's no going back to who you were before. The before-you will never again exist. In order to survive, you must accept whoever you are on the other side.

Nothing but love filled Aidan's face as he watched our daughter move around our living room. The house – fortress – he had designed to keep us safe. No one could get to her there, not even the serial killer we hunted. Heather laughed, and I struggled to figure out what was happening on their end until Ryan's face filled the screen.

"Time for a nappy change; Heather will take care of it. Ainsley's as smitten with her grandmother as grandma is with her."

My daughter is safe, if only I can protect every child. "Dad, did you get extra guards?"

"Yes, my girl. The property looks like a military base. No one is getting to Ainsley. Lizzie is working from home until you get back. She didn't ask any questions."

Lizzie stopped asking questions a long time ago. Now she understood the immensity of what her husband, sister, and the Walkers do. But more than anything, what it does to us. We needed her to remain our safe place, the one person other than Nathan outside of Fortius. I missed my sister, but all I thought about were the victims and their families. The Walkers had welcomed Lizzie, Eli, and Levi as part of the family. If anything happened to me, Lizzie would have them. A comforting thought. Now she had her own family. But the bond between sisters, especially after everything we went through, was forged in fire and is unbreakable.

"How are you feeling, old man?" I asked.

Aidan bumped his shoulder against mine as he sat down on the couch. "He's still the boss and he'll fire you for calling him old," he whispered.

I pressed my lips to his ear. "I'm his favourite, he won't."

"Call me old man again and I'll order you to redo basic training." He stared at me with nothing but love in his eyes. Ryan Walker never replaced my father, but I loved him as if he had taught me how to handle a gun.

"Did you tell Mom?" Aidan asked.

Ryan nodded. "She didn't even put up a fight but keep the news to yourselves until we can hold a meeting and make it official. Taking care of Ainsley is good for her, and Ains is such a delightful child compared to the four sons we raised. She sleeps through the night, has no issues when we put her down for a nap."

Isn't this how all children behave whenever their mother isn't around?

"How are you two holding up? Working together isn't easy for any couple."

Aidan and I looked at each other and shrugged at the same time. "I can follow his orders; he respects my opinions and decisions. We'll be okay in the long run."

Ryan laughed and the couch filled the screen behind his face. "Don't lie to me. The two of you are like an atomic bomb in a hurricane."

"Let me guess, I'm the hurricane?" Ryan nodded. "I defied one direct order and saved two of your sons' lives by doing so. Aidan laughed when I told him my idea to break into Black Dolphin. At least we didn't fight either time."

"This is the reason your mother and I want the two of you to take over command of Fortius. You know when to operate as a team and when to be lovers. Rowan said you've made him consider giving up his cover as Rob Granger. He's ready for a normal life."

I laughed so hard it's a miracle the people at the reception desk didn't hear me. "Normal life? Nothing about our lives is *normal.* Although, I think Rowan learned from Nathan's mistake." I turned to Aidan. "Don't even start with me now about our conversation the other day about *normal.*"

"Thank you for whatever you said to Liam, Finley. I'll be watching from the office, and for the record your idea would've been more fun. Damn whoever designed the prison and put a roof over the exercise yard. Then again, Russian winters isn't the season for being outside."

"Thank you." I lifted my arms, palms up.

My idea had been simple, elegant, and fun. Easy to execute. A helicopter. Aidan shooting from inside the helicopter and darting the guards with tranquillisers. From past operations, I knew he can do it. Rowan and I would've been lowered to the top of the cages; we could've burned through the steel bars with something – Aidan would've known what – and we could've lifted Ivar and Vladimir out. Marika knew two of the guards; they could've ensured that both men exercised at the same time. Easy-peasy. If not for that damn roof over the exercise area.

"Dad, can we trust Ivana? I suspect she has her own agenda. Piotr being here one minute and then the next he's heading to Toro. Something doesn't feel right."

"Of course she has her own agenda. Ivana hates that entire family and she has very good reasons for it. Let it play out, Aidan. Now, go do what you do best." Ryan ended the call.

"They trained Piotr to infiltrate the Stein family, Ylva is just his ticket in. Pretty face like his, the whole bodyguard/ protector of the royal damsel cliché. Why is he then helping Szymon kill?" I jumped to my feet. "Aidan, what if the serial killer isn't Szymon, but Ylva?"

The carpet tickled my bare feet as I made my way to the window. "Everything about this says we're looking for a male serial killer, despite the use of poison and hands-off kill methods. A man got the female victims' faces tattooed on his back. It can't be Ylva. While we wait for Ivar and Vladimir to die, I need to learn everything there is about the Stein family."

Aidan ordered room service and asked Rowan to join us for breakfast. After a quick shower, I got to work. *Why didn't Queen Katja send her male offspring as far away from King Mikolaj as she had the female members of their family?*

Forty

Krakow, Poland
Friday, 29 January, 2:49 p.m.

White filled the screen; inside the suite we remained warm. *Poor Liam.* "In position." His voice filled the room even though he stood almost 3000 kilometres away.

"See, I told you this would be boring." I leaned my head against Aidan's shoulder as we sat staring at the laptop's screen.

For a change, Ivana paced, Rowan sat on the armrest of the couch. Even though my eyes were on the laptop, my focus remained on Ivana. I wondered about her motives and what she hoped the outcome would be. Piotr had returned to Toro, and whether he warned the killer that we were closing in, remained to be seen. I didn't want to kill a man who infiltrated the family – because they had destroyed his own. *What is his objective and how big a hand does Ivana have in this?* In my gut, I knew they were trying to steer our operation. I've never liked playing by others' rules. I had reminded Aidan of this before Ivana joined us. He told me to trust his father, and that I did.

Aidan and I glanced at each other at the same time. "I love you," I mouthed. We didn't need to say it every hour of every day or when ending every phone call. Our love was born in our darkest times and here we sat, side by side, hunting the depraved and righting wrongs. Soon we would be responsible for the entire organisation. The strength of our shared vision, and what we as a couple brought to the table would be instrumental in future operations and the overall success. More people depended on us than Ainsley, but none of them more important than our daughter.

My husband pressed his mouth to my ear and kept his voice

low. "I told my dad we're taking a family vacation in March. Nothing will change that. I promise."

I lifted my mouth to his. We clung to these moments, if we didn't the darkness festering inside both of us would win. The biggest wars Aidan and I wage are with ourselves. "No matter what happens, let's try not to get killed. I have a feeling things won't end well with this one, not when we're up against an enemy with an army behind him."

Ivana excused herself and headed to the bathroom.

Aidan touched the back of his fingers to my cheek. "So do we. Eighty-five percent of the people employed by my parents' companies are ex-military. I don't want to pull them back in, but they'll do whatever it takes when the lives of innocent children are at stake."

"I don't trust her."

Rowan reached over Aidan's head and patted the top of mine. "Good, neither do I."

"We have a common enemy. The saying 'my enemy's enemy is my friend' holds truth. Her precious son is on the inside, and as long as Liam has Ivar, we have leverage over her."

I stared at my husband; my mouth fell open. "Commander Walker, are you saying what I think you're saying?"

Aidan nodded. *Always a hundred steps ahead.* My husband, even more intelligent than he's handsome, sexy, and the best sniper in the world. Off the record, of course. A single phone call to Szymon and Piotr's true identity could be revealed. In Russia, anything could go wrong. Aidan's sleeves filled with muscular arms – and aces.

I grabbed my mobile phone and scanned through the photos Princess Ylva had posted to her social media profiles. Piotr's hand covered by a black glove in each where his right was visible. None of the photos suggested they were in a relationship, other than damsel and protector. I wondered how and when things changed between them. Did she know about the tattoo on his hand? Did she even realise it's the dragon of the BSS?

Ivana returned as I dropped my mobile phone screen down on the couch. "This is boring. My apologies, Ivana, this must be a very stressful and emotional day for you."

She laughed. It sounded forced. *Did it?* This woman had been in the game her entire life.

"May I ask how you came to join the BSS?" Aidan brushed his elbow against my ribs. I ignored his subtle warning to back off. "Mikolaj had been in power for a few years before you joined. By then most citizens already feared him and grew tired of his constant wars on the neighbouring countries. Why then, did you join?"

Ivana pulled the desk chair closer and lowered herself onto it. "I didn't sign-up, we weren't given any other option. Orphans don't have the luxury of choice. From the moment we arrived at the orphanage, no matter how young, they turned us into super soldiers. Everything they did, said – even the food they fed us. Katja was the first person to show me any kindness. Ironic – the queen became the orphan's best friend."

"Not Ivar?"

"There's a difference between a lover and a friend." She crossed her arms over her chest.

Aidan tapped his middle finger against my thigh; for the time being, I followed his order and backed down. *Something isn't right.*

Forty-one

Krakow, Poland
Friday, 29 January, 3:27 p.m.

Liam lifted the rifle and the van's rear tyre rolled into his line of sight. A single shot, unheard by anyone in the vicinity. The driver tried to keep the van on the road. Seconds felt like minutes. The van crashed into a snowbank. Marika and Dmitry advanced, yanked open the front doors, and shot the two men. With tranquilliser darts, not bullets. We'll never hurt innocent bystanders, civilian or not. Liam opened the van's back doors and jumped in. Two black body bags lay on the gurneys.

He unzipped both and pressed his middle and index fingers to the throats of dead men. "Pulse," Liam said. Twice.

Dmitry helped him carry the sleeping men to the awaiting vehicle. We watched through the lenses in Liam's eyes, and the body cameras mounted to Dmitry's and Marika's chests. It all took less than a minute; I timed them.

For all his faults, Liam's one hell of a soldier. And even though I'm hard on him, I love that insufferable man. He just needed to spend more time with Dr Finley Williams-Walker, for unofficial counselling sessions. One soldier helping another; and I know better than anyone what it's like to not fit in. Aidan might've been the best person to talk to Liam, but he never grasped what every day failure feels like for others. His self-perceived failures are wins in most people's books.

"Exciting enough for you, Fin?" Liam asked.

"No, but I'm impressed. I enjoy seeing you in action; who knew you can shoot the tyre of a moving vehicle?"

Liam laughed. "One shot. How many did it take you the

other night?"

"There, you said it yourself, *at night.* You did it in broad daylight. You can't compare strawberries and cream to haggis."

Aidan pushed to his feet. "Enough, both of you. Liam take care of the patients; administer oxygen the way I told you to. A doctor will assess them when you reach the safe house. Once he, and I, have decided their lives aren't in danger, we can discuss our next steps." He turned to Ivana. "I'm sorry, but you knew using tetrodotoxin comes with risks. I explained the same to Vladimir's wife when I spoke with her."

Vladimir's wife was more than willing to risk her husband's life. He was, after all, incarcerated for an act which should've made him an international hero. Not a day went by that she didn't worry about a paedophile seeking revenge for the death of a fellow monster. She had already been given a new name, passport, and was moved to a classified location. As soon as Vladimir was given the all clear by the Russian doctor and Aidan, he would join his wife. Her new name, and the country where they would start a new life, a handful of Fortius' operatives knew. Myself included.

"Liam, you've got company. Two vehicles approaching; one from the north, the other on your six." Rowan stared at another laptop screen. The image relayed from the same drone we had used in the desert outside Dubai.

Aidan and I moved as one. The barrels of our guns lifted to Ivana's face as we shot to our feet. "Call your men off!" My SIG pressed against her forehead.

"No. As long as your brother doesn't shoot first, your team won't get hurt." Ivana's cold eyes stared up at me.

"Take them out." Aidan ordered Rowan.

Rowan dropped to his knees in front of the laptop and started typing at Eli's speed. Liam had launched the drone while waiting for the mortuary van to leave Black Dolphin, but once airborne Rowan took over the controls. I added 'learning how to fly a strike drone' to my long list of things I wanted to do – now that I was officially part of Fortius. Being able to fly one will allow me to assist our teams from the command centre in our house, while my daughter sleeps in her crib, her mother close by.

"Call off your men or you'll watch them die." The SIG pressed harder against her skin, my finger on the trigger. No one takes over my operation or puts my brother and squad's life in danger. Working for Fortius brought back all the memories from my time in the military. What it felt like to be a part of a team, to fight with them, and watch them die. Perhaps I needed to talk through all the emotions with someone; starting with Aidan. *Later.*

Ivana stared at me, the emotion in her eyes unreadable. As fast as possible, I tried to analyse the situation but with Liam's life in danger, my brain didn't want to work. I tried one last time. "Call off your men. Now! We can sort whatever issues you have with Ivar out face to face. Last chance."

"No."

"Engage." A single word from Aidan turned the situation around.

Liam, and our presence a few kilometres from Black Dolphin, wouldn't be under the radar for much longer. Strike drones aren't for sale over the counter. Let alone one this small – custom built for Fortius – but every bit as lethal as its bigger counterparts.

The vehicle closing in from behind came to an abrupt stop as bullets ripped into it. A white cloud lifted from the ground around the Humvee as snow filled the air. The same happened to the other vehicle ahead of our team, and the two poisoned men. The drone circled back. More bullets ripped into both Humvees.

Through Liam's eyes we watched as he ran to check on the occupants in the Humvee not 500 metres from where our van had stopped. On another screen, Marika and Dmitry did the same. The Humvee stood 300 metres away.

"Damn, Ro, you're good." I winked when he looked at me and raised my fist.

He bumped his fist against mine and continued typing on the laptop. "I need to get the drone out of there. Where do you want it?"

Aidan closed his eyes and took a deep breath. "Bring it back here. We might need it again. Soon."

This drone one of a dozen owned by Fortius. The others waited in strategic locations across the world. Of course, in secure facilities. No one can control it without the right thumbprint. The thumbs in question all belong to persons with Walker blood in their veins. The drones small enough to fit in the cargo hold of the Dreamliner. *Size always matters.* With an unlimited range, thanks to the satellite owned by my in-laws, the drone would be in Krakow in record time.

Aidan returned his focus to Ivana. "You're done." When she tried to stand, he placed a hand on her shoulder; his SIG remained in his other hand. "No, you're not leaving and you won't be retiring somewhere tropical. This little stunt of yours caused unnecessary bloodshed. Whatever your issues are with Ivar, it can wait. From now on, you're no longer part of Fortius. Your status has changed from operative to prisoner."

I took her mobile phone and patted her down, removing all kinds of weapons and placing them on the desk. I tied her hands behind her back and waited for Commander Walker to give me further instructions. He didn't.

"Liam, get to the safe house. I'll make a phone call and sort out this mess." Aidan marched into the bedroom and shut the door.

"Why didn't you wait until you can kill him yourself? Did you think we're so focused on our hunt we didn't realise you have your own agenda? Aidan prepares for everything." I sat down on the couch, my SIG rested on my lap, pointing towards the former BSS operative and the mother of Ivar's child. "Is Ivar even Piotr's father? Did he rape you?"

Ivana didn't look at me. "Yes. No. More than that, I won't tell you. It doesn't matter. Piotr knows the truth and unlike me, he won't fail."

The answer dangled in front of me like a piñata. No matter how hard I tried to hit it, I couldn't get the truth to come tumbling out. I shrugged, stood, and made myself a cup of coffee. While I waited for the coffee machine to do its thing, I ran through everything I learned in the preceding days. One thing stood out.

"The assassination attempt on Volkov, the one that got Ivar arrested and thrown in Black Dolphin. You tipped off Volkov. Why?"

Ivana shook her head, pursing her lips.

"Fine, keep your secrets. The truth will come out. Maybe I'll *make* Piotr tell me—"

"If you touch my son, I'll rip your heart out."

"Impossible to do, unless you cut her open first. Good luck getting her to lie still." Aidan walked out of the bedroom and pressed his lips to my hair.

"Situation contained?" I asked.

He smiled and I kissed him hard.

"You two have no idea what working together will do to you. One day one of you will stab the other in the back. Remember this day, this moment, because it will fuel your hatred for each other. You've never seen each other at your lowest, darkest, most desperate moments. Those are the moments that define us, and break our relationships, trust, and hearts."

"Sweetheart, stop projecting. You just told me everything about your relationship with Ivar and all I did was kiss my husband." I wrapped my arms around Aidan's waist. "Inside information – we've been to hell and back, on our own and together. The sad thing is you never got over what Ivar did or tried to do. You never remarried or had a relationship with another man. His betrayal destroyed you. It's going to be fun putting the two of you in a room together and watch you tear each other to pieces without laying a hand on each other. Ivar's betrayal involved Piotr because you've never cared about anything, or anyone, other than your son."

I walked to Ivana and stared down at her. "You may have

more experience in the field than I do, because you're old, but no one reads people better than I do. You've told me what Ivar tried to do without even saying it. Maybe, it will all depend on my mood, I'll let you kill him. He deserves to rot in Black Dolphin for what he tried to do. But sometimes death isn't enough."

She smiled up at me, and I wondered who would win our little game. Then again, I wasn't the one tied to a chair. Neither did hatred cloud my judgement.

Forty-two

Krakow, Poland
Friday, 29 January, 9:45 p.m.

History had been one of my favourite subjects at school, when I absorbed what my teachers said as fact, unlike now. On paper the Steins appeared like any other royal family, but the truth was a different matter. As most royal families throughout the ages, they had waged wars, married their cousins, and whether the citizens thrived or withered away depended on who sat on the throne. Of all the Steins, Mikolaj had been the worst. The paper version of him wasn't much better. Szymon brought economic stability, and tourism flourished under his rule. Why people wanted to travel to Bergia was beyond my understanding. Except for one lake, it doesn't offer much in terms of sightseeing. Oh, and of course skiing in winter.

I spent hours learning as much as I could about the family; as far back as the internet allowed. Aidan filled the bedroom's door, but I kept my focus on the Stein's family tree.

"I admit, the extraction turned out not too boring. Still, not as exciting as my plan."

Aidan made himself comfortable on the bed, placing his hands behind his head, and studied me. "Now isn't the time to just be Aidan and Finley, is it?"

I shook my head. "No, dude, my brain's fried, and we need to take turns watching Ivana. Guess no one will sleep tonight."

"We can hog tie her and put her in the closet." Mischief played in Aidan's eyes.

"Commander Walker, you're stepping on my toes. Breaking prisoners is my job." I stood, climbed onto the bed, and snuggled into Aidan's arms.

Aidan pulled me closer and threw his leg over me, I struggled to breathe, but didn't complain. We both needed a moment to be nothing more than us. Safe in each other's arms, yet evil kept gaining ground in the world around us and across the globe. The battles will never be over.

"I love you, Wife."

The stubble on his chin pricked my lips, but the sting reminded me how lucky I am to call this man mine. "I love you more than there are stars in the sky, or sand and rocks on the earth. I love you more than all the drops of water in all the oceans, rivers, lakes, streams, swimming pools, hot tubs, dams, fountains, bird baths – all of it combined."

Aidan laughed. The sound filled my heart and forced the darkness to retreat into her corner. A never ending dual between the light and the dark and somehow, I had to let it clash to find the grey. *The place where I can be who I am.* The position I was destined to take since before I had even met Aidan. From a young age I knew war and protecting the innocent is my life's calling. In Aidan's arms I found something else, and so much more. Life. A home. A daughter.

"Do you think Ivana realises you called her bluff?" Aidan rolled me onto my back and settled between my thighs.

"Who?" His body on mine always makes me forget everything. Even my name.

He pressed his lips to the hollow of my throat. I wanted nothing more than the feel of his skin against mine, to make love to him, and forget about the faces of the children. I couldn't. The children's faces weren't the only images playing through my mind; twenty-five other faces joined them. I kissed Aidan hard and promised to make it up to him.

"Why didn't the Stein sons also get sent away to boarding school? The paedophiles didn't prefer girls, they destroyed any child they could get their hands on." This I said once Aidan returned to his former position and pulled me back into his arms.

"Tomorrow. All of your questions, and mine, will be

answered. I can't believe Szymon is a serial killer."

I pressed up on my elbow and placed my other hand on Aidan's face. "Szymon might not be our killer. The Crown Prince of Bergia is at the top of my suspect list."

"Ragnar? He's a playboy who prefers spending his life partying all over the world rather than attend to any royal matters."

I smiled and waited for him to make the connection. Aidan's brain works with figures, variables, and other things I don't understand. Mine is fuelled by emotion; people's actions and reactions. The masks they wear don't hide their true nature from me. Although, my intuition had let me down in the past. Not the time to dwell on it. Lives were at stake. The dead waited for me to avenge them.

Aidan let out a deep breath. "I can see how you came to this conclusion, but we can't rule out Szymon."

"I haven't, my love. There's something else we need to discuss and I can't get the words out if you keep looking at me like that."

Aidan's smile anything but innocent. "I'm just looking at my wife, not my fault if you're seeing things that aren't there."

I glanced down at his crotch and back at his face. "My friend tells no lies, Mr Walker. Unlike you."

Aidan grabbed a scatter cushion and covered the bulge in his pants. I sat up straight, crossed my legs and intertwined our fingers. "I promise to make it up to you, but tonight I can't make the mental switch. Not after seeing all of those photos and videos of Mikolaj with children at fundraisers and events. All the signs were there, but people didn't pay attention. Or they ignored the truth. In some videos you can see the fear in the children's eyes, as if they saw the monster behind the facade." Children and dogs are the best judges of character.

Aidan pushed himself up against the headboard. "I understand, but that's not what's troubling you most. Tell me."

I did. We hunted a serial killer; one we couldn't take out without the rest of the world noticing. There would be hell to pay if the King or Crown Prince of Bergia disappeared or died under suspicious circumstances. We needed an A, B, and C plan. And a contingency plan. Despite Bergia not being a big country, their military didn't consist of a bunch of tree-huggers. They meant business; Aidan had seen them in action during the war.

Rumour is Mikolaj had procured more than one atomic bomb during his reign; their location remained a mystery. Aidan suspected they weren't in Bergia, as all countries have to declare the number of bombs they have and routine checks are conducted by the IAEA. Whether the number countries put on paper is truthful, is another matter.

"I need eyes on all the people we have linked to the paedophile ring. We need to take them all out in a coordinated strike. This isn't something we can take to the media. The predators will lawyer up and bury all of their depravities faster than the media can orchestrate something else to draw people's attention away from this. So many high-profile people are involved. My head still spins every time I see the list. And these are the ones we know about."

Aidan grabbed his mobile phone and started executing my plan. For the time being, the operatives were to keep out of sight and await further instructions. He returned his phone to the bedside table and came to stand behind me as I stared out the window. "This is taking you all the way back to your days as the Hangwoman. Are you sure you want to do this?"

I turned and placed my hands against his chest. "I don't have a choice. The people involved are too powerful, court cases will be dragged out, and if they are arrested, they'll be murdered while awaiting trial. We know these people make it look like suicides. We've seen it before with other high-profile cases. The surviving victims deserve justice. I wish I can give them their day in court. A day where they can take back their power by facing the men and women who preyed on them. Nothing will come of it if we leave it up to official channels. More children will be abused for the sick pleasure of these horrid human predators. I can't allow it, Aidan, I won't."

I fell to my knees and cried. It didn't matter if Rowan, or Ivana, heard as torment, frustration, and anger tore through me.

None of the tortures or deaths brought me any joy. I'm not like those I hunt. In fact, I'm the complete opposite. Because there isn't a thing I won't do to protect the innocent, the victims, the ones who aren't in a position to fight back. For four excruciating months, even I hadn't been able to fight back.

Every day I face the reality of the choices I've made over the course of my life.

Do I regret it? No.

Do I lose sleep over it? No.

Will I ever stop fighting for the victims? Never.

Years ago, I decided to do whatever is necessary despite the personal cost. Now I had a daughter to think about; she needed me to be her mother and not only a huntress of evil.

Light and darkness swirled around me, and inside me they duelled. In all the chaos a simple truth remained – those in positions of power can make any charges, or people, disappear. They've done it for years. I've never been blind to the truth, unlike most people who choose to not see. In the process of them looking the other way, they belittle the horrors the victims endured.

A small number of people across the world refuse to sit on their hands while men, women, children, even babies, are raped and murdered every single day. I'm one of them. And I will be, for as long as there is breath in my lungs.

Forty-three

Toro, Bergia
Saturday, 30 January, 1:50 p.m.

Aidan placed his hand on my thigh and I covered it with mine. Adrenaline danced in my stomach – the tango of the huntress. A single row of trees on either side of the cobbled road took us to one of the two men at the top of my serial killer suspect list. We weren't sure of Ragnar's location. The burner phone Piotr carried put him in Toro. Ivana told us the truth; Princess Ylva had contacted him in Krakow. Together they had travelled to Toro the previous day. The DNA from the condom found in the Zurich victim's mouth didn't match Piotr's.

"We haven't seen Ainsley in almost a week. This needs to end. Today." Aidan lifted my hand to his warm mouth. I kissed his shoulder and wrapped my arms around his left arm. "I love you, Aidan Walker. I wish I could send you home and continue this fight on my own. If anything happens to you, I—"

"Stop this, nothing is going to happen to either of us. We'll be heading home soon, and the world will be a safer place for our daughter. Besides, Ains is having more fun with her grandparents and Mom is a different person compared to last week."

"This driveway is long."

Aidan's laughter filled the interior of the SUV and for a moment I breathed, taking in the snow-covered landscape. I focused my eyes on everything other than my handsome husband, who wore his newsie cap. Aidan had told me his preferred term for it after the second time I asked him to wear it every day, no matter the heat or humidity in Marcel. Of course, he said no. I can't fault him for not wanting to sweat like a race horse every day.

"Szymon knows I'm always armed, so our best bet is if he doesn't realise you're carrying."

I turned to my husband and touched my fingers to his cheek. "I don't need any of these weapons to protect you, my love. If someone threatens your life I'll bite their throats and rip them to pieces with my teeth and hands."

"Perhaps watching a horror movie last night to decompress wasn't the best idea. You sound very *murdery* today."

I patted his cheek and placed my hand on his thigh, moving it high enough to make Aidan laugh and almost send the Range Rover skidding off the road. "I love the sound of you laughing. It was the first thing I noticed about you, even before I saw your beautiful face."

"Can you please stop talking as if someone might die today? It's my job to worry about my operatives, Fortius, my wife, and my daughter. Not in that order. Nothing is more important than keeping you and Ainsley safe."

I didn't know why I wanted to tell him how much I love him or cherish our life together. Not to mention the beautiful miracle child we share. Perhaps it came down to an entire week of being surrounded by nothing but evil, depravity, and death.

If not for the Kevlar under his shirt, I wouldn't have allowed my husband to lunch with a potential serial killer. Not that Commander Walker took orders from me. Aidan Walker is by far the more reasonable of the two.

While we spent the afternoon with royalty, Rowan kept watch over Ivana. They weren't far away and within the hour another Fortius operative would arrive in Toro, in case Aidan and I needed Rowan's help. Liam waited close by. Aidan moved all of us around like chess pieces. He didn't share his every decision or strategy with me, he was after all the boss, or would be in a matter of days. If someone had to decide my next move, I prefer it be Aidan. Marika and Dmitry remained with Ivar and Vladimir until the doctor decided the patients have recovered enough to travel. A part of me hoped Ivar didn't, despite not knowing what he had done to make Ivana's love for him turn into full blown hatred.

The Stein's country home looked nothing like I expected, but somehow it did. I've visited many castles and palaces across Europe on the many family vacations my parents had taken Lizzie and me, but this building seemed less grandiose than most.

"Not what you expected?" Aidan asked as he pressed his foot on the brake.

"I expected more castle, and less mansion."

Aidan unbuckled his seat belt and turned to me. "This isn't the official country residence of the King and Queen of Bergia. Mikolaj left the main property to Ragnar. When you see it, you'll understand why it was for the king's use. The place is a fort."

"How many times have you visited Bergia?"

"I spent a week here after Mikolaj passed away. Szymon invited me to his coronation ceremony and made time to show me around his country."

I reached for Aidan's hand. "This weighs heavy on you. Keep in mind I'm not sure he is, or isn't, the killer. The murders aside, he knew his grandfather was a paedophile and asked you to take out the BSS operatives. He has done nothing to shine a light on Mikolaj's crimes. Instead, he buried them by having Fortius act as a death squad for him. The BSS operatives were well aware of what they were doing for king and country and probably deserved to die for the things they did. I dug into their backgrounds and from what I can gather most were orphans like Ivana and Ivar. As children they might not have had a choice, but as adults, carrying weapons and travelling across the world, they did."

I took a deep breath. "Eli contacted me earlier. He's been digging into the paedophile ring. He found a detective who worked a missing children's case a few years ago. They found the thirteen-year-old boy, but he refused to say where he had been, or what was done to him. The detective told Eli that a doctor confirmed the boy was raped. The only piece of evidence the detective had – a picture the boy kept drawing. A dragon. The end of its tail always nine lines. This confirms that at least one of the BSS operatives deserved to die for reasons other than the long list of crimes Mikolaj made them commit."

"Could the rapist be Ivar?"

I shook my head. "Ivana has a picture of the two of them hidden in the sole of the left boot she lent me. Below Ivar's dragon is a bear. Something that distinct, I think the boy would've drawn it as well."

"You and Rowan did a thorough job going through her things if you even checked the soles of her shoes."

"She's an assassin. I won't leave my brother with her without ensuring his safety. Cavity searches are not for the faint-hearted."

Aidan laughed, placed his hand on my neck and pulled my mouth to his. "Are you ready to meet a king and queen?"

I rolled my eyes and sent a text message to Rowan. Within seconds both he and Liam would see what we saw and hear every sound around us. "They're no different from us, except Szymon received life on a gold platter. Astrid worked for everything she has, including the company she still owns. The first commoner to marry into the Stein family. Point is, they bleed like the rest of us. No one is untouchable."

Forty-four

Toro, Bergia
Saturday, 30 January, 2:05 p.m.

The King of Bergia opened the front door and took my coat after Aidan made introductions. I didn't bow in front of Szymon, neither did I in front of Astrid. It struck me as odd when a butler didn't meet us at the door, but I bit my tongue. Things have a way of coming out even without me putting people on the spot. In order to assess the probability of Szymon being our killer, I needed him relaxed enough to lower his guard. People who live in the spotlight are masters of deception.

"It's an honour to meet you, Finley. Aidan hasn't told me much about you. Then again, I guess neither of us have much time for friends these day, not after he decided to be a doctor." Szymon motioned us towards a sitting area. The interior of the royal house as understated as the exterior.

"I love this room; it's so homey, and warm," I had to compliment them on something, as the things I wanted to say weren't polite.

Astrid's smile reached her eyes. "Thank you, I did the interior decorating myself. Can I offer you something to drink? Lunch will be ready in an hour. I put the lasagne in the oven about five minutes before you arrived. I had some emails to catch up on and lost track of time. My apologies."

"Please don't apologise; we had a late breakfast. We would both love some of your famous coffee." Aidan turned to me; the emotions in his eyes forced. "I've been telling her about it since we arrived. It reminds me of the coffee we had in Vietnam."

"Might be because I import it from Vietnam. Please make yourselves at home, I'll be back with the coffee." Astrid nodded with a smile but before I could offer to help her, Szymon said my name.

"Finley, I know little about you. Aidan is very secretive about his life and said nothing more than that he married the perfect woman. Any children yet?"

Why do people always feel the need to ask? It isn't anyone's business. I lost count of the number of times people asked Aidan and me about our family planning, when we had suffered a miscarriage, and while we went for IVF.

"No children," Aidan said. "We don't want any either."

Aidan's denial of Ainsley's existence was to protect her from a possible serial killer, and the person who hid his grandfather's crimes.

"How are you, old friend?" Aidan asked and took my hand as we sat down on a chocolate-coloured leather couch across from Szymon. The fire in the hearth offered welcome relief from the cold outside.

"Life is good. My wife and children are healthy and the country's economy is getting back on its feet." Szymon stood when Astrid returned with the coffee. He took the tray and placed it on the table between us.

The darkness kept screaming for me to lunge over the table, put a blade to Szymon's throat and ask him if he murdered twenty-five people across the world just for the fun of it. I needed to be specific because he had killed during the war, and a serial killer might've enjoyed it. Even if it didn't tick all the boxes of his fantasy.

Instead of indulging my darkness' request to play, I pushed to my feet and picked up two mugs. "My apologies if this seems rude, but don't you have any help?" If I didn't say or do something inappropriate, I wouldn't be me.

Astrid sat down next to her husband and studied me. "Not rude at all, I'm asked much more intimate questions during interviews. We do at our official residence, but out here, it's just us. I wanted our children to experience life the way I had growing up. They make their own beds, help with dinner, and washing up. Even at Stein Palace I always made them do their own laundry, since they were old enough."

This I learned from the magazine articles I had read on Astrid, the first non-blue blood to become a Stein. The world's media adored her and I understood why. People want to be able to relate. *If only they knew the truth.*

"You're a true inspiration to us common folk." I lathered honey to my words.

Aidan returned his mug to the tray and complemented Astrid on it. I couldn't disagree, it was delicious.

"While we're on the subject of your children, how are they doing? I often see Ylva's name in the newspapers with all the humanitarian work she does." Aidan returned to his seat and placed his hand on my thigh.

Astrid and Szymon glanced at each other. "We've been friends for years and I trust your wife will keep what we're about to say private." Szymon looked straight at me, perhaps through me.

"His wife is the gate keeper of all secrets. Whatever you say will stay between the four of us." The secrets I kept were what I planned to do to them and everyone else involved. A little careful wordplay on my side; Aidan didn't miss it as he gently tapped his fingers on my thigh.

"We love Ragnar but wish Ylva can ascend the throne one day. Of the two, she's what this family, and country, needs to move us forward into a new era. We fear Ragnar's love for partying and women will destroy everything Astrid and I built over the years. Every decision we've made has been to eradicate my grandfather's legacy and create a new image not only for this family, but for Bergia as a country." Szymon took Astrid's mug and leaned forward, returning it to the tray. I caught a glimpse of something on his chest, as his shirt pulled down ever so slightly, but couldn't make out the black design.

"Would he abdicate?" Aidan asked.

Astrid shook her head. "He sees it as his birthright, which it is, but we hoped—"

Szymon squeezed the mother of his children's hand. "Perhaps if he meets the right woman he'll grow up and become the man we hope he can be."

I willed my eyeballs to remain in place. No person ever has changed for another, true growth comes from oneself, and for yourself. If not, such a relationship would go down in flames and be on the cover of every tabloid for weeks. "And Ylva? Is she dating?"

Astrid smiled a mother's smile. "Yes, but we asked them to keep it private until they're sure how serious their relationship is. Dietrich is a wonderful young man, but we worry Ylva will one day realise that physical appearance and feeling protected isn't everything. He needs to be a worthy partner and her equal in all aspects."

Dietrich? I guess Piotr never told them the truth. Then again, why would he when he planned to destroy them?

"You'll meet them; they're on their way to join us for lunch." Astrid pushed to her feet. "If you'll excuse me, I need to go check on our lunch."

"Will Ragnar also be joining us? I haven't seen him since my last visit." Aidan squeezed my thigh and I took it as my cue.

"Astrid, is there anything I can help you with?" I didn't wait for her to answer and followed her into the kitchen.

Through the earpiece I listened to Aidan and Szymon's conversation while Astrid and I spoke about anything and nothing. If she knew the truth about Mikolaj and Szymon's order to have the BSS operatives assassinated, I would hold her accountable. Astrid lived most little girls' dream – she married a prince, became a princess and later queen. The world adored her because she kept working as an interior decorator. That's how she and Szymon had met when she remodelled his first apartment. Astrid sent her children to local public schools and she never allowed them to wear designer clothes. And as she mentioned earlier, taught them to do things for themselves. On top of it, the media described her as a classic, natural beauty.

Alarm bells sounded. Everything about her seemed too perfect. Astrid reminded me of a tower of Jenga blocks, but a colourful one. Together it formed an exquisite image. But if I pulled on the right one – the entire thing will collapse. I studied her, listened to her every word, and paid attention to the things she didn't say. One block was the lynchpin and I suspected they tried to throw it in Aidan's face while drinking the delicious coffee. Szymon had manipulated and lied to my husband once before in order to get someone else to do his dirty work. Never again.

I'll yank out the block and watch the entire castle crash down on them.

Forty-five

Toro, Bergia
Saturday, 30 January, 2:58 p.m.

Before lunch I asked to use the restroom and as I wondered up the stairs and down the hall – the wrong direction to which Astrid gave me – it became clear they kept this house free of Mikolaj. Not a single photo of him hung among the others on the walls leading to the bedrooms. *Chambers?*

Katja's face a prominent feature, but no sign of the tyrant who had ruled this land for far too long. In every photo Ragnar wore a shirt, even when the family were on holiday somewhere tropical. This house was their sanctuary. A place where they could be like any other who didn't live in the spotlight or have a legacy of wars and evil.

I bumped into something solid as I exited the restroom and stared up at a face I hadn't seen this close since Dubai. "My apologies." I held out my right hand towards him. "I'm Finley."

The man shook my hand, his covered by black leather, and stepped aside. "Please to meet you, Finley. I'm Dietrich, and this is Princess Ylva."

I greeted the princess but didn't curtsy or whatever commoners are expected to do.

Ylva spoke in Polish, and Dietrich left us without saying another word. I wondered if she wanted to add her own blocks to the tower her parents had already constructed for us. My focus remained on her but I kept an ear on Aidan's conversation with Szymon and Astrid. To wear a mask isn't easy for him, but I couldn't be prouder of my husband. He held his anger, bit his tongue, and spoke as if one of his most trusted friends and allies hadn't stabbed him in the back or used him as a pawn. Aidan has a long fuse, but at the end is an atomic bomb. The countdown started the moment he had learned the truth.

"These are wonderful photos. Looks like you've had quite adventurous family holidays. Why aren't there any photos of your brother?"

Ylva pointed with a perfectly manicured finger to Ragnar's face. "That's my brother."

I forced a shrug and a humiliated smile. "I assumed he's one of your bodyguards as he's the only person wearing a shirt."

Ylva and Astrid lay on sun loungers; both wore bikinis. Szymon and Ragnar stood behind them, Szymon's torso uncovered. The tattoo on his chest an eagle. The Stein family's coat of arms.

"Ragnar never takes his shirt off in front of my parents. He's worried about what they'll say about the tattoos on his back." Ylva hooked her arm through mine and guided me further down the hallway, pointing at more photos. "See, in none of these he's ever without a shirt, but I've seen it. Faces. Women's faces. I don't know if he has a grading system, that only say the number ten's make it onto his back. Ragnar has slept with *a lot* of women, since high school."

Ylva didn't drop breadcrumbs at my feet. She threw them in my face. "Perhaps they mean something to him; more than just how good they are at the act of sex."

The princess let out a deep breath. "Of course, they do, but he won't tell me. Not even when he got the first one after his trip to Mexico almost a year-and-a-half ago."

Aidan listened; he's always aware of everything around him. In his right ear, he heard the truth – his friend wasn't a serial killer. A question answered. My prey now had a face and a name. Another question took its place – did Szymon and Astrid know their son is a murderer? Probable, as they kept grandpa Mikolaj's vile secrets.

For the time being, I played dumb. "Why aren't there photos of your grandfather on the walls? Your grandmother was a beautiful woman."

"Mikolaj doesn't deserve to be in this house." Ylva touched a finger to Katja's face on a photo of her taken a few years before her death. "*Babcia* is my role model. She was everything a woman should be. Strong. Resilient. A protector."

"Babcia means grandmother," Rowan said to me.

Ylva used the Polish word for grandmother when talking about Katja yet called Mikolaj by name. *Now or never.* "Did your Babcia protect you against Mikolaj when you were a teenager?"

Ylva straightened her spine and pressed a finger to the corner of her right eye. "Come, lunch is ready."

Without realising it, or perhaps she did, she answered my question. Mikolaj, or one of his friends, had infected Ylva's young life with their depravity. *Why aren't you screaming it from the rooftops?* A person in her position has a voice and a platform countless victims would give anything for.

I followed her down the stairs and into the dining room. Outside the window snow fell, creating a picture-perfect winter wonderland. Perhaps not the beauty of the white landscape, but my curiosity and thirst for the truth caused goose bumps to spread across my skin.

Aidan stood and placed his hand on my lower back, above the Glock 43 Gen4. "What took you so long, honey?"

Never before had Aidan called me *honey.* This was his mask talking and not my husband or Commander Walker.

"I got lost. Remember when we went to Scotland and I got lost in Edinburgh Castle, despite all the direction boards and tour guides? I have no sense of direction." I shrugged and sat down when Aidan pulled out a chair for me.

Piotr's head tilted to the right as he took a seat across the table. "Getting lost can be dangerous. I hope you don't plan to go hiking while you are in Bergia. Snow is much more treacherous than sand."

My mask didn't move. *Ivana warned him.* She made a big mistake thinking I won't make her son suffer for standing by while Ragnar murdered twenty-five people. *Time to play with your prey*. "Now that you mention sand, Piotr, when last did you visit Dubai?"

Ylva covered the glove on his right hand with her left hand. "Dietrich, not Piotr. You don't speak Polish?"

I nodded. "Apologies, Dietrich. Not fluently, only a few words which aren't suited for your young ears. How long have the two of you been in a relationship?"

Aidan bumped his shoulder against mine. "Sweetie, what's with all the questions? Did you leave your manors in Dubai?"

"I'm sorry, darling, just trying to get to know your friend and his family. You've spoken so highly of them and I'm curious by nature."

"Tomorrow is our two-year anniversary." Ylva stood and dished lasagne for her boyfriend and herself. She said something to Astrid in Polish and I waited for Rowan to translate for me.

"Ylva, we never speak in a language our guests don't understand." Astrid handed me the salad. "Please excuse my daughter."

I took the salad and wondered why Astrid bothered making it with such a big lasagne and bread rolls on the table. In this cold weather I wanted to carbo-load. "Please, don't apologise." After eating nothing but hotel food and takeaways, I welcomed a home cooked meal.

"I asked my mother why she didn't cook a decent lunch instead of taking lasagne out of the freezer. I keep telling them they must hire a chef to cook over weekends. It will give her more time to focus on her precious business."

"I also cook big batches and freeze it for days when I don't have time to cook." I wondered how high this ranked on the list of biggest lies I've ever told. Lizzie is the chef in our family. Whenever I want to make something special, she needs to be on speaker phone and give me clear instructions. My talking cookbook, even though she had bought me a stack of the ones you need to read for Christmas.

"What line of work are you in?" Szymon asked before stuffing his mouth with a fork-full of layered pasta.

I placed my hand on Aidan's thigh. "I'm a criminal psychologist. My field of expertise is serial killers, but I hunt all kinds of serial offenders. Most people refer to me as a profiler."

Even though my eyes were on Szymon, my focus remained on Piotr. He choked, and Aidan pushed to his feet. Ylva grabbed her lover's arm but made no attempt to save his life.

"Stand." Aidan commanded the patient and performed a Heimlich manoeuvre.

I poured Piotr some water once the food dislodged from his trachea. Over the years I learned a few things from Aidan, but Biology had also been my favourite subject at school. It appeared Ivana hadn't dug deep enough to learn what I brought to Fortius' table.

"So, you arrest serial killers and they are sent to jail?" Astrid asked once Aidan returned to his chair and continued eating.

"I'm a freelance profiler, so whatever happens to the serial killer once the local authorities arrest him or her, isn't my concern. In some countries they get the death penalty, in others life imprisonment. I worked a case this week in Moscow. Such a sad story. For the victims, of course."

Aidan placed his hand on my arm. "Honey, they don't want to hear about your work. It's hard enough for me to listen to your cases. Please don't tell them about what happened to Oleg Petrov, the paedophile."

Szymon and Ylva both stopped chewing when Aidan said Jefferson's assumed name.

"You're right, darling. Please excuse me everyone, I'm very passionate about my work and forget most people don't have the stomach for it." I continued eating and waited for the ball to drop. It didn't. These people were good at covering things up, even their emotions.

After lunch Ylva helped me clear the table and once we were alone she asked, "What happened to Oleg?"

I did better than tell her. Ylva lifted a hand to her mouth; tears streamed down her face. We both turned when Astrid walked into the kitchen.

"What's wrong now?" Astrid asked and started loading the dishwasher.

Ylva grabbed the phone from my hand and held it up to her mother. "The man Mikolaj allowed to rape me is dead. See who it is, Mother? Look at is his face! You dined with him, danced with Oleg even after I told you what he did to me. Babcia begged you to send me away, but you refused. If you had listened to her, none of it would've happened." No translation needed, Ylva spoke in English.

Astrid looked at me. "Not in front of our guest, Ylva."

"Why not in front of me? Scared I might learn the truth about Mikolaj? I already know *everything*, Your Highness. Don't worry about your public image. The world won't learn about your despicable family secrets. Because I'm going to do *that* to every single person who knew about the rapes, and murders, and didn't do a damn thing about it. *You* just made my list."

Astrid glanced at the knife on the cutting board. I showed her my teeth. "Your Majesty, I don't want to hurt you. Not before I tie you to a chair like I did your buddy Oleg. Do you want to see what happened to Volkov?" I took my phone from Ylva's shaking hand and showed Astrid.

The queen screamed. Dare I say she attempted to scream her head off?

I wedged myself between the refrigerator and the kitchen door. With my Glock in hand, I waited for Piotr to come do his job. He rushed through the door; the barrel of my gun pressed against his temple. "Don't do anything foolish, *Piotr*. We have the same enemy, remember?"

Forty-six

Toro, Bergia
Saturday, 30 January, 4:19 p.m.

Aidan shook his head as he took Piotr's weapons from him. He asked Szymon and the rest to sit down while I fastened Piotr's hands and feet with plastic flex cuffs. Once his hands were secured behind his back, I removed the glove.

My husband winked when our eyes met and again shook his head. The latter might've been Commander Walker. It had to be hard for him to work with me when he never knew what I would do next. Neither do I most of the time.

"This isn't sticking to the plan."

In my ear, Rowan laughed. "Bro, you knew the moment she smelled blood she would go in for the kill."

"Orcas can't smell blood. Never compare me to a shark."

A line didn't appear between Astrid's brows, but she squinted. *Her Botox is good.* "Who are you talking to?"

"Just one of our team members, he's trying to remind me how much I love hunting criminals." I held up a hand and stared at nothing in particular, as if listening. "Yes, and I also hate those who enable sexual predators to prey on innocent children. The people who allow these horrid creatures to destroy that which we should protect at all costs. People like *you*."

Ylva smiled and snuggled into her father's arms. Szymon pressed his lips to his daughter's blonde hair. "I told my mother but she didn't believe me. My father was fighting in the war when it happened. Babcia confronted Mikolaj; that's when he ordered one of his BSS operatives to murder her."

I threw my hands in the air. "Why did you not protect your

daughter?" Aidan grabbed me when I lunged towards Astrid.

Her eyes grew bigger when she realised she couldn't get away from my wrath.

"My father tried to protect me. He sent someone to kill Petrov and Volkov."

Szymon hugged her tighter.

"Ivar failed his mission because *someone* tipped Volkov off. Why did your mother do it, Piotr?" I asked.

Ylva pushed out of her father's arms but before she got to her feet, I instructed her to remain in her seat for the duration of the evening's festivities.

"Why do you keep calling him that?" she asked.

I gestured for him to tell the truth to the woman he had deceived from the first day they met. Instead, he kept staring at his feet.

"Okay, I'll tell her the truth, seeing as you don't have the balls to do it. Ylva, meet Ivar and Ivana's son, Piotr. Look at his right hand? Do you know what it is?"

Ylva shrugged. "Of course, I'm not stupid."

Aidan crossed his arms over his chest. "No, stupid, you're not. Fin, what's the word I'm looking for?"

I smiled at my brilliant husband. "You're going to need more than one. Manipulative, narcissist, psychopath, diabolical, as this conversation progresses I'll add more to the list." His neck warm against my lips as I joined him. I stood by his side in more ways than one, and will for as long as we can avoid death.

Szymon tried to push to his feet, but the barrel of my gun showed him the way back down. "Take a nice deep breath and relax. This is going to take a while." I handed my Glock to Aidan, removed another from my right boot and disappeared into the dining room.

Out of the royals' earshot I asked, "Okay, boys, it's time. ETA?"

"Fifteen minutes. Quinn can't join us, so it's just the four of us," Rowan said.

I nodded and stared at my reflection in the oversized mirror hanging on the wall. Not yet time for Botox. Although, it felt as if the week's events had added fifteen years to my face. "Do you have everything?"

"Of course, Mrs Walker, your husband gives very precise orders. Szymon's free-pass made it much easier bringing everything into the country. Poor fool." Liam chuckled. To hear him laugh lifted a weight off my shoulders.

"Right, I'm going to get this party started. Eli, I need Ragnar's location. This all goes down the porcelain throne if I can't put a bullet between his eyes." I tapped a finger to my lips. "That's the contingency plan. Please remind me why Commander Walker didn't approve my kill request?"

"Woman, I can hear you," Aidan said in my ear.

Eli cleared his throat. "I can't give you his exact location, but he's in Bergia. I've set up alerts for all the ports and borders. If a camera catches his face, I'll know."

"Thank you. Keep Lizzie at home and please go check on Ainsley."

"Your property looks like a military base, Fin. Same as mine. No one is getting to them, I promise you. Ryan is armed to his teeth, and so is Heather. They're keeping Ains indoors; lucky for you it's raining. Her screen time might not be at a mommy-approved level today."

I didn't care, nothing mattered as long as the ones I love remained safe. Those in Marcel, and the three Walker brothers with me. Nothing is more important than family. How could Astrid turn her back on her own daughter and allow Ylva to be raped? How many times? Once, twice? It didn't matter. I cursed like the soldier I am.

"Finley, don't." Rowan warned.

I ignored him, ran full speed in to the sitting room and used the added momentum to slap the queen. Perhaps bitch-slap is the correct way to describe it. Screw playing chess when I can go in for the kill. This mother didn't protect her child; she deserved whatever I decided to do to her.

Szymon didn't flinch or try to stand up for his wife. A

sly grin spread across his face. I nodded when our eyes met. "You're welcome. Now, where were we? Oh yes, Piotr's tattoo."

Aidan placed his arm around my shoulder when I returned to his side. "How many of you are there?" he asked Piotr.

The silence sucked the air out of the room. I dropped to my haunches in front of Piotr. "Your mission is over. Ivana begged us to offer you a position in our organisation, of course we complied, but we lied." I laughed at my little rhyme. "This won't end well for you. You'll suffer for your part in the murders of twenty-five people. Here is where you hold some power. Talk, and I'll gift you with a quicker death. If you don't, let's just say it's going to take me longer to cut you open than it did with Petrov. Don't worry, Ivana will be right there with you. Aidan and I can tag team a blood eagle. As for Ivar, I haven't decided what I'm going to do to your daddy. It all depends on what you and mommy tell me."

"If you touch my mother, I'll kill you."

I pushed to my full length and patted the top of his head. "Now that's how family should feel about each other. Good for you, Piotr. Even though she didn't raise you, the bond is still there. I respect both of you for it." I did.

"How many?" Aidan growled. The sound made me turn to him and nod my approval. The man keeps on getting sexier. For a split second I wondered what a psychiatrist would say about me, and the bond between Aidan and me. The things that turn us on, the way we react to certain situations. Then again, it didn't matter if people didn't understand, they haven't survived, or seen, what we have.

I tapped the barrel of the Glock to my forehead and stared down at Piotr. "Last chance, before I make you bleed. No, wait. I'm going push a funnel down your throat and force organophosphate poison into your body." I counted the other methods on my fingers. Poison from the golden poison frog. Bury him alive. Hack off his hands. A lethal dose of insulin. When I extended my left pinkie I added, "Burn you alive."

Eli cleared his throat. "Voice recognition confirms it. He

placed the call in Abu Dhabi."

Where's Ragnar? "I believe Commander Walker asked you a question."

Piotr stared at the coffee table.

Szymon spoke first. "Aidan, you're a guest in my house, a man I considered my friend. What's going on?"

I almost slapped Szymon for trying to appear aloof and confused as to the true reason for our visit. An elaborate, and very loud song chimed through the house. "Fantastic. Right on time as always. Ladies and gentlemen, the reaper has come for your souls. Ylva, I'm still a little on the fence about you."

I sashayed to the front door and pulled it open. Rowan handed me more guns than I needed, at that moment, and stepped past me into the house. Liam carried my laptop bag over his shoulder and pressed his lips to my cheek. "Rowan's the reaper, I'm the *angel* of death."

"You're no angel, brother. Neither am I." I hugged Liam hard and returned to where our guests waited. No, they weren't our guests in their own home, but I was about to put on a show for them. Not a pretty one, or one they were likely to tell their friends about.

While I connected my laptop to their television, Aidan answered Szymon's earlier question. "You betrayed me. For that alone, I should put a bullet between your eyes. However, I'm not as quick to act as certain people in this room. Yes, Fin, I'm referring to you."

I giggled, and pressed my palms to my eyes, not caring if it smeared the mascara. "Touché, dude. Perhaps it will be in their best interest to know who's the crackerjack in our team."

"That's not the correct use of the word *crackerjack*." Aidan pursed his lips when I turned to give him my death stare.

"English isn't their first language. Thank you for undermining me in front of them, Professor Walker. Answer the king so we can get this show on the road. I've waited a week to kill their firstborn."

Szymon tried to push to his feet but sat down hard when

Rowan and Liam lifted their rifles, aiming at his chest. So much for being the ruler of the land and commanding officer of an army when you can't even do as you please in your own home.

Forty-seven

Toro, Bergia
Saturday, 30 January, 5:16 p.m.

Aidan stood at the sliding doors with his back to the room. "Not only did you use our friendship to manipulate me into assassinating the BSS operatives for you, but you also covered up Mikolaj's crimes. I'm not referring to his war crimes. I'm talking about the things he and his friends did to children. To your own daughter."

Aidan turned to face his former friend. Rage swirled in his eyes. "You knew their names, what they did, yet you left them to continue destroying even more children. On top of it, your son, the Crown Prince of Bergia, is a serial killer. Not only did Piotr aid Ragnar in the murders, but he's also head of a paramilitary group set on overthrowing you and putting Ragnar on the throne. The moment the crown touches his head, he'll continue right where Mikolaj's reign of terror ended on the people of this country, and the neighbouring countries as well."

Piotr lifted his eyes to Aidan. "You're better than my mother thought."

"Ivana thinks she knows the workings of our organisation and family. She gobbled up the scraps my parents threw her way. She knows nothing we didn't want her to. Also, she overplayed her hand when she tried to have your father killed in Russia. Patience is a virtue very few of us possess, myself included, unlike you. No, you've been waiting, setting everything up to take them all down. The condom in the Zurich victim's mouth, you placed it there. The victim in Abu Dhabi, you ensured she survived. Did you tire of watching him kill for fun when all you want to do is cut off his head?"

"That will be too quick." Piotr grinned when his eyes met mine.

I pulled out the Ka-Bar TDI and wondered who should bleed first. It didn't matter, DNA is DNA. Astrid had made the choice for me, the day she turned her back on her daughter. She screamed when I nicked her finger, and again when I took a sample of her blood. I handed it to Rowan.

Silence returned to the room while we waited for the results. Astrid's blood confirmed it. The DNA retrieved from the sperm inside the condom was her son's.

"Do you have any other sons we don't know about?" I asked. She shook her head. "Well then folks, this confirms it. Ragnar is a serial killer. Let me show you the faces of the people he murdered. You might not care, seeing as they were commoners, but I do. A lot." While they stared at the crime scene photos, I studied their faces. Their every reaction I deciphered; one person's response spoke volumes. It didn't surprise me in the least.

"Ylva, when we were looking at the photos in the hallway earlier, you tried to tell me your brother's a murderer. Why didn't you just say it?" Before she could answer, I continued. I like talking for people. "This is all part of your little game. Every person in your life is nothing more than a pawn on your chessboard. And when you win, you'll be queen. Sorry, princess, I'm going to stick C-4 under your chessboard and blow it to hell."

Szymon grabbed the back of Ylva's neck and forced her to look at him. "What have you done?" Aidan translated for me and placed the device we used with Sanchez on the coffee table.

"After everything I've been through, I deserve to be queen. Ragnar is a murderer, and every bit as evil as Mikolaj. With an army I can hunt down the perverts who Mikolaj called his friends. The ones he brought into his house, to do things to me, to the other children."

The device translated her words and mine. "Ragnar didn't kill until you introduced him to Dietrich. The moment you placed Dietrich as a pawn on the board, it was the last push Ragnar needed."

I lowered my bum to the coffee table and took her hands. "I'm sorry for what you had to live through, the pain and anger you still carry. Ylva, I understand what it's like to feel powerless. I was a soldier, a human weapon, and still, I couldn't protect myself. The difference is, I use my anger to hunt down those who hurt others. Unlike you, I don't see it as my right to anything, because I was a victim once. You're still a victim, Ylva. You're not a survivor. The moment you take back power of yourself, you become a survivor. What you plan to do comes from a victim's fear."

I brushed the tears from her cheek and it saddened me to understand, yet see the evil lurking in the shadows of her being. Ylva is a narcissist. And in my professional opinion she was born one. Rape didn't turn her into a vengeful woman who hates everything and everyone around her. It added fuel to the fire already smouldering inside her.

"Ragnar has wanted to kill since we were children; it was a matter of time." Ylva sat back and crossed her arms over her chest.

Szymon covered his face with his hands. "This family is cursed."

Aidan leaned forward, resting his elbows on his knees. "No, not cursed. For centuries, the Steins have believed you're above everyone else. Your actions, and that of your children, prove my point. Ylva could've used her position to expose an international paedophile ring, yet she remained silent. Because she wants to be queen. Every day she kept her mouth shut the very people Mikolaj welcomed into his home, your country, kept on brutalising children. You knew, and you kept quiet."

I pushed to my feet. "I might as well cut out their tongues, it's not as if they use it."

In unison, they all pulled their lips back. *Idiots.* I couldn't cut out their tongues, not until they gave me Ragnar's location.

Aidan tapped his fingers on his chin. "We have a problem. Ragnar isn't fit to be king, and he'll die for his crimes. Ylva isn't any less evil than any of her predecessors, and therefore not fit to rule either. Astrid is a terrible mother and a horrible cook. If we kill all of you, it will draw too much attention to Bergia and I won't risk exposing our organisation. What would you do in my position, old friend?"

Forty-eight

Toro, Bergia
Saturday, 30 January, 5:58 p.m.

"There's activity at the castle Ragnar inherited," Eli said.

I unplugged my laptop from the television and switched to the live feed. Heat signatures of at least twenty individuals moved across the screen. We had studied the layout of the castle from the blueprints I found online. In Bergia building plans for alterations to the royal residences must be submitted, I doubted we studied the final version. No one can be that stupid or careless. Then again, the Steins had thought themselves above the law for centuries. *It ends tonight.*

Aidan snapped his finger at his once upon a time friend. "I'm waiting, Szymon. What will you have me do to you? We both know you're not above killing innocent people. What about your own blood? Your wife? Or are they above the law? They sure aren't above mine or that of the rest of the world."

I made myself comfortable on the armrest next to the man in charge, my husband. "I'm going to shoot Ragnar. Because if I don't, the other question I've been pondering for the past week will go unanswered." Rowan kept his face devoid of any emotion, even when I stuck my tongue out at him. "As for Astrid, she'll die from a heart attack upon hearing the news of her son's death. It will appear natural. We won't tell the media of Ragnar's execution. A simple twist of the truth, such as a skiing accident. Piotr can take the place vacated by the one we don't talk about; white will go well with his complexion."

It was exciting telling them what awaited them. I continued, "The princess will die in an aeroplane crash, seeing as she loves doing humanitarian work in isolated places. What happened to the money, Ylva? There are no refugee camps or schools who have ever heard your name, let alone seen your face. As for you Szymon, Aidan will perform a vasectomy on you, thus ensuring the evil gene ends with you. We'll allow you to mourn the deaths of your wife and children and then you'll become an advocate for the rights of children abused by people in positions of power."

I pushed to my feet and walked around the couches, circling my prey. "Piotr, how long do you think you'll remain sane when exposed to nothing but white? I'm pretty sure Ivana and Ivar never trained you for white torture."

"I'll go if you let my mother free. She needs to kill Ivar."

Ivar, not father? "What did daddy do?"

Piotr went mute. The last drop of my patience evaporated. The Glock's barrel connected with his jaw. I spared my fists for Ragnar. "Hey, man-who-likes-to-dry-hump-women-in-the-desert, this won't end well for you. How many times do I need to repeat myself?"

Still, he said nothing. Ylva's saliva ended on her mother, instead of her lover. "You touched another woman? We agreed to be exclusive until we got what we wanted."

"You won't blame him if you saw the woman in question," Liam said, and repositioned the rifle's strap over his shoulder.

"Who is she? I'll kill her!"

I laughed and raised my hand, waving it in the air. "Oh, silly princess, you're not going to pee again, let alone get the chance to kill *me*."

Aidan placed his hand on my thigh. "Good one, Fin."

I thought about what I said and then it clicked. I had read the story to Ainsley when she had a fever while teething and wanted nothing but to be in her mother's arms. My arms. I stared at the gun in my hand. Light and dark duelled, their battle never ending. I needed to return to the light soon, or the darkness would pull me back in. It was time to redefine myself. Finley D. Williams-Walker. Wife. Mother. Warrior. Sister. Daughter-in-law. Huntress of evil. Lover. Killer. Although, all of my kills were justified and those who would still die by my bullets will deserve it.

"Okay, people, let's wrap this up. There are other evil predators and tyrants we also need to focus on. Is my plan a go?"

Aidan pushed to his feet and stared down at his friend. I placed my hand on my husband's back. A comforting gesture. His heart isn't as dark as mine. "Szymon, we faced war together because our countries are allies, but you became my friend. For your denial of Mikolaj's crimes and for manipulating me into doing your dirty work, I'll never forgive you. Astrid will die, as will Ragnar, and Ylva. After six months of grieving you'll marry your mistress. It's not as if the world frowns upon it anymore; they do for a week and then carry on with their lives."

Astrid's neck twisted and gave away her true age. "You bastard! I ended my relationship, yet you kept your mistress?"

"Calm down, drama queen, soon to be dead queen. His mistress is such a well-kept secret not even he knows her name."

Aidan glanced back at me, mischief and approval in his eyes. "She'll arrive any minute and has received a kill order. One foot, one wrong breath, and she'll end you. Am I making myself clear or do I need to repeat it in Polish?"

Szymon covered his face with his hands. Liam stepped forward. "She's younger than the horrid old hag you call wife now. And far more beautiful. She speaks fluent Polish and is an amazing lover, not that you'll ever experience her skills. The cherry on top – she's happy to chop off heads. Her blade ended Volkov. Would you like to see her work?"

I lifted my mobile phone in front of Szymon's face and showed him a photo of the head and the hearth. *Great name for a story.*

"Please, don't make them suffer. For all they've done wrong, they're still my children, my blood. You can do as you please with Astrid. I fell out of love with her even before

Ragnar's conception."

I tried to remember how many months after their wedding they lifted the baby prince into the air at Stein Castle. "Five months," Aidan whispered.

I squeezed his bum. He knows me better than anyone and because, well, his bum is one of his most beautiful parts and was right there in front of me. "Is my plan a go, Commander Walker? Come on, I've wanted to stab Astrid since I learned the truth. A mother is the last person who should ever turn her back on her children."

Commander Walker nodded, and I grabbed the syringe from the backpack. I lowered myself onto the coffee table and stared at Astrid. "You fought your way out of poverty to become queen. Yet, when you held the power to do something good, you chose not to. Instead, you allowed your daughter to be raped, and her rapists to go unpunished. Your death won't be quick and in no way painless. If I had more time, I would've made you suffer. Duty before fun."

I grabbed the back of her head and plunged the needle into her neck. "Say hello to Mikolaj, Volkov, and Jefferson. Don't worry, their other friends will join you soon enough. Hell might even get a little crowded, who knows? Oh yes, you will, firsthand. And she didn't live happily ever after."

"Thank you." Ylva sat unmoving, not a single tear formed in her eyes.

I patted her cheek. "Sorry, princess, I have *no* sympathy for you. I told you earlier, you could've used your international platform to raise awareness of the plight of millions of children. Unlike you, when they speak up few people listen. I do. I hear their silent screams in my sleep. Their faces play like a movie reel through my mind every time I close my eyes. I'm a nobody, yet I do what I can to protect them. Instead of doing something good and worthwhile, you manipulated your way through life, and look where it got you?"

Astrid grabbed the couch, her throat, her eyes wild with fear. She fought for her last breath as the front door opened.

Forty-nine

Toro, Bergia
Saturday, 30 January, 6:49 p.m.

My stomach growled. "Do you think we can order takeout? I'm hungry."

Aidan grabbed my shoulders and pulled me against him. He lowered his mouth to mine. For a moment I forgot we were being watched and what my question was. My boss released his hold on me. "Liam, check the kitchen. We're in for a late night."

I floated towards my laptop. No further activity at Ragnar's fortress. Over the centuries, it withstood many enemy attacks. Lucky for us, we weren't trying to get in with arrows and swords.

"Piotr, Dietrich, whatever, tell me what your daddy did to make your mommy hate him?" I tried again. One day curiosity might put me in danger. I checked his restraints and added another pair of flex cuffs. "Ylva, you can feed him."

Her eyes narrowed when she looked at her lover. "He can eat with his hands behind his back. He destroyed our plan. I told you, let him kill thirty people and then leave evidence."

The device translated the ensuing conversation.

"I grew tired of you and playing this game of yours. You're a despicable woman. I couldn't take faking a relationship with you anymore. While we're on the subject, Ragnar is even more self-involved than you are. He loves talking as if he has been in war or faced real danger."

Piotr turned to me and said in English, "You'll find him hiding in the dungeons. Mark my words, as soon as the first bullet exits a barrel, the prince will hide like the coward he is. Couldn't even take someone's life by getting his precious hands dirty. Look at the way he kills; like a woman."

My offence must've shown; he apologised and continued. "All because Astrid told him he doesn't deserve to be king. Let's not forget when she told him no woman will ever want him. For a royal notch in their belts or the crown yes, but not as a man because he isn't interesting, educated, successful, or brave like Szymon had been by going to war."

"That explains a lot." Oh, the damage parents do to their children. Whether or not intentional.

Liam handed me a plate of leftover lasagne. I ate enough to quiet my stomach's whale call, but not too much to make me sleepy. I had a prince to slay. Everyone else ate in silence. I ended up feeding Piotr. I'm not a monster, and a well-fed prisoner lasts longer.

Szymon placed his plate on the coffee table. "This isn't the life I envisioned growing up. You're right, I should've done more."

Aidan placed a hand under his plate and lifted it to his shoulder. I grabbed his arm. "No, dude. The new queen will end up scrubbing the sauce out of the carpet. Do you want to lose your head?"

My husband lowered the plate.

"I told you she's beautiful, Szymon." Liam bumped his shoulder against mine. "Too bad she won't sleep in your bed."

Marika said something in Russian and Szymon answered her before Liam could. They both laughed. I glanced at Aidan, my full stomach in my throat. What if she turned into a Stein? With her skills we would spend the rest of our lives searching for body parts. Aidan winked and my nausea settled.

Rowan took the plate from my hand. He devoured the remaining lasagne. "My work here is done. Time to tie up the king and princess. Marika, you take it from here. Jay will arrive soon. Sorry, Piotr, Ivana won't be joining you tonight. I tell you what, let's make this interesting. Szymon, how would you like a front-row seat to your son's execution?"

I liked Rowan's way of thinking. Szymon's lack of a more paternal response upon hearing his son is a serial killer, and his daughter a master manipulator, bothered me. Although he asked us not to make them suffer, but it didn't sit right with me. It's not the way a loving parent would react. If someone threatened Ainsley, I'll tear them apart using nothing but my hands and teeth. I'll rather be tortured to death than see my daughter hurt.

"Szymon, I have questions for Ragnar. If he isn't forthcoming with the truth, I have no option but to *make* him talk. You think you saw stuff during the war, it's nothing compared to what I'm going to do to the person responsible for the deaths of twenty-five innocent people. Victim number twenty-six survived because of Piotr." Another thing which kept me perched on the fence. I hated not knowing which way I would fall when it came to him.

The king stared at all of us. "I knew this day would come. What Mikolaj did left a trail. Too many people were involved. As for Ragnar, growing up he spent more time with Mikolaj than with me. If I hadn't tried to play hero by going to the war..."

I waited; he didn't continue. "Mikolaj groomed all of you to one day take over the true depravity of the crown, didn't he?"

Szymon nodded. "I got away by going to university in Munich, then joining the army, and the war. My greatest regret is that I had trusted Mikolaj when he promised not to expose Ragnar to his dark ways before Ragnar's eighteenth birthday. I had hoped by then my son would be far away from Bergia, and Mikolaj."

Dark ways? Eighteen? Rage coiled inside me and as I leapt forward with my hands extended, ready to throttle the life out of him, Aidan grabbed me by the waist. "Let me go."

"Stand down, that's an order."

"He knew what Mikolaj would subject his son too. He didn't stop it. Ragnar could've gone to boarding school in far, far away land. Nothing! What kind of father allows a paedophile access to his children, *knowing* that Ylva would be raped, and Ragnar groomed into being just as deprived as Mikolaj?"

Ylva laughed, the sound bitter and filled with contempt. "My father tried. Ragnar got on a train and came back. What you don't realise, although Ragnar isn't a rapist and hated Mikolaj as much as I do, Ragnar fed on the fear of the victims. He loved it. After he told me I stopped screaming. I stopped fighting and I would just lay there with my eyes closed and wait for whoever to be done."

Bile rose in my throat and I allowed myself to feel empathy for the young girl Ylva had once been. "Ragnar watched?"

Ylva nodded. "When he went to university he kept flunking out because hosting extravagant sex parties was more important than learning anything which would better equip him to run this country. Don't you understand? Everything I did is for the people of Bergia."

I placed my hands at my sides; the empathy evaporated. "Twenty-five people didn't have to die for you to make a point. Instead of getting Piotr to help Ragnar murder innocent people, you could've killed your brother. You play this game very well, *princess*, but not good enough."

Szymon's eyes fixed on me as I moved around the room. Perhaps he worried I would defy Commander Walker's earlier order. "Your Highness, you knew what your son is capable of, yet you chose not to protect anyone against him. You're as despicable as your forefathers, Szymon. No amount of bravery on the battlefield can ever overshadow the veiled evil inside you."

I tapped a finger to my mouth. "No, let me rephrase: you're a coward. A true ruler won't let anything, or anyone, stand in the way of doing what's right. You'll watch when I make your son bleed and Marika will cut your throat if you as much as breathe wrong. All the presidents of your neighbouring countries are ready to take over Bergia. If you think about it, there's no need for kings and queens when people can elect their own leaders. In case you haven't heard the word before

– democracy. It's not perfect, but it's better than what your family has done for the people of this country. Tonight, we'll right the wrongs of the Steins."

The front door opened and Jay walked in, while Rowan and Liam tied up the king and princess.

I glanced at Piotr, defeat visible in his eyes. "I'm sorry you won't get your revenge."

"Let me go with you, I can help. You're outmanned, outgunned, and you don't know the layout of the castle. Take me with you. I'll show you where Ragnar will hide."

"No can do, desert-man. You and mommy have your own mission and I won't let it interfere with ours. To be frank, I don't trust you. Let's not forget you helped murder twenty-five people."

Aidan repositioned his thigh holster as he came to his feet. "You're the head of the Neo-BSS. The twenty plus individuals at Ragnar's castle are under your command. Sorry, son, but you're not going anywhere. You recruited them, trained them, taught them everything Ivar, Ivana and your years in the Wojska Specjalne taught you. Your adoptive parents gave you an out, an alternative life to the one Ivana indoctrinated you with. You made your choices, Piotr, and you'll carry the consequences."

"Neo-BSS?" Szymon asked, and I was grateful he did as I didn't have a clue what Aidan referred to.

Aidan let out a deep breath. "Szymon, in order to govern a country, one must know everything, anticipate anything. If you hadn't assassinated the BSS, you would know about the Neo-BSS's existence. You command an army and a police force, yet you never considered forming a new secret service.Perhaps the best thing I can do for the people of Bergia is to put a bullet in your head. You're incompetent, spineless, and as self-involved as every other member of your family. It sounds to me Katja was the only person worthy of being in a position of power. Why didn't you investigate her death? You could've exhumed her body, and proved she didn't die from natural causes."

I slipped my hand into Aidan's. "Are you sure we shouldn't borrow a tank from Szymon's army? It will make it easier getting into Ragnar's fortress of perversion."

"We discussed this. Your plan B isn't mine." Aidan pressed his lips to my hair.

Ylva shook her head. "How can you people be so calm when you're about to die?"

"We're all about to die if you want to get philosophical about it. Don't worry about us, princess. We're not the ones who will die tonight." Aidan placed his arm around my shoulder. "Szymon, old friend, if your name comes up even once as we keep digging into the paedophile ring, I promise to come visit you again. I don't care about any political or international fallout. What we did to Max Jefferson, aka Oleg Petrov, will look like a children's birthday party compared to what I'll do to you."

I wrapped my arms around my husband's neck and stared up at him. "Dude, you just used one of my sayings. How is it even possible to love you more than I already do?"

"Wait until you hear what I plan for phase two."

Before we left, Ylva asked to speak to me in private. I refused to be alone in a room with her, on account of how badly I wanted to snap her neck. After she pouted for a full minute, she told me the true depth of the relationship between Mikolaj and his grandson.

Fifty

Toro, Bergia
Sunday, 31 January, 00:26 a.m.

I didn't say it, but I thought it. *I'm too old for this crap.* Tree climbing is for children. Yet there I sat, perched on a branch, cold bark pressing through my cargo pants and into my bum. I waited, watched, eager to get this over and done with and return home to my daughter.

Aidan had filled me in on the Neo-BSS during the drive from Szymon's country house to Ragnar's castle. While I had listened to his every word, I realised the immensity of the responsibility which would rest on his shoulders once he became the official head of Fortius. I vowed again to be by his side and help him in any and every way possible. Our work involves much more than just taking down the bad guys. My life had always been about the battle; now I needed to consider the strategic moves, the behind-the-scenes protection of the innocent. At Aidan's side my life might involve less bloodshed than I first thought, which isn't all together a bad thing. However, Aidan had promised to let me hunt down those who prey on children. With them, I can do as I see fit.

"Sitrep," Aidan's voice filled my ears.

"I'm sitting, and if we don't move soon my butt is going to freeze to this bloody branch." I kept my voice low, but ensured he heard my irritation and boredom. "Send in the strike drone and light this place up. We can take them out as they come running out."

"Again, your Plan C isn't mine."

"Commander Walker, I'm just going to say it: I'm bored. Piotr told you about the secret tunnel. Let's go."

Rowan cleared his throat. "The tunnel is rigged. Tripwire five metres in. You were right, Fin, he has his own agenda."

"How much longer?" I asked.

"Sight tight, Williams-Walker."

"You're making me crave a cigarette, F-one."

Aidan laughed. "F-one?"

"Yes, like bravo one. I'm shortening it as we aren't special forces, but we are a force. So, f is for force, not foxtrot or Fortius. You're F-one, Rowan is F-two, I'm F-three, and Liam is F-U."

None of them laughed out loud, but they did, I heard them. Of course, they all denied it later.

"F-U?" Liam's voice filled my head.

"Movement in the east corridor." I lied. Liam's come back would've made me laugh loud enough for the guards to hear.

"Initiate phase one," Aidan ordered.

"Copy that," Rowan and Liam said in unison. In time, I learned how to use all of Fortius' toys. *Not the time to ask for on-the-job training.*

I watched on the screen mounted to my left arm as the mosquito sized drone thingies took off and headed into the castle. Small enough to fly unseen, no irritating buzz sound either. We familiarised ourselves with the interior layout. The alterations weren't included in the 'official' building plans submitted. This building might've been a fortress during the Middle Ages, now it was impenetrable. To most. Not us.

Thirty minutes later, the tiny drones returned to their masters. Adrenaline pulsed through my every muscle fibre; it had been years since I last ran into combat. And my first time storming a castle. The darkness awoke from her slumber. If only she could've turned into a dragon, letting me ride her into battle instead of having to do it the boring way.

I stared into the black night. To my left, Aidan sat in his own tree. No giant eagles swooped down to help us.

Instead of voicing my disapproval of Aidan's plan, I held my tongue and rubbed my hands on my thighs. Gloves kept my hands warm; the rest of my body warmed by the familiar call. The darkness' battle cry.

I wondered how many people can say they had annihilated or apprehended a crown wearing serial killer. Then again, I'll never say it either. Whatever happened in the next few hours wouldn't be spoken about beyond those who needed to know. Myself, the three Walker brothers with me, Eli, Ryan and Heather. Oh, and Quinn. I had to tell my new best friend about this night. *She's going to be so jealous.*

Movement on the screen mounted to my arm caught my attention. Every hour, on the hour, the guards did their rounds and rotations. Their heat signatures visible on my arm, thanks to the strike drone circling high above us. Eight out of twenty wanna-be soldiers down gave us a much better chance of success. Piotr did a good job recruiting the members of this ragtag team called the Neo-BSS. Delinquents with no strong family ties. They spent most of their youths in prison or reform schools. The chips on their shoulders he lathered in a salsa consisting of hatred, perceived invincibility, and their chance to 'stand up to the man'.

The guards dropped like flies. Aidan's bullet never misses its mark. "Advance," he ordered.

I dropped to the ground and sank a few centimetres into the snow. I wished Bergia lay further south on the world map. Perhaps somewhere tropical where we could sip frozen margaritas after completing the mission.

With the butt of the rifle pressed to my shoulder, I scanned the surrounding area. I moved as fast as possible towards the eastern wall. What I did wasn't running; the soft snow didn't allow for a sprint.

Aidan placed his hand on my shoulder before we dropped to our knees and stuck two small gifts for the prince to the left and right sides of the iron gate. On the western side, Rowan and Liam did the same.

Aidan and I headed back into the darkness. The trees, the only living things aware of our presence. My heartbeat violent in my ears. We were outmanned, but not outgunned. On the other side of the stone walls a serial killer hid, as he had his entire life behind a title, money, and perceived power. The truth is – no one is bulletproof. There isn't a person alive who is above the law. If only those who hold the power to take such evil down had bigger balls or weren't themselves involved.

"Initiate phase two." Aidan grabbed the back of my head and pressed my cheek to his chest. The night no longer quiet. The heat of the explosion reached us, warming my face.

I lifted my eyes to my husband's and for a second, I considered shooting him in the knee and storming the castle without him. Nothing is more important than Aidan and Ainsley's safety.

"We're both coming out of this alive, that's an order, Mrs Walker. Now, go slay the prince, my lady."

"I'm no lady." I pressed my mouth to his and stormed the castle.

My primary objective for this mission? Keeping Aidan safe. To do that, I had to be through the C-4 created hole in the wall first. If the Neo-BSS aimed their bullets at me they might not see Aidan on my six.

Twenty-five people deserved to have their deaths avenged. Images of their faces, in life and death, filled my mind every time I squeezed the trigger. I didn't slow down. Bullets whizzed past me. One grazed my thigh. I ignored the pain. A single image held my focus – my daughter's face.

Rapid gunfire filled the quiet of the night; the silencers on our rifles didn't add to it. The screams of the men who swore to see Ragnar on the throne, and Bergia return to waging countless wars, became deafening. I ignored them; not that I understood their last words.

"Dammit, Fin, you're supposed to be behind me." Aidan breathed hard in my ears.

With my back against the wall, I pressed the release and reloaded. "We don't have time for this. Thank me later for the bullet I took for you." Liquid warmed my left leg. No time to assess the wound. If fatal, I would know soon enough.

"Sitrep," Aidan's voice hard.

"Three hostiles down," Rowan said.

Liam grunted. "Two."

If not for the bullets pounding into the other side of the wall I used as cover, I might've laughed. "Four."

"Two hostiles still active." Aidan cursed. "Grenade!"

I crouched down, using my arms to shield my head. Pieces of rock and wood rained down. To distract myself, I tallied our combined total. Aidan took out the eight guards and killed one more. If I didn't storm in ahead of him, his tally would've been higher. *Look at me counting in the middle of combat.*

I peeked around the corner; a gun barrel stared back at me. The man's words I didn't understand, but his intentions I did.

Fifty-one

Toro, Bergia
Sunday, 31 January, 1:59 a.m.

The gun barrel pressed against the back of my head. He kept taking it away and slamming it against my skull. My nostrils flared, my thigh burned, and my rifle hung over my captor's shoulder. I walked in the direction he pushed me. His palm connected with my back. I didn't stumble. I waited. The darkness flapped her majestic wings. *I won't be at anyone's mercy again.*

"Sitrep," Aidan's voice filled my ears and heart. *Better me than him.*

Two fast taps to the receiver mounted to my chest got me another blow to the head. Aidan, Liam, and Rowan now knew I wasn't free to explore the castle. *They won't let anything happen to me, neither will I put them in danger.*

Instinct kicked in. It took full control of my body.

My right hand reached behind my head; my fingers wrapped around the rifle's barrel. My left hand closed over the Ka-Bar hidden underneath my Kevlar. I spun around. The blade sliced through the air and my enemy's throat. He fell backwards, gripping his bleeding neck. His rifle skidded over the stone floor as I kicked it out of reach. A single bullet ended this young man's life. It was either him or me. Neither of us should've been there.

"Finley!" Aidan's voice caught.

"Everything's under control, my love. One hostile remains. And the evil prince hides somewhere inside this vile place." The putrid stench of depravity hung heavy in the air. This place unlike any other castle or palace I had ever set foot in. It suffocated me, as if the souls of those who were destroyed here still lingered. Mikolaj's death hadn't set them free.

A sound to my left. I grabbed a grenade from my belt, pulled the pin and tossed it. "Flash out!" I warned the members of the team. My family.

My feet pounded over the original stone floor. Number twenty didn't have time to reach for his gun. A bullet entered his left temple as he lay crumpled on the floor. To be on the receiving end of a flash grenade isn't fun.

"Ragnar! Come out, come out, wherever you are!" I lowered the night vision goggles over my eyes and scanned the surroundings. The mozzie drone thingies had made this much easier. But I wasn't naïve enough to believe taking down a royal serial killer would be this easy. I pressed my hand to my thigh and cursed, then smiled. *Not tonight, Reaper.* "I'm not in the mood to play hide-and-go-seek with you!"

"Finley, stay in position. That's an order. You're not going down there without us."

I did as Commander Walker ordered, watching their positions on the screen mounted to my arm. Three dots closed in on my location. I stood as Aidan stepped through the antique wooden doors. A fitting place to end a tyrant – the throne room. "We drag him back here. This is where he dies."

"A little dramatic, don't you think?" Aidan placed his left hand against my cheek, the tactical glove kept his skin from mine.

"Maybe."

My husband grabbed the back of my neck and pulled me against him. I pursed my lips and breathed through the pain. Aidan did the same. I grabbed the flashlight from my belt and inspected him despite his protests. Blood stained the spot between his Kevlar and belt on his right side. With trembling hands, I ripped his shirt. My heart lodged in my throat. It stopped beating.

"Through and through, I'll live to fight another day and make love to you soon." He shut his eyes but smiled when

I lifted the flashlight to his face. "Here, put one on the exit wound. I can manage the front."

Aidan handed me QuickClot Combat Gauze. "It will stop the bleeding and help for the pain. Not that it's hurting." Aidan winced as I pressed the gauze to his back.

"Oh, you're *so* strong. You're staying up here. I'm not taking any chances with you being wounded and all."

Aidan pressed his lips to my ear. "I've survived far worse *and* I'm married to you. Being your commanding officer is much more life threatening than a through and through."

"I can't lose you, Aidan. I love you. You're my life, the light to my darkness."

"Fin, I'm not dying. Stop talking as if someone is going to die. Besides, I killed more people than you did tonight, so calling me *the light* is reaching."

Rowan and Liam joined us. "Are you two done with whatever this is? Foreplay, fighting? Who knows with you?" Rowan placed his hand on the back of my neck. "You okay?"

I nodded. "I'll be better once Ragnar's blood soaks the throne's velvet covered seat." It stood where it had for centuries. The butts of too many vile human predators had warmed it. Warmongers, tyrants, a paedophile and a serial killer. *What a family.*

The door to the dungeon stood ajar. I stepped closer, my rifle extended in front of me. "Oh, Prince Ragnar! Play time is over. You have two options. One, take your life before I get down there. Two, make this hard for me. I've been waiting a long time to see you bleed." I shouted into the shadows.

"Did you think it would be this easy?" His voice bellowed out of the dark. Footsteps became louder. Not two feet, but twenty-four.

I stepped behind the throne, dropped to my knees, and positioned the barrel of the HK416 A5 on the armrest. Movement behind me as Aidan, Liam and Rowan took cover.

What followed? Carnage.

The instant a head became visible, four bullets tore through it. I didn't count the heads. I kept squeezing the trigger and reloading. Setting a new personal best in the process.

"Fin, enemy on your six!" Rowan shouted.

I grabbed the SIG holstered at my left thigh. The rifle kept firing into the darkness as I ended the life of two young men with the SIG in my left hand. Their lives didn't matter to their future king. He sent them into battle to be slaughtered, just as his forefathers had done.

How long before Ragnar realised he couldn't hide, retreat, or escape? The exit route he counted on no longer there. It had caved in at the same time we took out the eastern and western gates.

"That's all of them," Aidan said. "Ragnar, I'm going to count to three. If you do not show your face, your next breath will fill your lungs with mustard gas."

"You're such a dad." Liam bumped his shoulder against Aidan's as he walked around the room, ensuring the bodies laying on the floor weren't playing possum.

"One!" Aidan reloaded.

I found the light switch and wanted to plunge the room back into darkness. The dead didn't bother me as much as the over-the-top royal kitsch did. The BSS dragon carved into the wooden ceiling, stared down at us and the dead. A stuffed bear stood in the corner, its teeth and claws out. I've never understood the need to kill an innocent animal, stuff it or whatever taxidermists do, and then put the poor thing on display. Perhaps a case of small penis syndrome or something. As if killing an innocent creature shows your manliness. I doubted any of those hunters can do what we just did.

"Two!" Commander Walker removed a grenade from his belt. It didn't hold mustard gas or any biological weapon. "Don't make me say it, Ragnar."

Out of the shadows, the blue-blooded serial killer's face appeared. He made his way over the bodies of the men who sacrificed their lives for him.

Not once did he look at them. Instead he stepped on their

bodies as he made his way to the middle of the room.

Ragnar raised his arms at his sides and smiled. "What a mess."

Fifty-two

Toro, Bergia
Sunday, 31 January, 2:38 a.m.

Ragnar tilted his head to the right and left as he studied our faces. “You’re supposed to kneel. Idiots.”

Laughter echoed down the stone walled passages. The Walker brothers turned to me and shook their heads. I shrugged. “I don’t bow. Not in front of any man, woman, statue, or the bear in the corner. Least of all in front of you. That bear deserves more respect than you do, *Your Highness.* Sit. Let me explain life to you. The only person who will end up on their knees is you. When I slice your back open, crack your ribs, and pull out your lungs.”

“You can’t touch me.” Ragnar stepped forward but stopped when my SIG moved into his line of sight. “My father will have you killed for this.”

“Oh, that’s precious.” With my left hand, I retrieved my mobile phone and showed him his family’s current situation. Szymon and Ylva bound, their mouths covered with duct tape. Astrid’s lifeless body remained on the couch; blood trailed from her eyes. Ironic as she had never cried for her children.

Piotr grinned when Marika moved the mobile phone in front of his face. “My only regret is not being the one to kill you.” Aidan translated for me and admitted he left out a lot of swear words.

“Don’t worry, they can see you as well.” I pointed at the body camera mounted to my chest. “In case you missed it, your mommy is dead. I gave her the death penalty for not protecting Ylva. Remember all the times you watched your own sister being raped? You stood there and did absolutely nothing to protect your own blood. Except, her just lying there with her eyes closed woke something in you. It birthed the fantasy of the sleeping princess. The very fantasy you recreated when you murdered innocent women. Sit, *Raggie*, you and I are going to have ourselves a little chat. I promised your daddy that if you talk, I won't make your death painful. I lied. Whether or not you talk, it doesn't matter. You. Will. Die. And so will every person linked to grandpa's sick circle."

"They killed them. I had nothing to do with it." Ragnar moved closer to the throne.

Bullet after bullet tore into the wood; splinters flew into the air and fell to the floor. I repositioned the rifle over my shoulder. "No. You'll sit in the blood of the men who died trying to protect you."

Ragnar didn't move. Defiance got him only one thing – a bullet in the knee from my husband's SIG. Gravity and pain did the rest.

"Big, bad, evil prince, crying like the pathetic loser you are. Come on, Raggie, show some self-respect." I shook my head and marched to where he sat. Blood soaked his jeans from the ground up and from the hole in his knee. I studied his face, trying to look past the pain carved into it and the tears streaming down his cheeks. "Mommy was right. No woman will ever want you; you can't even take a bullet like a man. Pathetic."

"I didn't kill anyone," he whimpered.

I turned to Aidan. He answered with a slow blink. My fist connected with Ragnar's solar plexus. He tried to breathe but couldn't. A minute or two later, once Ragnar caught his breath, my right boot connected with his nose. The prince cried some more. I had hoped this would be more satisfying, instead of pathetic. I wiped my forehead with my free hand.

This moment – reality. Men and women who prey on the innocent are pathetic, whiny, little nothings when they're on the receiving end.

Aidan took me by the arm and steered me towards the

oversized doors. "Finley?" He pressed his lips to my hair.

"Nothing he says will bring them back or undo the pain their families have to live with. The one thing that came from this is we learned about Mikolaj and his *friends.* Eli has found more names and added them to my list. I'm tired, Aidan. Tired of waging a war against an evil which will never seize to exist."

Aidan cupped my face in his gloved hands. "Are you going to stop fighting?"

I shook my head and brushed my lips against his. "Never."

"Do you want me to shoot him?"

"No, if I don't put a bullet between his eyes my other question will remain unanswered."

Rowan laughed. "You're still on that? I promise to tell you; just shoot the sonofabitch."

"You can't kill me! I'm the future King of Bergia."

Without looking at Ragnar, I squeezed the SIG's trigger, not caring where the bullet entered. Hollow-points don't exit. More screaming from the serial killer. *Dammit.*

I turned to him. My aim had been a little to the left and too low. Instead of his forehead, blood oozed from his right shoulder. "Ragnar, I had big plans for you. Unlike the ones your parents had the day you were born. I wanted to blood eagle you and make you die an excruciating death. It won't undo what you did. It won't bring back twenty-five people."

"I didn't kill anyone. Dietrich did."

Aidan addressed Ragnar in different languages, to each the serial killer responded without a hint of an accent. Even I could tell, but Aidan nodded.

Eli's voice filled my ear. "Voice recognition confirms it. He placed the other calls."

"Oh, you mean Piotr. That's his real name, by the way. You should've been more careful about the people you trusted. Including your sister. Besides, the forensic laboratory in Zurich found *your* semen inside the condom left in the victim's mouth. We have linked your voice to the calls placed, except the one in Abu Dhabi. Guess you needed to hurry to make it in time to have dinner with your parents, so you left it to Piotr, or as you know him, Dietrich. Grandpa's perverted friends found victims for you because you blackmailed them. *Boring.* Your mother couldn't have been more right about you."

Ragnar failed to get to his feet, unsteady as a newborn foal. He tried to reach for the gun at his back. Liam took it from him and bumped the barrel against Ragnar's head. "Oops," Liam said and tossed the gun out of Ragnar's reach.

I stepped behind the murderer. Aidan and Rowan grabbed his arms and kept him down. The Ka-Bar TDI made light work of slicing through his clothes. The faces of twenty smiling women stared at me, including Alicia Rideout's. "Your victim in Abu Dhabi didn't die."

I dropped to my knees and removed their faces from his back. The prince screamed and pleaded for mercy. I showed him none.

For more than a week I yearned for this moment. Now, I wanted it to be over. I stepped in front of Ragnar. "Any last words? Don't even dare spit in my face. You do not want to see me pissed off."

"I'm the crown prince of Bergia! You can't do this to me."

Time for one last monologue, I decided. "Life was given to you on a gold platter. Your grandpa was a paedophile and your mother a self-involved gold digger with a heart as pure as decomposition. Instead of being worthy of the life you were privileged enough to be born into, you consider everyone and everything yours to control, to destroy. Your little title means nothing to me. Thank you, though, for exposing Mikolaj's friends. It's the one good thing you did with your life. Your attempt to pin the murders on them is pitiful. For once in your life, man up to your actions. Of course, they'll all be dead before this day is over."

"Do you know what Mikolaj did to me?" Ragnar didn't even attempt to wipe the blood streaming from his nose. Or his tears.

"Yes. He shouldn't have exposed you to his depravity, but

you asked to watch. Or are you going to tell me Ylva lied? As children we don't have control over our circumstances, but as adults we do. At thirty you're not a child, Ragnar. I have empathy for you and Ylva as children, but I have nothing but contempt and hatred for the people you are today. The choices you two made destroyed the lives of countless people." I raised my arms at my sides. "Look at all these unnecessary deaths. This is because of *you*."

"Mikolaj made me do terrible things for him. I hated him. Not even animals rape; it's despicable. Unnatural." Ragnar stared up at me with cold eyes.

"That's rich coming from a serial killer. Let's not forget you brought your high school girlfriends and female friends to him, knowing what Mikolaj would do to them. You *invited* them here. And you watched. Please spare your last breaths and don't lie to me. I see what you are. Nothing else."

Ylva told me about the steady stream of young women Ragnar had brought his beloved grandfather. *No love lost between these two siblings.*

I hunched down, out of his reach. "The saddest thing? You weren't even creative with the murders. Mommy read you a bedtime story every night, the only time Astrid ever spent with you and Ylva. A different story every night, but always the same six stories. I bet if I go into your bedroom, I'll find the book on the nightstand."

One last shake of my head and I came to my full length. "I'm done. Marika?"

Two siblings. Two bullets. Marika and I fired at the same time. The Stein's evil legacy over. Well, the legacy ended when Aidan performed a vasectomy on Szymon. Which he did before we left Bergia.

Fifty-three

Marcel
Monday, 1 February, 2:01 p.m.

With my shoulder pressed against the door frame, I watched my husband cradle our daughter to his chest. The most beautiful and tranquil smile on his handsome face. Ainsley slept without a care in the world. We had made it a safer place for her and countless other children. It was well worth not being able to sleep on the flight from Toro to Marcel, and all the times I ran to the lavatory to empty my stomach. Depravity stays with you. It changes you if you don't process it. We all have our ways of doing so. When I heard all the members of Mikolaj's circle were annihilated, I stopped needing to run to the onboard porcelain throne. A car accident here. A heart attack there. A broken neck after a fall down the stairs. An overdose on prescription pain medication, or fentanyl the predator had in his home. It's easy to cover up the truth.

The world learned of Ragnar's death and blamed Mikolaj for it. Everyone suspected he had an arsenal of biological weapons and bombs hidden somewhere. Who would've thought to look in the castle he had left his grandson? It seems no one in Bergia ever did. Astrid had suffered a heart attack upon hearing the news of her beloved son's death. Of course, the country mourned for both of them. Szymon had asked the world's media to give him and Ylva privacy to grieve for his wife and son. For now, he walked the line.

The princess didn't die with her brother; we never intended to kill her. However, in a few days Ylva would die in a small aeroplane crash in a remote area in an African country. That's what the media will report, but she will spend the rest of her days taking care of the poor, the sick, and the dying. It's amazing what plastic surgery can do to alter one's appearance. No one will ever know she's royalty. Except the person in charge of the organisation she'll be working for. An undercover Fortius operative.

"You didn't have to do it," Aidan whispered as I snuggled up next to him and pressed my lips to his cheek.

I stared at my beautiful daughter, her red hair not long enough to attempt her first ponytail. Heather had bought clips, a tiny glitter covered crown clipped into Ainsley's hair.

I didn't have a choice. "They deserve the truth. The worst part for any parent is not knowing where their children are, or what is being done to them. To tell the parents of the twenty-five victims the man responsible for ending their children's lives can never do it again, is the least I can do. They deserve closure."

I made untraceable and anonymous calls to every living parent, mother and father. They deserved to know justice was served, even though I didn't give them any specific details. Who would believe such a thing? A prince capable of murder. A princess who introduced her brother to the man who helped him fulfil his darkest fantasies. Piotr's involvement baffled me. In time he told me the truth; after we moved him out of the white room. He lasted two weeks, Ivana three. Ivar sat in hell with Mikolaj. Dmitry took care of him once we learned the truth about the man Ivana once loved. A man capable of trying to trade his own son to his paedophile boss in order to have a chance of getting out of the BSS didn't deserve to breathe.

Alicia Rideout would return to Ireland and finish her degree in Psychology. An anonymous donor had paid enough money into her account for her to fulfil her dream of becoming a psychologist. On the condition that she help other survivors of violent crimes.

"What's next for you, Mrs Walker?" Aidan turned to me and dropped his forehead against mine.

I didn't know, but I wasn't about to give up the fight. It's not who I am. Despite being a mother and a wife, I'll always be a warrior and a protector of the innocent. "I'm going to continue doing what we do best, but first Rowan owes me an answer." I brushed my lips against Aidan's and smiled against his mouth. "Commander Walker, I believe there's still the matter of me defying your direct order in Vienna. We haven't *undressed* it yet."

Mischief played in Aidan's eyes. He laughed without making a sound. "Working with you is going to be a challenge."

"Yes, it will be. We make one hell of a team, Commander Walker." I bit my bottom lip.

"That we do. And you're a good influence on Rowan and Liam. They both respect you as an operative and love you as a sister. They deserve to find what we have in each other."

"And they will, as will Quinn. I love you, Aidan Walker. Thank you for our life."

I leaned my head on my husband's shoulder. Ainsley's hair soft underneath my fingertips. Even though Aidan and I both came from good families and money, our parents had ensured we understood the importance of using our talents, abilities, and opportunities to better the world.

As I stared at my daughter, I hoped we can instil the same in her. The world is filled with people who look the other way. We must never be like them. Through our work and dedication to the vulnerable, Ainsley will see first-hand what it is to be a protector. If she decides to one day join Fortius, the decision will be hers to make.

After dinner Ryan and Heather informed the rest of the family – Fortius was Aidan's to command, with me by his side.

This was the first of a very long list of wars Aidan and I would wage against those who prey on the innocent. Men and women set on destroying nations and people.

They don't know Fortius exists, or that we are heading straight for them. We won't stop until their carcasses drift in our wake. One predator at a time.

No one is untouchable.

Acknowledgements

To my husband, Jeremy, for always believing in me and pushing me to pursue my dreams. Thank you for thirteen years of unconditional love. I am who I am because of you. You will always be my muse; my everything. I love you. I miss you. Always.

How do I even begin to say thank you to my family and friends for their continued support. You're always first in line to buy my books and send commentary on Finley's adventures. My first pass readers: Maricka, Nicolina, Tania, and Yolanda. Thank you for continuing to share in Finley's life and mine.

Maricka Jansen, thank you for taking it in your stride when I named an assassin after you. You might not be as lethal as Marika, but you're every bit as impressive. Also for helping with the German words and sharing your knowledge of Russian cuisine.

Nicolina Pieterse, you never flinch when I ask for your help killing characters, no matter how disturbing my questions are or how late at night I get a new idea. Your medical knowledge is a cornerstone to making my novels more realistic.

To the following individuals for allowing me to use their names for some of the victims in this book: Dana Ichilov, Vesta Lamont (Merwe), Donovan Peo. A special thank you to Alicia Rideout for your enthusiasm about having your name in Fortius, even though you had no idea whether your character would be a victim or a villain.

Rolandi du Toit, I may have altered your name in such a way that very few people will realise a certain detective is based on you. You know, and I know, that's all that matters.

Mariaan Opperman, thank you for helping me find the perfect spot to dig a shallow grave outside of Cape Town. May neither of us ever have to make use of this knowledge.

Marcel Koortzen, my editor and proofreader. Thank you for being with me every step of the way.

Shannon Jump, thank you for your constant support as a fellow author and friend, and for being the last pair of eyes on this novel.

Jana Barclay, thank you for helping to finish the cover design and for continuing with Jeremy's legacy. His work is in good hands.

Thank you to the readers for being a part of Finley's journey, as well as mine.

Most of all, to God. All I can ever offer in gratitude is my life, and it will never feel that it's enough.

All mistakes are my own.

About the author

Mariëtte Whitcomb studied Criminology and Psychology at the University of Pretoria. An avid reader of psychological thrillers and romantic suspense novels, writing allows her to pursue her childhood dream to hunt criminals, albeit fictional and born in the darkest corners of her imagination.

When Mariëtte isn't writing, she reads or spends time with her family and friends.

Visit www.mariettewhitcomb.com or find her on Facebook or Instagram.

www.ingramcontent.com/pod-product-compliance
Lightning Source LLC
LaVergne TN
LVHW091115080826
845145LV00008B/1926

* 9 7 8 1 7 7 6 2 8 2 3 1 9 *